"I don't suppose you're the welcoming committee."

"Don't think so." He smiled. No man should have a smile like that—charming and unhurried, but with a dash of devil-may-care.

"I'm the new doctor in town, and—"

"Now, isn't that a coincidence," Tim Miller interrupted. "So happens I'm the new doctor in town, too."

Laurie stared at him. "I wish you'd stop joking—"

"No joke." His drawl had vanished.

"You're a doctor?" she asked in dismay.

"So they tell me."

"The *town* doctor?"

"One and the same."

"No," Laurie said emphatically. "There's some misunderstanding. Because *I'm* the new doctor. I have a contract, dammit."

"How about that. So do I."

ABOUT THE AUTHOR

Ever since winning a national short-story contest when she
was in high school, Ellen James has wanted a writing career.
Doctors in the House, Ellen's seventh Superromance title, is
actually her sixteenth novel, so Ellen obviously has her wish.
Ellen and her husband, also a writer, share an interest in
wildlife photography and American history.

Books by Ellen James

HARLEQUIN SUPERROMANCE
613—TEMPTING EVE
641—FORBIDDEN
651—A KISS TOO LATE
685—MOTHER IN THE MAKING
708—THE MAN NEXT DOOR
738—LISA

DOCTORS IN THE HOUSE
Ellen James

Harlequin Books

TORONTO • NEW YORK • LONDON
AMSTERDAM • PARIS • SYDNEY • HAMBURG
STOCKHOLM • ATHENS • TOKYO • MILAN
MADRID • WARSAW • BUDAPEST • AUCKLAND

ISBN 0-373-70757-6

DOCTORS IN THE HOUSE

Copyright © 1997 by Ellen James.

Printed in U.S.A.

DOCTORS IN THE HOUSE

CHAPTER ONE

"WHO IS THAT *hunk* on our front porch?"

Laurie Russell didn't have an answer for her daughter's question. Certainly she wasn't acquainted with the man who had emerged from the house onto the porch. He was carrying a box packed so full of stuff it looked as if it would spill over at any moment. That didn't seem to bother him, though. He moved at a leisurely pace down the steps and toward a rusty pickup parked in the drive. The box was slid unceremoniously into the bed of the truck. He turned then and glanced across the yard to where Laurie stood with her daughter. A "hunk," perhaps. Handsome, assuredly. He had red hair so vivid it made Laurie think of maple leaves turned fiery in autumn, and his eyes were the most startling crystal blue.

"Mom," Alyson whispered, "who *is* he?"

"I don't know," Laurie muttered back. "I guess we'll just have to find out." She'd been told she could take possession of the house today. She and Alyson had rented a moving van and driven all the way out here from Detroit, and she didn't want any delays when it came to settling in. Unfortunately this man had the look of a delay.

She went up the walk toward him. "Hello," she said.

He took his time looking her over. "Hello," he finally said. His voice took its time, too, deep and slow with a hint of a Western drawl. Laurie was uncomfortably aware of the man. She found herself taking in every detail—the soft flannel of his shirt fitting comfortably over his shoulders, legs long and lanky in weathered denim, cowboy boots so scuffed the leather had worn to a sheen. Too late she realized she was staring at his feet. She lifted her gaze.

"I'm Laurie Russell," she said.

"Tim Miller." He shook her hand and gave the faintest of smiles.

"I don't suppose you're the welcoming committee," she said.

"Welcoming committee...don't think so." His smile broadened. No man should have a smile like that—charming and unhurried, but with a dash of devil-may-care. Laurie glanced back at Alyson and saw that her seventeen-year-old daughter was staring at him with a starstruck fascination. It was definitely time to move this encounter along.

"Mr. Miller, I'm not quite sure what you're doing here," she began, but then his smile distracted her all over again.

"Mizz Russell, I might say the same about you." The Western drawl had deepened just a little. Laurie pulled her gaze away from his disconcerting blue eyes and studied the pickup. It was so mud-spattered she couldn't even guess at the original color. But it was an older model, built back when trucks had high cabs and big curved fenders and seemed meant for bouncing along country roads. The pickup was like Tim Miller—charming but disreputable.

Laurie saw a scattering of tools in the back. "I don't suppose you've been doing repairs on the house," she said.

He seemed to give this some thought, then nodded. "Sort of like the local handyman?"

Laurie looked at him in exasperation. "I don't know. *Are* you the local handyman?"

"Mizz Russell, no. I am handy around the house, though."

Laurie wondered if she'd heard right. The man, it seemed, had just called her…"Mzzz." And he'd done it with a sinful glint of humor in his eyes.

"Mr. Miller, what do you say we cut this short? I'm the new doctor in town, and—"

"Now, isn't that a coincidence," Tim Miller interrupted. "So happens I'm the new doctor in town, too."

She stared at him. "I wish you'd stop joking—"

"No joke." Something in his voice had changed. The drawl had vanished. And when she gazed into his eyes this time, the humor had vanished, too.

"You're a doctor?" she asked in dismay.

"So they tell me."

"The *town* doctor?"

"One and the same."

Laurie shook her head. "No," she said emphatically. "There's some misunderstanding. Because *I'm* the new doctor. The town council gave me the job."

"Old Doc Garrett gave me the job," said Tim Miller. "Now this could be a problem. Even with the clientele from nearby towns like Edgewood, Hickory and Brayton, there's only enough work for one physician in Grant." He didn't sound disturbed. He didn't sound upset. He just sounded very matter-of-fact.

Laurie suddenly found she needed some support, and without thinking she leaned against the grimy pickup. "This doesn't make any sense. I was hired to take over Dr. Garrett's practice. No one said a thing about another doctor."

"This is the first I've heard of you, too, Dr. Russell." His voice had taken on a hard edge, and Laurie decided she liked the drawl better. Then her daughter came to stand beside her.

"Two doctors," Alyson said reasonably. "What's wrong with that?"

"Everything!" Laurie burst out. "Mr.—Dr. Miller is right. There isn't enough work in this area for two of us. It's a one-doctor practice. And I have a contract, dammit."

"How about that," Tim Miller said. "So do I."

They stared at each other again. When Tim Miller wasn't smiling, he had a determined look on his face. It was not the look of someone who yielded easily. Laurie had the unsettling suspicion that when he went after something, he usually got it.

Until now, she told herself. Because she never gave up, either. To raise a child single-handedly and earn a medical degree at the same time, you couldn't be the kind of person who gave up. Or the kind of person who gave in.

"Dr. Miller," she said more calmly than she felt, "obviously we have a major misunderstanding here. I suggest we get together with the town council and straighten it out right away."

"Hmm...never did much like decisions by committee,'' he said. He started back up the porch steps. ''Hate to break this up just when we were gettin' to know each other, but I promised Doc Garrett I'd clean out the rest of his place. The old guy's a real pack rat, you know.''

''I *didn't* know,'' she said grouchily. ''And it was never really his house, was it? This place is town property, meant for the town doctor—nobody else. I have the key.'' She fished in her pocket, pulled out her key ring and held it up for his perusal.

''One coincidence after another. I have a key, too.'' He held up his own, and it glinted silver in the late-afternoon sun. Laurie told herself this couldn't be happening. Any minute now Tim Miller would drop the act. He'd confess to being the local handyman and tell her it was just a practical joke. *Please let him tell me that,* she prayed. But Tim didn't say anything at all. With another leisurely appreciative glance at Laurie, he disappeared into the house.

Alyson gave a heartfelt sigh. ''He really is gorgeous, isn't he?''

''For goodness' sake, Alyson, the man is old enough to be your father.''

Her daughter waited just a fraction of a second before she said, ''Well, I don't know much about having a father, do I?''

Laurie told herself not to say anything more, not to react to that rigid tone in her daughter's voice. Lately whenever the subject of fathers came up—in any shape or form—Alyson would get that accusing resentful tone. Over the years Laurie had explained as gently as possible about Alyson's father—about his absence in their lives. And Alyson had appeared to accept the explanations. It was only now that she seemed dissatisfied with everything Laurie had told her.

Laurie gazed at her daughter. Alyson had inherited not only Laurie's dark brown hair, but her easily readable dark brown eyes, where every emotion rippled to the surface for all to see. If Laurie and Alyson had always been a team, it was all too apparent from the look in Alyson's eyes that the team was in danger of breaking up.

Laurie thought back to the way things had been before. During the years she'd plowed through medical school and her hospital residency, she and her daughter had shared the same dreams. It had been their plan that when Laurie finally got her medical degree, they'd move someplace that would be a real home. There were other parts to the dream of course. Despite a financial situation that could only be called precarious, over the years Laurie had painstakingly built up a college fund for Alyson. She and her daughter had been a team there, too. They'd planned and hoped for the future, sharing a genuine closeness, creating their own special world—a family of two. So why, lately, had Alyson begun pulling away? Why did she seem so restless and troubled, and so unwilling to confide in Laurie?

"Don't worry," Laurie told her now. "I'll take care of this mess with Tim Miller. What I have to do is call an emergency meeting of the town council."

"If it's all the same to you," Alyson said, "I'll just go explore the town on my own."

"But you don't know anybody here."

"Right," Alyson said with exaggerated patience.

"So maybe I *will* get to know somebody. Isn't that the general idea?"

Laurie controlled the irritation she felt whenever her daughter spoke to her as if she'd had brain damage. "Okay," she said evenly. "What do you say we meet back here in a couple of hours? I should have the Tim Miller situation resolved by then, and we can call for pizza."

Alyson gave a wry grimace. "Sure, Mom. Takeout pizza. Some things never change." That was another of Alyson's subtle digs—a reference to all the nights Laurie had been so exhausted from marathon shifts at the hospital that picking up the phone had been her best effort at dinner.

"Some things do change," Laurie countered now. "That's why we're here."

"Sure. See you later, Mom." Alyson went down the sidewalk. Laurie watched her go, tempted to call her back—wanting to hold her close as she'd done so often before. Something really was troubling Alyson, and Laurie had to find out what it was.

Meanwhile, however, other problems beckoned. Laurie glanced down and saw a big smear of dirt on the side of her blouse from leaning against Tim Miller's pickup. She tried to brush it off, but it seemed determined to stay.

"Not on your life, Dr. Miller," she muttered under her breath, frowning at his rusty old truck. "This place is mine. This job is mine."

LAURIE SPENT a very unsatisfactory two hours trying to mobilize the town council. Afterward she trudged back to Grant's small medical clinic, crossing the gravel drive that separated it from the doctor's house—*her* house, she reminded herself firmly. Glancing around, she saw that the rented moving van was still parked just where she'd left it, her car hitched behind. Tim Miller's deplorable truck still commanded the drive. Alyson, however, was nowhere to be seen. It was near evening now, shadows of dusk drifting over the mountains which rose above Grant. Not just any mountains—these were the Rockies, stern yet majestic snow-capped peaks. Laurie gazed up at them for a long moment, then walked toward the house. It was a charming old place, with a white picket fence, gabled windows, redbrick chimneys and even an ivy-covered gazebo nestled in the side yard. Lights shone from the house and, for some reason, that made Laurie feel a sudden loneliness.

Her discussions with the town council had not gone at all as she'd hoped. First of all, it had been impossible to round up the entire council. Two members were on vacation, another had gone to visit his parents in Durango, and yet another had resigned in some sort of tiff. That had left Beverly Davis and Harold Lattimer, both well-meaning individuals who claimed to have no authority on their own. They had been suitably sympathetic and distressed for Laurie without being able to offer any solution to her predicament. Of course, as soon as a quorum could be gathered, the matter would receive top priority...but who knew when *that* would be? No, old Doc Garrett was nowhere to be found, either. Seemed he had a new lady friend in Digby, and everybody knew what *that* meant.

Laurie didn't care about Doc Garrett's high jinks

with his new lady friend. She only cared about getting Tim Miller out of her house—out of her life. She marched onto the porch and raised her hand to knock on the door.

Just in time she realized that would be a strategic error. She tried using her key instead, but the door was unlocked. She opened it and stepped inside. The wooden floor of the hallway creaked under her feet, and automatically she tried to step more lightly—a habit developed during the years she'd stayed up late at night to study, keeping quiet so that Alyson could sleep.

Now Laurie heard Alyson's voice, drifting down the hall. She must be in the kitchen. "...Roxy. What a great name. Wish I could meet her."

Another voice answered—Tim Miller's, deep and easy. "My brother's keeping her for me, so I know she's in good hands. But still, I miss Roxy."

Laurie stayed where she was, battling a slew of emotions. She didn't like that her daughter sounded so friendly and relaxed with Tim Miller. But then something else sneaked its way in—plain simple curiosity. Who on earth was Roxy?

Alyson spoke. "I'll bet she's beautiful."

"Darn right she is. Prettiest little thing you ever saw, all dappled gray. And fast, too. Damn, but I do miss saddling her up and taking her for a ride."

So Roxy was a horse. The mystery had been solved, and Laurie knew she ought to make the two of them aware of her presence. Instead, she stood where she was, picturing Tim Miller on that horse of his out riding the range somewhere. The image was far too appealing.

"I love horses," Alyson said fervently. "I always have."

It was the first Laurie had heard of any such devotion. She found herself caught by the enthusiasm in her daughter's voice. It had been such a long time since she'd heard that tone from Alyson—excitement, pleasure. Tim Miller seemed to have brought it out naturally.

"Your brother's ranch sounds wonderful," Alyson went on. "New Mexico...I've always wanted to go there."

"It's officially Hallie's ranch, but my brother adopted the place once he married her. Gabe's a doctor, too. I never figured him for much of a rancher, but he took to it just fine."

"Don't you want to go back there?" Alyson asked. "I'll bet it's a lot more exotic than here."

"New Mexico..." Tim said. "No, I won't be going back anytime soon." He sounded grim, as if New Mexico held memories he'd rather not dwell on. Laurie wondered what they could be and then chided herself for eavesdropping like this. It made her feel extremely foolish. She went down the hall and entered the kitchen.

The scene before her was one of carefree domesticity. Dr. Miller lounged back in a chair, his feet resting on the battered oak table. He held a slice of pizza in one hand. Alyson sat opposite him, presiding over the near-empty box of pizza. She didn't seem to have any complaints about take-out food when it came to Tim Miller.

Alyson glanced at Laurie. It almost seemed as if a mask came over her face, liveliness replaced by a guarded indifference. "Hi, Mom. There's still some left."

Laurie wasn't hungry. Her gaze strayed back to Tim Miller, and she felt that disturbing little shiver of awareness. Tim, however, simply looked amused—as if he knew full well she'd been lingering in the hallway, purposely overhearing the conversation.

Laurie flushed. She didn't feel any better when Tim swung his feet down, stood and pulled out a chair for her with all the gallantry of a Southern gentleman. She didn't want to sit beside him—but somehow she ended up doing it, anyway. The table seemed too small and cozy, too intimate.

"How is the venerable town council?" Tim asked.

"Disorganized," Laurie admitted reluctantly. "It seems they recently had some sort of altercation. One of them quit, a few others went off on vacation...but I'm sure they'll sort it all out." She knew how unconvincing that last statement was, and obviously so did Tim.

"Doc Russell," he said, "it's like I was tellin' you. Never wrassle with a committee."

"Wrassle?" she echoed in disbelief. She gazed straight into his eyes and saw that abiding humor. But underneath it, she detected something else, perhaps a warning that Tim Miller's drawl and devil-may-care attitude were merely a front—disguising something a whole lot more complex.

Laurie wrenched her gaze away from him and focused on her daughter. "How was your tour of the town?" she asked too brightly.

"There's not much to see," Alyson said.

Laurie wasn't unrealistic. On her first visit to Grant, she'd evaluated the town's limitations, as well as strengths. She'd liked the feeling of a small community, the way everyone seemed to know each other. But she'd also seen that the place lacked many of the advantages of a larger town—it possessed only one small bookstore, one movie theater, one really decent restaurant. For that matter, it was only supposed to have *one* doctor.

Laurie faced Tim Miller again. "I was hired for this job in a very straightforward manner. The town council reviewed my credentials and then set up an interview. They even paid to have me flown into Denver and then driven here to Grant."

"Took out a newspaper ad, did they, all the way to Detroit?" Tim said.

She frowned. "Of course not. One of my colleagues at County has a friend whose mother lived here, and—"

"Word of mouth," Tim murmured. "Not so straightforward, now, is it? Certainly not sophisticated. A colleague's friend's mother..."

"The council is hardly unsophisticated," Laurie said.

"That must be why they're so...well organized. You know, the little matter of coming up with an extra doctor and all."

"The point is, Dr. Miller," Laurie said, "I went about getting this job in a very aboveboard fashion. But when I visited town for my interview, no one said a word about *you*."

"Not even Doc Garrett?"

"He wasn't available when I was here. Something about a cruise in the Caribbean."

Tim gave his slow grin. "That's where he met Estelle."

"I'm not concerned about Dr. Garrett's social life."

"You oughtta be. Everyone else in town is. See, here's how it happened. Old Doc went on that Caribbean cruise with a bunch of seniors from Cortez and Digby. Estelle happened to be along for the ride. And everybody's in an uproar because Estelle doesn't behave like any senior citizen you've ever seen. Very dashing lady, Estelle."

All Laurie could do was stare at Tim Miller. He had a way with a story, spinning out the words. Just the way he savored "Caribbean" could make you forget your train of thought.

Alyson was staring at him, too, her expression rapt.

"Dr. Miller," Laurie said, "could we forget the town gossip and get back to the point?"

"Darlin', town gossip is about the only entertainment in these parts."

Laurie couldn't believe he'd called her "darlin'." "How do you know so much about Grant?" she asked dryly. "Are you a native son?"

"Hardly. Let's just say Doc Garrett's an old family friend. He offered me the job—so here I am." The edge of steel had returned to his voice.

"You're not going to back down easily, are you?" she asked.

"Neither are you. This could be an interesting fight." His gaze held hers. But she didn't want a fight.

She just wanted to know she'd finally found a permanent home for herself and her daughter.

She pushed back her chair and stood. "One way or another I'll get this resolved. And meanwhile, Dr. Miller, you're in my house."

"I could say the same."

"Look, you'll just have to find somewhere else to stay until we work this out."

"There isn't anywhere else," Alyson contributed. "The tourist season hasn't started yet, so the hotels are closed. A few places do the bed-and-breakfast thing, but they're not open, either."

Laurie glanced at her daughter in surprise. "How did you find out all that?"

Alyson shrugged. "There's not that much to find out in a place like this."

"She's right, you know," said Tim Miller. "This town is shut down tight till after the first of June." He settled back in his chair, swinging his feet up on the table again. His scuffed cowboy boots had a particularly rakish look about them. "Well, Dr. Russell," he said, "seems you and I are goin' to be... roommates."

CHAPTER TWO

TIM MILLER SHIFTED position again, but it still didn't help. The floorboards of the porch seemed to be pressing into his back, aggravating that old rodeo injury. His ancient sleeping bag didn't provide much of a cushion, either. Over the years it had flattened in some places and gone lumpy in others. Maybe he ought to buy himself a new one. Then again, maybe he ought to ask himself why the hell he was sleeping on the front porch of his own damn house.

Laurie Russell was the answer of course. It had been her vulnerability, as if her very life depended on living in this house. He'd surprised himself by volunteering to sleep on the porch—this first night at least.

He shifted position yet again, even though he knew it was useless. This was going to be a long uncomfortable night. He turned his head and stared at the stars glimmering in the Colorado sky. And then, for some reason, the image of Laurie Russell intruded on his thoughts once more.

She was beautiful, no doubt about it. Intriguingly beautiful—dark hair falling in waves to her shoulders, a provocative tilt to her chin... Not that Laurie Russell intended to be provocative. He was pretty sure of that. She had the air of someone who wanted to protect herself. Tim had a feeling she was the kind of woman who bruised easily—and who didn't like to admit it.

He sighed in exasperation. Why was he speculating about the woman? She was an obstacle in his life, nothing more. All he had to do was get her out of here so he could be the town doctor—and if the idea of being town doctor didn't particularly thrill him, he had only himself to blame. He should have considered that before he'd accepted the damn job.

Grumbling, Tim unzipped the sleeping bag and got to his feet. He rubbed the sore muscles in his back, then went to lean against the edge of the porch. That midnight blue sky arced above him, and he sensed the bulk of the mountains, half-seen shapes that seemed to anchor the night. He didn't have anything against Colorado personally. What pressed on him was the knowledge of where he could have been right now—Chicago. The Jacobs Institute, where just about the most exciting advances in viral research were being made. Yes, he could have been there right now if he'd accepted the fellowship he'd been offered. Instead, he'd accepted *this* job—small-town doctor. And he still couldn't explain why. That was the hard part.

He went over it again in his mind, trying to find some connection he'd missed before. He'd been so close to everything that mattered. The fellowship his for the taking, the chance for real success before him at last. All he'd had to do was reach out, grab hold of the chance and in so doing wipe out a lifetime of failure. The past wouldn't have mattered anymore.

And he *had* reached out, had almost taken hold of the future...

Next came the part Tim couldn't explain. He'd gone to that medical convention in Denver, run into his dad's old friend Jonathan Garrett. He'd always liked Doc Garrett. The two of them had shared a couple of beers in the hotel bar. Then they'd shared a couple more. Doc Garrett had told him he was retiring and his small-town doctorship was up for grabs. He wanted Tim to have it. Couldn't think of anyone better for the job. All Tim had to do was say yes and it was his.

He'd said yes. Afterward he'd tried to blame it on the alcohol, a few too many shared with an old family friend. But that wasn't good enough. No excuse was good enough to explain why Tim had passed up the research opportunity of a lifetime for a dead-end town like Grant, Colorado. Maybe failure was a habit he didn't know how to break. His dad would sure as hell agree with him on that.

Tim paced from one side of the porch to the other, but the view wasn't any different. Maybe he'd pull on his boots, go downtown and find out what was happening in Grant around midnight. He suspected it wouldn't be much of anything.

Behind him, the front door started to creak open. He turned, feeling a pleasurable anticipation that didn't make any sense. Nothing in his life made a lot of sense, but he still looked forward to the thought of Laurie Russell making an appearance. Maybe she was starting to feel guilty about leaving him out here.

It wasn't Laurie. It was Alyson, the daughter, poking her head through the doorway. "Dr. Miller," she whispered, "are you all right?"

"I'm fine," he said to Alyson. To himself, he tried to explain the stirring of disappointment he'd felt upon seeing the daughter, instead of the mother, but no luck there. Explanations weren't his strong point these days.

Alyson slipped out onto the porch, giving a shiver in spite of the parka she wore. "It's cold out here. How can you stand it?"

He'd noticed the cold only as something peripheral. Even though it was already May, nighttime in the Rockies was bound to be chilly.

"I'm fine," he repeated.

"If it were up to me, you'd be inside," she said fiercely. "There's plenty of room."

"I appreciate the concern." He wished the kid would go back inside, leave him to his own dour thoughts.

"I don't think there's anything wrong with two doctors in town. Why all the uproar?" Her tone implied, why was her mother causing all the uproar? Tim had already sensed it, the unspoken tension between Laurie Russell and her daughter. No way did he want to get involved with that. *Don't ever get too involved.* That was how it had always been for him.

"The problem with two doctors…it's something to do with economics and logistics," he said. "But your mother and I will work things out." He thought about Laurie and the stubborn look in her lovely dark eyes—a competitive look. A competitive spirit. He knew about that himself, having only recently pushed his way through medical school and his residency in record time. His competitive spirit had been responsible for helping him land that fellowship. Maybe he'd turned down the fellowship, but the competitiveness remained. It seemed to be kicking in now as he thought about Laurie's stubborn dark brown eyes. He had a suspicion he was going to enjoy fighting Laurie Russell for this job. In the dead-end town of Grant, at least it was something to look forward to.

"Why don't you just come inside?" Alyson said. "It's stupid for you to be freezing out here."

He smiled a little to himself. "No, thanks," he murmured. "That's not how you play the game."

"Game?" Alyson echoed with interest.

"Nothing to worry about. I'm fine, kid. You'd better go inside yourself and get some sleep."

She seemed to stiffen at the way he called her "kid," but it had been a deliberate choice of words. After a second or two she mumbled a good-night and retreated back into the house. Tim stretched out in his sleeping bag again, the floorboards as hard and unyielding as ever. But as he closed his eyes, he gave another smile at the thought of Dr. Laurie Russell.

GRANT'S SMALL CLINIC did not have the latest in medical technology. Laurie listened with a growing sense of impatience as the staff nurse explained the rather convoluted process for obtaining lab results from Durango.

"It's inefficient," Laurie said. "I can't be dependent on a lab that faraway just for routine workups."

"That's the way Dr. Garrett has always done it," Bess Thompson said icily.

Laurie studied the nurse who had worked with Dr.

Garrett for close to forty years, and realized that she'd already managed to alienate the woman. Bess might be a small-town nurse, but she was surprisingly elegant. Her silvery hair was long, caught up in back in a rather complicated coil. She wore a fitted dress that showed off her trim figure, and she also wore heeled pumps, not the customary white orthopedic shoes. Looking quite a bit younger than her sixty-five years, she gave the impression that she took very good care of herself. She seemed the type who'd be up on the latest diet and exercise advice, so why did she so willingly accept the clinic's outmoded technology? More than that, Bess Thompson appeared ready to defend every one of Dr. Garrett's long-standing idiosyncrasies—whether it was his refusal to install a computer system or his animosity toward pharmacy sales representatives. This morning Laurie and Bess had already undergone a strained conversation about *those* matters.

Laurie had taken this job knowing that Grant was a bit backward when it came to medicine, but that didn't mean she had to accept the status quo. That was the whole point, wasn't it? New person on the job, new techniques.

"I'm sure Jonathan Garrett is an excellent doctor," Laurie said, "but it won't hurt to review the clinic's procedures." She congratulated herself on being diplomatic, but Bess hardly looked convinced.

"I don't think we should discuss this any further," she said stiffly, "not until Dr. Garrett decides exactly *who* is going to take over his practice."

Laurie controlled a surge of irritation. "I've already told you—it's not up to Dr. Garrett. The town council is—"

"According to my understanding, Timothy Miller has been offered the job. Dr. Miller has a superb academic record and the very best of references." Bess gave Laurie a disparaging glance, as if to imply that *her* academic record and *her* references could not possibly measure up. Then the woman turned to fuss unnecessarily with a rack of patient charts.

The last thing Laurie needed was a staff nurse already firmly on the side of Tim Miller. Bess was clearly a fixture in this place. She was experienced and from all reports, very competent. Certainly Laurie would have preferred to hire her own nurse, but she had a feeling applicants wouldn't flock to Grant for the job. Somehow she had to get Bess Thompson on her side.

The door of the clinic banged open. "Mornin', ladies," said Tim Miller. As he came in, the place seemed to take on added life and color. Laurie found herself staring at him, just as she had yesterday when they'd first met. And again she felt that unwilling awareness of his every inch.

"Bess, I hope you didn't get the doughnuts already—I'm buyin' today." He set a box of doughnuts on the counter. Before Laurie's eyes, the older woman's countenance appeared to soften.

"Doughnuts..." Bess objected, but she treated him to a smile. "And just tell me, how am I going to eat all these by myself?"

"I'll help. So will Dr. Russell." He took the box, opened it with a flourish and presented it to Laurie. "First pick," he murmured. "By the way, hope you slept well last night knowin' I was locked safely outside.''

She flushed. The truth was, she'd slept badly. With her moving van still unloaded, she'd been obliged to take the one bed in the house—the bed where Tim had already slept. It seemed he'd arrived in Grant some twenty-four hours before she had. That didn't qualify as much of a head start, but she'd felt she was evicting him from his own home. Although Tim had "wrassled" up some fresh sheets for her, his masculine presence had seemed to linger long after he'd retreated to the porch.

Then of course, there'd been her daughter. Alyson had decided to sleep on the shabby couch in the living room, but she'd stayed up for the longest while. She'd sat by herself, reading, as if she would retreat as far as possible into her own world. Laurie had lain awake, watching the lamplight that spilled from the living room and wondering why her daughter seemed so faraway these days. Eventually Alyson had gone out on the porch, and Laurie had heard her talking for a few minutes to Tim. That was just one more worry, the way Alyson had seemed instantly taken by Tim Miller. At last she'd come back inside and settled down—but she'd been up and out of the house almost at dawn, muttering some vague excuse about exploring the town some more. It had definitely not been a restful night.

Then this morning, when Laurie herself had left the house, she'd had to step over Tim's prone form on the porch. He'd appeared to be asleep, but she'd had the uneasy sense he was guarding amusement behind his closed eyes. She saw the amusement now—it was unmistakable.

"Try one of the jelly ones," he told her. "Made up fresh at the bakery. That's one thing about Grant—best doughnuts in the state."

"A connoisseur, are you?" she said.

"In all the things that matter." Here came his slow grin, his gaze traveling appreciatively over her features. She wondered how many women he'd looked at like that and how many women had fallen for it. Probably too many. Laurie found herself taking one of the jelly doughnuts and then almost dropping it on the floor, as if she'd grown clumsy in Tim's presence.

He was the one who broke the moment between them. He set the doughnuts back on the counter and leaned against it himself.

"Bess," he said, "heard from Doc Garrett lately?"

The older woman got a funny look on her face. "No," she said quickly. "And if he's in Digby, it's certainly none of my business."

"Too bad," Tim said. "Maybe the doc could shed some light on this two-doctor situation of ours."

"Unfortunately I'm sure he's been much too busy to think about that," Bess muttered. "He'll just have to resolve the situation when he has…more time."

Tim gave her a thoughtful look. "Well," he said, "got any new pictures of the grandson?"

Bess seemed relieved to have another topic of conversation. "I was only waiting for you to ask." She fished a wallet from her purse and flipped it open for Tim's perusal.

"Good-lookin' boy," Tim said. "It's time you got him on a horse."

"No bronco-busting for *my* grandchild," she protested. "Don't you dare put any ideas into his head, either."

Laurie stood there with her jelly doughnut, listening to the two of them. She knew she could go over and marvel at Bess's grandson, too, but somehow that felt like conceding some sort of defeat. On the other hand, she couldn't just wait here, relegated to the sidelines.

"I gather you know each other from some time back," she said at last.

"Way back," confirmed Tim. "When I was a kid, I spent some family vacations up here."

"I remember the first time you came," Bess said. "You weren't more than eight or nine. Your poor dear mother was still alive—" She stopped abruptly, as if afraid she'd said too much. But Tim's easy manner didn't change.

"You spoiled Gabe and me rotten," he said.

Bess gave a sigh. "Hard to believe your brother's married with children of his own."

"Don't act like he grew up all of a sudden. He's already passed forty. Come to think of it, so have I."

Laurie took a bite of her doughnut. She figured Tim didn't have anything to worry about—he'd be turning female heads for a long time to come. Just as long as he didn't turn *hers,* she'd be fine.

He addressed Laurie again. "Bess here thinks I should settle down like my big brother, start a family. I keep tellin' her I haven't found the right girl yet."

Laurie couldn't picture Tim Miller settling down— ever. She looked at him in his well-worn cowboy boots, his faded jeans and his rumpled flannel shirt, and she could imagine him riding off somewhere on his dappled gray horse Roxy. But settling down...no, she couldn't picture that.

Suddenly Laurie realized she had jelly all over her fingers. Usually she was a neat orderly person, but Tim Miller had a strange effect on her. Worst of all, he seemed to know exactly what she was thinking. He fished a bandanna out of his back pocket and handed it to her solemnly.

She cleaned her fingers and then gazed down at the vivid blue-and-white cloth. "You really are a cowboy, aren't you?" she asked.

"Doctor, remember?"

Unfortunately she did remember. But now she had a jelly doughnut in one hand and a bandanna in the other. Maybe it was time to be a doctor herself.

"I'm surprised no patients have come in yet," she said to Bess.

The older woman gave her a cool glance. "A lot of folks only want to see Dr. Garrett. They won't accept that he's retiring. I've also had some cancellations. People are confused about the rumors flying around—two doctors in town."

From what Laurie had seen so far, Grant, Colorado, seemed to thrive on rumors. "We must have *some* appointments today," she said.

Bess gave a deliberate shrug. "Not so far."

"Doc Russell," said Tim, completely deadpan, "you could always go wrassle up some patients of your own."

"Right," she muttered. "And maybe at the same time I could *wrassle* up a little common sense in this town." Laurie couldn't believe she'd just said "wrassle." She glanced at Tim and saw the way his mouth quirked engagingly at one corner. She glanced quickly away again and headed for the door.

"I'm sure you and Bess can hold down the fort, Dr. Miller," she said caustically. "But I'll be right next door if you need me."

"Giving up so soon?" he asked with mock disappointment.

"Hardly." She left the clinic and went across the gravel drive. Much to her displeasure, Tim came right along with her.

"You haven't finished your doughnut," he pointed out.

"Don't you have something better to do?"

"You saw it yourself, Doc Russell. No patients."

She stared at him. "Doesn't this situation bother you in the least?"

"I'm always up for a good fight. Especially when I know I'm going to win."

The determination was back, solid as rock underneath the easy grin and the nonchalance. Laurie headed toward her moving van. She finished off her doughnut, wiping her sticky fingers once more on Tim's bandanna. She frowned at the bandanna, then stuffed it into her back pocket. She took her keys from her front pocket and started to unlock the chains fastening her car to the tow trailer.

Without Laurie knowing quite how it happened, Tim appropriated the keys from her and took over the job. Here she was, suddenly standing off to the side again.

"Dr. Miller, I'm perfectly capable—"

"No doubt you are, Doc Russell. But I used to do this kind of thing for a living. I was a trucker once."

"I thought you were a cowboy."

"That, too. Guess you could say I've been around."

None of it seemed to fit. She was supposed to believe that Tim had been a cowboy and a trucker and who knew what else—and now he was a doctor. Not the usual career path, but then, she hadn't taken the usual career path, either. Unwed mother at nineteen, for starters...

Her mind veered away from that thought. She didn't dwell on it a whole lot anymore; no reason to do so now. She watched as Tim climbed into her car and backed it off the tow trailer. The little hatchback seemed far too tame a vehicle for him. He was much better suited to that disreputable pickup.

He parked her car, then opened up the back of the moving van. He untied the ropes anchoring her bureau and began hauling it out.

"Wait," Laurie said at last.

"I got the idea you wanted to move your stuff inside."

"Yes, of course, but—"

"I don't have anything better to do, Doc Russell. Might as well take advantage of me."

She wished his rich deep voice didn't have such an effect on her. And it didn't seem right, Tim Miller helping her to move her things inside the house. He should be objecting to the plan—he should be trying to stake out his own territory. Unless, of course, he was so confident of winning this job that he figured he could afford to be magnanimous.

She felt uneasy. It was very clear that Tim already had connections in town. He'd spent summer vacations here as a boy. Dr. Garrett was a longtime family friend, and Bess Thompson acted as if she wanted to adopt him. Where did that leave her, Laurie?

With the town council behind her, she reminded herself. So what if the council was temporarily in disarray? She'd been offered the job. She'd accepted. It was hers.

"Those must be some thoughts," Tim remarked.

She turned away, not wanting him to read anything more. It would be safer if she could pretend to be casual and unconcerned. But the truth remained—this job meant everything to her. This was what she'd been working toward all those years. This was the dream she and Alyson had planned together. She finally had the future in her hands and she couldn't let Tim Miller take it away from her.

She could feel him waiting behind her, waiting as if he had all the time in the world. She spoke. "Alyson will help me unload as soon as she gets back. That should be any minute now."

"Not likely. When she stepped out this morning, she said she'd probably be gone past lunchtime."

Laurie couldn't avoid glancing at him again. "She told *you* that?"

"It's enlightening, the conversations you can have on your own front porch."

"I do realize Alyson went out to speak to you in the middle of the night," Laurie said.

"Figured you would. You keep your eye on the kid pretty good, don't you?"

Laurie wondered why he made her feel so defensive. "If you're implying I'm overprotective, I'm just concerned, that's all. And I don't see how Alyson is going to wander around this town for hours with nothing to do." She glanced down the street as if she could make her daughter materialize.

"You don't need to worry about her," Tim said. "There aren't any ax murderers in Grant. This town's too dull for that."

"If you dislike the place so much, why on earth did you accept Dr. Garrett's offer?"

Tim didn't answer for a minute. A look of discontent flickered across his face, and once again Laurie had the sense that his carefree humor hid depths she couldn't even begin to fathom. But the look was gone almost as soon as it had come.

"My dad's a small-town doctor," Tim said. "So's my brother Gabe. Maybe I just wanted to follow in their footsteps." From the subtle irony in his voice, Laurie suspected that the story was a whole lot more complicated than that. And what about Tim's mother? Bess had started to speak about her, making clear that she'd died. How? When?

Laurie caught herself. Curiosity about Tim's personal life was not something she could allow herself. Right now what she had to do was get her furniture into that house, claim it as her own. She began tugging on the bureau.

"See you later, Dr. Miller. I can handle the small stuff by myself. Alyson will help me with the rest of it later."

He lifted the bureau and carried it down the ramp

of the moving van. "Don't forget—I used to do this kind of thing for a living." And with his lackadaisical grin he went up the walk to the house.

CHAPTER THREE

A FEW HOURS LATER, it was Laurie's couch that caused trouble. Together she and Tim had managed to get all the other furniture inside. But her brand-new oversize couch simply refused to fit through the front door. It loomed there on the porch, bulky and unwieldy and bright orange.

"Hell," Tim said, "you could always leave it out here, a deterrent to door-to-door salesmen."

"Very funny," Laurie muttered. She was sweaty from hauling and lifting and pulling, but Tim still looked fresh and relaxed. There'd been no stopping him—he'd persisted in helping her unload the van. He'd handled every piece of furniture with an ease she'd secretly admired. Watching Tim Miller engage in physical tasks had been...satisfying. Tantalizing, too. She'd never thought that watching a man bend and lift could be so interesting. More than once she'd caught herself simply gazing at him, observing the way he moved. He'd rolled up the sleeves of his flannel shirt and she'd seen the strength in his arms...

Now Tim surveyed the orange sofa. "Big sucker, isn't it."

"We're getting it into the damned house if it's the last thing we do!"

"I'm game for anything," he said. "Here, maybe if we turn it this way. No, that way…"

They strained. They heaved. They pushed. And slowly, tipped on one end, the couch began to inch through the doorway. Laurie heard the upholstery snag on the doorjamb, but she didn't care. It had become a point of honor, getting this sofa into the house. It would be a symbol of her permanence here. After all, once they got it in, how would anyone ever get it out?

Unfortunately, about halfway through the process, it stuck. Tim gave it a manful shove, then reached behind to rub his back.

"Did you hurt yourself?" Laurie asked, immediately the professional. "Let me see—"

"It's nothing," he said. "Fell off a bull once, that's all."

"Is there anything you haven't done?" she asked.

"Could be I've finally met my match with this orange monster." Another mighty shove and the sofa advanced another fraction of an inch.

Laurie was feeling defensive again. "I know the color is a bit…hideous. But it's incredibly comfortable and it was on sale. I thought if I draped a few blankets over it or a shawl…"

"It sure as heck needs something," Tim muttered, straining until the muscles stood out on his arms. The sofa budged another inch. Laurie joined Tim in pushing the behemoth. After some twenty minutes of slow excruciating effort, the sofa finally cleared the door.

It now sat in the living room, dwarfing the shabby sofa where Alyson had spent the night.

"Yours?" Laurie asked.

"Doc Garrett's. He agreed to leave it here for me. I didn't bring any furniture."

That didn't surprise Laurie. Tim Miller seemed like a man who would travel light. She went to the kitchen, poured two glasses of water, came back out and handed one to Tim. Then she collapsed onto her orange sofa.

"It really is comfortable," she said.

Tim sat down at the other end of the sofa, stretching out his legs and taking a long swallow of water. "Have to agree with you," he said. "The damn thing *is* comfortable."

Laurie glanced around at her possessions scattered here and there—the plasterboard bookshelves she'd painted to disguise their cheapness, the futon she'd purchased at a garage sale, the pillows she'd bought at the bargain store. Every item seemed a testament to the enforced frugality of her life. Even the new sofa represented her limitations. She'd bought it to celebrate her new job in Grant, but she hadn't been able to afford a more tasteful color. Orange had been the only color on sale. Now, when she thought about the mountain of debt still hanging over her from medical school, apprehension tightened inside her. She needed this job. If she didn't start pulling in some money soon, she'd really be in trouble.

"I'm here to stay," she informed Tim.

"Yeah," Tim said casually, "me, too."

"I wish I knew why you found this whole thing so amusing," she muttered. "You're treating it like some kind of, I don't know, a match of wits."

He gazed at her speculatively. "Can you think of a better way?"

"Yes, I can. A straightforward decision from the town council, for one thing."

He didn't answer, just sat there looking perfectly at home on her orange couch.

"I wonder where Alyson is," Laurie said. "She should have been home by now."

"It's not even lunchtime yet."

"If you're implying I'm overprotective again—"

"You're the one who keeps saying that," he pointed out. "Not me."

Laurie made a gesture of futility. "It's just that...lately Alyson can't even seem to sit still. She takes these long walks."

"Nothing wrong with walking," Tim said.

She wondered why she was telling him any of this. She was seized by a restlessness of her own and she stood. "It's one thing to take a walk in order to go somewhere. And quite another to walk as if you're trying to get away."

"All teenagers want to get away," Tim said. He didn't sound like someone who wanted to hear Laurie's troubles. Why had she even started?

"Look," she said, "thanks for helping me unload the van. The town council has arranged for someone to drive it to Denver for me. They can turn it in there. At least that's something." She wished she could ask Tim to leave. But her rights in this situation were more than a little muddied.

He got up and crossed to her. "Your daughter seems like a decent kid," he said gruffly. "Maybe you shouldn't worry so much about her."

He still sounded like someone who didn't want to hear her problems. But then she looked into his eyes, and the startling blueness of them made her forget logic.

"I do worry," she said in a low voice. "Maybe that's what's driving her away from me." It was all she could do to keep her expression blank. But something must have shown, anyway. There was a flicker of concern on Tim's face. Then he reached up his hand and gently, very gently, brushed his fingers over her cheek.

It was the briefest of touches, over almost before it began. But it made Laurie tremble. She stepped back quickly.

"Don't," she said, her voice harsh.

He didn't say anything, just stood there gazing at her quizzically for a long moment. And then he seemed to sense her need to be alone.

"I'll let you get settled," he said almost too kindly, and left her.

SOMETIMES WHEN ALYSON was around her mother, she felt like she just couldn't breathe. It was the way Mom looked at her these days, that probing concern. Even when Mom didn't say anything, the questions were there, hovering unspoken between them. *Why are you so quiet, Alyson? What's troubling you? Does it have something to do with the father you've never known? Let's talk about it. Let's talk about everything that's bothering you, and then let's go back to the way we were before. Just the two of us against the rest of the world.*

When her mother gazed at her with that worried expression, Alyson had to get out—she had to get away. That had been a lot easier in Detroit, where you could actually go someplace. Here, in Grant, Colorado, you could circle the town again and again and never end up anywhere.

This morning Alyson had already seen everything. Grant was laid out in an unimaginative grid pattern. There were residential streets, row upon row of Victorian houses, some with the paint peeling and others with fresh gingerbread trim. Most of the businesses and stores were on Main Street, where there were brick buildings with ornamental fronts and fancy awnings, but hardly any customers that Alyson could see. The entire town was cupped in a narrow valley, the mountains jutting up all around. And that was the only spectacular thing about Grant—the way the mountains towered over it, the green of the forest hardly seeming to soften the forbidding rock faces.

Now Alyson walked down Main Street for what seemed the tenth time. She didn't want to go home, so she finally ended up at the small diner she'd visited yesterday. She slid into a booth next to the window, using her coat sleeve to brush away the crumbs left on the table. The middle-aged waitress came over.

"Back again," she commented.

So much for anonymity in this town. There weren't any other patrons, and the waitress left the menu and then hovered, as if expecting Alyson to strike up a conversation. But Alyson was getting very good at killing a conversation before it had even begun. All you had to do was keep quiet, not give in to the temptation to fill the uncomfortable silence. It worked this time. At last, with a shrug, the waitress wandered off.

Alyson stared at the menu. Nothing sounded very appetizing: miner's biscuits-and-gravy, strike-it-rich omelettes, silver-dollar pancakes. The whole menu was a pathetic play on the town's mining history. Alyson shut it and pushed it aside. She didn't have much money on her, anyway, and she ended up ordering just a cup of coffee.

She sipped the bad coffee and stared out the window. She tried to imagine what it would be like if she chose her own place to live, her own town. Of course, in a way she'd done that already. Early last January, she'd picked out her favorite colleges and mailed applications to them. A few answers had already come back: one acceptance, two refusals. Her mother had been more upset about the refusals than she, Alyson, had and had given a long speech about not getting discouraged. She hadn't seemed to realize that Alyson wasn't even sure anymore about going to college. Mom insisted you could talk to her about anything, but there were really only certain things she wanted to hear.

Mom seemed to have it all figured out. Alyson would go off to college in the fall, but she'd always have a home to return to, here in Grant. They'd spend every school vacation together, and they'd go on being what they'd always been: Laurie and Alyson Russell, mother and daughter extraordinaire. No one else would ever be allowed to get too close.

Alyson wrapped her hands around her coffee cup. Sometimes all she wanted was to have things the way they'd been before, to believe she and her mother shared some special unique connection. But more and more Alyson found herself struggling against that connection, hating it almost. She'd look at her mother and see someone who worked too hard, someone who'd kept her mind on one goal all her life—being a doctor. Relentlessly pursuing that goal, letting it consume her so she missed everything else. Mom didn't seem to realize there were other things in life, other ways of living than being dedicated and alone. No one around except maybe a daughter who wasn't even sure she wanted to be with you anymore.

Alyson drank the rest of her coffee, the taste bitter on her tongue. All morning she'd been keeping a certain thought at the edge of her consciousness. Now she allowed it to take over. It was the thought of Tim Miller.

She could honestly say she'd never known anyone like him. It just seemed that he'd *lived* more than anyone else. He'd worked on a couple of ranches and been with the rodeo. All you had to do was look at him and you started picturing things like prairies and blue sky. Elemental things. Masculine things.

Other thoughts intruded now, such as the way Tim Miller looked at her mother. He didn't look at Alyson like that; instead, he treated her as if she was a child. It made her feel confused, uncertain. She'd been feeling confused a lot lately—about everything.

She went on staring out the window, but there was nothing to see in the street. No bustle, no excitement. Just a sleepy small town that no one seemed to care about much anymore. But then it happened. Someone strolled right by the diner, only a few feet away, on the other side of the glass from Alyson. A guy, maybe twenty years old. Maybe not as good-looking as Tim Miller, but almost. He had a rugged profile and dark blond hair that fell almost to his shoulders. Even though the weather was cool, he wore khaki shorts and a T-shirt. He looked like he could handle any kind of weather. As he walked past, he glanced at Alyson. Self-consciously she sat up a little straighter, suddenly wishing she'd done more than pull her hair back into a ponytail that morning. He gave her only a slight uninterested perusal before moving on. That was how Tim Miller looked at her, without interest. Suddenly Alyson felt more confused than ever, struggling against an obscure misery. She hated feeling like this, as if she were invisible. Didn't anyone really see her? But now she couldn't help herself. She watched the blond guy as he crossed the street.

The waitress drifted over, following the direction of Alyson's gaze. "Quite a specimen, isn't he?" she said.

Alyson tried to look bored, knowing she didn't succeed. "Who is he?" she found herself asking.

"The one and only Kevin Nichols. But let me give you a piece of advice, dearie. Stay away from him— stay well away. Kevin Nichols is bad news."

TIM BROUGHT his pickup to a stop right in front of the small, rustic cabin. The place hadn't changed much over the years. Doc Garrett kept making noises about remodeling it, maybe adding a room or two, but he'd never gotten around to the job. This was his hideaway, nestled far up the mountainside from Grant. He was known to retreat here when even small-town life grew too much for him. And he'd always planned to retire here when the time came. Well, the time had come—and one doctor too many was ready to take over the job.

Tim climbed out of the truck and went to knock

on the sturdy front door. After a moment it swung open and Jonathan Garrett himself peered out.

"Tim-o," he said, using the nickname he'd given Tim long ago, "step aboard!"

Tim ducked his head and entered the cabin, where early-evening sunlight streamed in through the deep-set windows. The place was snug—maybe a little too snug. It was cluttered, filled with the odds and ends Doc Garrett had collected over the years and never thrown away—musty books, outdated medical journals, fishing rods, leaky wading boots, chairs with uneven legs. The doc was famous for purchasing broken furniture he intended to fix up, but never did. The cabin was crowded with projects he just somehow never got around to starting. Tim shook his head and gave the old doctor a wry glance.

"I have another load of your junk from the house. Where am I supposed to put it all?"

"Hell, I don't know. Out back somewhere, I suppose. But forget it right now—let's have a drink." Jonathan poured a scotch for himself, another for Tim. Tim reminded himself that this was how he'd run into trouble with Doc the first time. Sharing a few drinks, getting mellow...accepting a job in the mountains of Colorado and then wondering why the heck he'd done it. But Tim took the scotch, anyway, and sat down in one of the chairs with mismatched legs.

Jonathan sat across from him. The Doc was much like the cabin itself—somewhat untidy and haphazard in appearance. He wore corduroys from a different era and a sweatshirt with a frayed collar. He'd never been a particularly tall or imposing man, and at seventy seemed to have settled into himself. He'd acquired a comfortable paunch—nothing too major, just something to rest a drink against. He'd gone bald over the years, and the look suited him. It seemed to appeal to women, at any rate.

"Didn't think I'd find you here," Tim said now. "From all accounts, you've been spending most of your time in Digby, with Estelle."

Jonathan looked disgruntled. "Don't tell me you've been listening to those stories, too."

"Why not? You and Estelle are providing the only excitement around here."

"She's not bad," Jonathan said.

"Getting serious, is it?"

Now Jonathan looked evasive. "Hard to say."

"Latest rumor is that you and Estelle are going to take another cruise."

"Not a cruise," Jonathan denied. "We're just going to hire a fishing boat, maybe down in Mexico. Oceangoing." A note of enthusiasm had crept into his voice.

Tim nodded gravely. "Sounds serious to me when you take a girl fishing with you. Oceangoing and all."

The doc looked displeased again. "Enough about me. What's the story *I've* been hearing, about the damn-fool council hiring its own doctor?"

"You heard right. She's pretty, too. Very pretty."

"A woman?"

"They do make lady doctors these days." Tim's thoughts lingered on Laurie Russell, a recurring habit. This morning she hadn't seemed particularly happy when he'd helped move her furniture into the house. Apparently she liked to be independent—or maybe it was just his help she didn't care for. He remembered

the shadowed look he'd seen in her eyes and the way
he'd wanted to make that look go away. Tim knew
he had to watch himself. He wasn't used to feeling
like this, as if he thought he could change something
for a woman. There was no reason to start now.

"They'll just have to send her back to wherever
she came from," Jonathan stated. "The job is yours,
Tim-o. Nobody else's."

"Afraid it isn't going to be that easy. Laurie re-
fuses to go anywhere." Tim had to admire her for
that—she wouldn't give up without a fight.

Jonathan uttered a curse. "Phil Cline has had it out
for me ever since he joined the damn council. I'll
wager this is his idea, sneaking around behind my
back, trying to hire my replacement. All because he
thinks I stole his girlfriend that time in 'forty-eight."

It was undeniable that Jonathan had a long history
of breaking women's hearts. Nothing had settled him
down, not even being married and divorced twice.
Estelle was only his latest fling.

"I don't think it's a conspiracy," Tim said.
"Maybe it's just as simple as a lack of communica-
tion. Face it, Doc, you let it be known you were going
to retire, but you didn't say anything about your plans
for bringing a replacement in. Here's how I see it.
The council members started to get worried—after all,
not that many doctors would be willing to come all
the way to Grant. They put some feelers out, found a
woman who's just finished her residency and who's
actually willing to relocate to this place. So they hired
her on the spot. Sounds pretty reasonable to me."

"Whose side are you on?" Jonathan demanded.

"Good question." Tim swirled his drink. The image of Laurie Russell came to him again. Lovely, dark-haired, stubborn. Prickly if he so much as reached out to her—guarding herself. From everything he could see, she'd raised her daughter on her own. That must have been rough.

"She'll have to go back," Jonathan repeated. "This job is yours. It can't belong to anyone else."

"You make it sound like fate," Tim said.

"Maybe it is—ever think about that?" Jonathan straightened and gave Tim a stare of unusual intensity. "You're following in your dad's footsteps. That counts for a lot."

Tim went still. "Don't start this again."

"Sooner or later you'll listen to me. You'll understand what I'm trying to tell you. Your father would be proud of you for taking this job."

Tim swirled his drink again without tasting it. "Proud," he said mockingly. "That's one thing Samuel Miller is never going to feel about me."

"Give him some credit," Jonathan urged. "He can change. He probably knows he hasn't been the best father—"

"Leave it, Doc."

Jonathan started to speak, then subsided. When it came to Tim's father, they couldn't agree. Jonathan had been Samuel Miller's friend for decades and had always stood up for him. At the same time he'd stood up for Tim. Over the years, he'd tried to be a sort of go-between for father and son. It hadn't worked, but at least he'd tried.

Tim remembered it all wearily. Until the time he was twelve, he'd lived what he considered a happy enough childhood. Maybe he'd been prone to trouble even back then, but somehow his mother had managed to keep him in line with a healthy dose of love. Through the years her face had faded from his memory, but he could recall the sound of her voice, the warmth and spirit in it. She hadn't been a compliant retiring woman—she'd let her husband and her two sons know exactly what an important place she occupied in their lives. But then, when Tim was twelve, his mother had died, and the family she left behind had seemed to spin out of control. First it was Gabe, rebelling for all he was worth, and then Tim following suit. Their father, however, had always seemed able to forgive Gabe. But not Tim. Never Tim. Over and over Samuel Miller had sworn that his youngest son would never amount to anything good. And Tim had done his damnedest to prove his father right—to prove with a vengeance that he *was* a failure.

There were a couple of people, though, who never did give up on him. His older brother, Gabe, was one. And Jonathan Garrett was another. When Tim was a teenager and really out of control, Jonathan had even taken him in a couple of times. Tim would always be grateful for that.

"Look," he said now, "I know you'd like the Millers to be one big happy family. It's just not going to happen. Isn't it enough that Gabe and I are finally okay with each other?"

"You told me to drop it," Jonathan said. "I'm dropping it."

Tim figured he'd hurt the old guy's feelings. It wasn't what he wanted, but when it came to discussing his father…there weren't any compromises.

"Anyway," Jonathan said after a moment, his

voice a little less brusque, "the job is yours. No questions, no excuses. No alternatives."

"Maybe you should ask Laurie Russell for her opinion," Tim murmured.

"I don't even need to meet her. She's gone. She's out of here."

Somehow Tim had a feeling that Laurie wouldn't agree.

CHAPTER FOUR

LAURIE SHOULD HAVE HAD a good night's sleep. She was in her own bed, surrounded by familiar objects—her stenciled bureau, the simple pine desk where she'd studied all through medical school, the blanket chest she'd inherited from her grandmother. Yesterday she and Tim had arranged these items in one of the house's pleasing high-ceilinged bedrooms. But maybe that was the reason Laurie hadn't slept so well, after all. Because Tim Miller had helped her to move in, and she felt his influence throughout the house.

She turned, bunching up her pillow. Morning light seeped through the windows, yet she felt as if she'd hardly closed her eyes at all. Tim wasn't even around—he'd said he would be spending the night up at Dr. Garrett's cabin in the mountains. That meant Laurie and Alyson had the entire house to themselves, front porch included. So why, then, did she keep thinking about the man?

At last, with a curse, she climbed out of bed and fumbled for her robe. Slipping it on, she padded out of her bedroom and across the hall. She glanced into the bedroom Alyson had chosen and saw that her daughter was fast asleep. Laurie stood there for a moment, remembering the countless times during Alyson's childhood when she had done precisely this—

watch her daughter sleep. Back then it had made her feel close to Alyson; now it just made her feel inadequate. She saw a mixture of child and adult in her daughter, and wanted to hold on to the child, keep the adult from taking over. At this moment it seemed to her it had all happened much too quickly, Alyson's growing up. If only the two of them could turn the clock back a little, do certain things differently...

Laurie sighed and went downstairs to the kitchen. Here Dr. Garrett had left behind ancient appliances, including a refrigerator that hummed too loudly and a pea green eyesore of a stove. She poured herself a glass of juice; yesterday she'd shopped for groceries and stocked up the fridge. She was going through all the motions at least, doing what was necessary to create a real home. There was only one minor detail getting in the way. This place wasn't really hers. Not yet.

Carrying her glass of juice, Laurie wandered through the living room and then, for some inexplicable reason, found herself going to the front door. She unlocked it, stepped outside—and almost went tumbling over the body lying on the porch.

"What the hell...?" Tim said.

She'd managed to hang on to her glass, although some of the juice had slopped onto Tim's sleeping bag. She stared at him in the pale morning light.

"I thought you were up at Dr. Garrett's cabin."

"I thought so, too," Tim muttered, "until I tried to find a place to sleep among all Doc's clutter. The guy gives new meaning to 'pack rat.'"

This was something new. Tim Miller actually

sounded as if he was in a bad mood. Laurie stepped over him and went to lean against the porch railing.

"You don't seem too chipper this morning," she said.

He gave her a sour look in response.

"Pressure getting to you?" Laurie asked. "Maybe Dr. Garrett had a solution to our little problem, something you didn't like." She felt a surge of hope at the idea. It was always possible that Dr. Garrett would be reasonable and cede to the town council—

"Doc had a solution, all right. Something about you packing up your bags and your orange couch and leaving town."

Laurie shook her head. "I'll talk to him myself just as soon as possible."

"If you think it'll do any good. Doc Garrett has a way of sticking to his decisions." Tim gazed at her from his sleeping bag, and she became aware of how she was dressed—long cotton nightgown, terry-cloth robe. Perfectly respectable attire of course, but not sexy. Plain cotton and terry cloth—she might as well just announce to Tim Miller that she hadn't shared her bed with a man in years.

"You're blushin', Doc Russell." Tim's tone was almost grudging. He was lying there prone and that should have put him at a disadvantage. Yet even with his hair rumpled and that stubble of russet beard outlining his jaw, he looked incredibly handsome.

Laurie made a concerted effort to focus on her juice. Tim started to climb out of the sleeping bag, then gave a grimace and sank down again.

"Damn," he said.

"What is it?"

"Nothing," he muttered. He started to rise again, turning awkwardly onto all fours.

"Damn. Damn. Damn."

Laurie had already set down her juice glass and stepped close to him. She probed his back gently. "Where does it hurt?"

"All over the damn place," he said through gritted teeth. "It's an old back injury."

"I knew I shouldn't have let you move that furniture for me. And I shouldn't have let you sleep on this porch."

"It was my own idea," he said, his teeth still clenched. "And I'm not a damned invalid. Like I told you, I fell off a bull once."

"We could be talking ruptured disk here. I need to get you over to the clinic for X rays. What I'd really like to do is a CAT—"

"I've already been through all that," he said brusquely. "Had it checked out years ago. Seems that tussle with a bull has left a legacy of severe chronic lower-back instability—only it comes and goes in spells. It'll be over soon. Real soon."

"Tim," she said, "you're a doctor. What do you think?"

At first he didn't answer as he crouched there awkwardly. But then he spoke. "All right. Just get me inside the house."

Laurie accomplished the next part as efficiently as possible. She woke a startled Alyson and brought her out to the porch. After a few terse instructions she had Alyson position herself on one side of Tim. Laurie took the other and gave her daughter further instructions.

"We have to move him very carefully. No jarring, no sudden motion of any kind. Picture yourself handling a crystal vase worth thousands of dollars. You can't possibly afford to drop it...."

Tim gave a groan. Maybe he didn't like her image or maybe he was just in pain. "I've been through this before, all right? It doesn't matter how you haul me in there. It's still gonna hurt."

Laurie ignored him. Together she and Alyson guided him cautiously through the doorway, supporting him so that he could almost glide along on his hands and knees. He was impressively solid and Laurie found herself straining just as she had yesterday moving furniture. But eventually she and Alyson were able to lift him and deposit him safely on the orange couch. More quick instructions and Alyson came scurrying over with pillows. Laurie tucked a few under Tim's knees, another under his head. Then she stood back to survey him.

The expression on his face conveyed his disgust with the entire situation. "I just need a few minutes," he said. "The two of you can leave."

"How bad is it?" Alyson asked.

"Bad enough," Laurie answered. "Apparently he fell off a bull and hasn't been the same since."

"I'm so sorry, Tim," Alyson said fervently. "What can I do to help?"

"Nothing, kid. You and your mother, just go about your business."

"This *is* my business," Laurie told him. "You're hurt, I'm the doctor. And I still think I should get you over to the clinic."

"Didn't you hear what I said? I've already been

through the whole damn routine—specialists, tests and more tests. This happens now and then. I get over it. I go on.''

Maybe the old saying was true—doctors made the worst patients. Laurie considered the options. Just down the hall was the bed where she'd slept the first night. But it was another relic left by Dr. Garrett, and it sagged deplorably. Tim couldn't climb the stairs, which left only one possibility.

"Very well," Laurie said, "you'll have to stay right where you are. If you won't go to the clinic, I certainly don't want you trying to move anywhere else.''

"I'll do whatever I damn well—''

"Dr. Miller," she said firmly, "what would you tell one of your own patients if they were curled up on a sofa suffering from severe chronic lower-back instability?''

"I'm not your patient, Dr. Russell.'' He scowled at her.

"As of about five minutes ago you are. You're going to stay there and do exactly as I tell you. Alyson, go find the heating pad. The ice pack, too. They're both in that linen closet upstairs.''

Alyson hovered for a second, gazing at Tim as if seeking confirmation.

"Alyson," Laurie said, knowing she spoke too sharply. But at last her daughter went hurrying upstairs. Laurie studied Tim again. He was wearing jeans and a denim shirt and wool socks with one toe worn almost all the way through. "Too bad you're not in something more comfortable," she said. "Sweats would be preferable.''

"I don't own sweats," he growled. "Now you're going to dress me?"

"I don't think we have to go that far," she said calmly.

"Makes you feel good, doesn't it, Dr. Russell? Having the upper hand and all."

"I hadn't thought of it that way. Do you really think I want you parked here in the middle of the living room?"

He looked more disgusted than ever. "It won't take me long to get through this."

"Right. A couple of days, maybe a week."

Clearly he wanted to argue, but he didn't. Alyson came down the stairs with the heating pad and the ice pack. Laurie plugged in the pad and slipped it under Tim's back—with no cooperation from him of course.

"We're going to alternate heat to relax the muscles and ice to reduce the swelling," she said. "Alyson, go make sure there's some ice in the freezer, will you? I remember seeing our trays somewhere."

Alyson hesitated one more time. "Mom," she said in a pained voice, "don't you think you should ask Tim what *he* wants?"

Since when were Tim Miller and her daughter on a first-name basis? "Alyson," Laurie repeated, "just see if there's ice in the freezer."

"Sure, kid," Tim muttered. "Ice. Sounds good."

Alyson went hurrying off again.

"You've missed your calling, Doc Russell," Tim said. "You should've been a drill sergeant."

Laurie cinched the belt of her robe a little tighter. "You'll be getting up only when absolutely necessary. In time you'll be allowed the occasional warm bath."

"Any other instructions?" Tim asked discontentedly.

"That's all for now."

"You have one helluva bedside manner, Doc."

It was what she had always liked about being a doctor—taking charge of a problem, figuring out ways to fix it. Admittedly with Tim Miller she'd come on a little stronger than usual. He affected her in ways she never quite expected.

The phone rang and she went to answer it.

"I have a patient here," Beth Thompson announced, "and no doctor. Now, you'd think with all the doctors running around this town, at least one of you could show up."

"I'm on my way, Bess." Laurie hung up and headed for the stairs.

"What was all that about?" Tim asked.

Laurie glanced back at him. "Seems we finally have someone needing our services. And since you're in no condition to do anything about it, looks like I'm going to do some real doctoring."

Tim started to lift himself up. She went and stood over him in menacing fashion.

"Tim, get real."

His head sank back on the pillow. "This really does make you happy, doesn't it?" he grumbled.

"Of course not. I don't like to see anybody suffer."

"I'm not suffering."

"I suppose it's part of the cowboy credo, not admitting when you're in pain."

All she got in return was another disgusted look. Alyson came wandering back into the room.

"I filled up the ice trays," she said.

"Good," Laurie answered as she went up the stairs. "I have to go to the clinic, but Dr. Miller should be set for a while."

"I'll look after him," Alyson said. "I'll get him anything he needs."

That was enough to stop Laurie in her tracks. "I really don't think you have to look after him."

"Well, you told him he couldn't move. We just can't *leave* him there. What if he needs something to eat or a book to read or—"

"I'll take care of everything before I leave."

"Mom, I *can* handle a little responsibility, you know."

"Alyson—"

"Ladies," Tim interrupted. "Number one, there's a patient waiting at the clinic. Number two, I don't need a nursemaid. Everybody satisfied now?"

Satisfied was the last thing Laurie felt. Her daughter was gazing raptly at Tim Miller and Laurie couldn't do a thing about it—she really did have to go see to that patient.

What a way to start her new life.

THE PATIENT TURNED OUT to be an uncooperative fifty-three-year-old woman with an itchy back. Laurie conducted a thorough examination, reviewed the woman's medical history, then began to ask what she felt were a few simple and pertinent questions.

"Have you changed your diet, Mrs. Patterson?"

"You think I'm fat?"

"How about your laundry detergent—any changes there?"

"Do my clothes look dirty?"

Laurie gave the woman her best bedside-manner smile. Mrs. Patterson sat there gripping her purse as if she expected Laurie to snatch it. The purse was a cheap vinyl. Mrs. Patterson's dress was outdated but didn't look as if it had been worn very often—perhaps she only dragged it out of the closet for such occasions as visits to the doctor.

Laurie jotted something down on her prescription pad, tore off the sheet and handed it to the woman.

"You have a slight rash, Mrs. Patterson. This cortisone cream should take care of the immediate problem. I'm also recommending a hypoallergenic soap."

Mrs. Patterson regarded the prescription with an air of suspicion. "Whenever I need any medicine, Dr. Garrett always calls the drugstore personally."

"If that would make you feel better, then of course I'll be happy—"

"I don't need to *feel* better. It's just the way he did things. I'm perfectly capable of taking a prescription to the drugstore myself."

Laurie's first patient in town, and already she was off to a bad start. "Why don't I just go ahead and call in the prescription for you?"

"I'll handle it myself."

Laurie controlled a grimace. "Very well, Mrs. Patterson," she said pleasantly. "Is there anything else I can do for you?"

The woman hesitated. "My husband is coming in next week," she said at last. "He has to have a physical for his job."

Laurie nodded, careful to appear noncommittal. She could tell Mrs. Patterson had something else on her mind.

"The point is, he's never gone to a female doctor before," she finally burst out.

Laurie gave a reassuring smile. "It will be just fine, Mrs. Patterson."

The woman looked very skeptical. "He's used to Dr. Garrett."

"We'll do everything we can to make your husband feel comfortable."

"Don't make him feel too comfortable," Mrs. Patterson said somewhat snippily.

Laurie revealed none of her frustration. "Female doctors are becoming more and more common."

"Not in this town they're not."

"As of now," Laurie said, "Grant has one female doctor. I'm sure it won't take too much getting used to."

"I'm not set in my ways," Mrs. Patterson said, "but far too many people in this town are. I think you should keep that in mind, Dr. Russell." With that she left the examining room.

Laurie closed the woman's patient chart with a smack. Then she sat down and stared at the jar of tongue depressors. It was true that all during medical school, the men had outnumbered the women. Same thing with her residency. But she'd rarely felt at a disadvantage because she was a woman. Her superiors had expected *all* students and residents to live up to impossible standards. Males and females had suffered alike, sharing a certain camaraderie as a result.

It had been a long time since Laurie had heard remarks like Mrs. Patterson's.

A few minutes later Bess poked her head in the door. "Coast is clear. She's gone."

Laurie hadn't meant to seem as if she was hiding. "She was harmless enough."

Bess raised her eyebrows. "Are we talking about the same person? The Shirley Patterson I know can't take a breath without causing a ruckus."

"I handled it," Laurie said.

"Indeed. I suppose that's why she informed me that she's changing her husband's appointment and having him drive all the way to Cortez for his physical."

Laurie gazed at the nurse in dismay. "We can't have patients doing that."

"I should hope not. But whatever you told her didn't seem to do the trick, Dr. Russell. She informed me in no uncertain terms that her husband is not going to wear his birthday suit in front of a female doctor."

"I don't believe it," Laurie muttered. "I just don't."

"Believe it." Bess didn't sound like she was commiserating. She didn't even sound like she was surprised at this turn of events. She sounded almost pleased. Laurie still didn't seem to be getting along at all with her staff nurse. Bess probably wanted to trot right over and show Tim some more photos of her grandson.

"I have a feeling the main reason that woman came in today was to check me out," Laurie said grimly. "Sort of an advance guard for her husband."

"Maybe she wanted to check out Tim. She had no

way of knowing he's temporarily out of commission." Bess seemed to be implying that Mrs. Patterson wouldn't have canceled her husband's appointment if Tim had been here.

"Any more patients?" Laurie asked briskly.

"No. But I did have two more cancellations."

"This is ridiculous," Laurie said. "People need medical care. They can't just refuse to come in for some idiotic reason."

"Is that what you told Shirley Patterson?" Bess asked. "That she was being idiotic?"

Laurie gave the nurse a repressive look. "I know how to keep my tongue, Bess."

Bess merely raised her eyebrows again. "I should hope so."

Laurie reflected that sooner or late she and Bess would have to come to some type of understanding. They'd have to learn to work together if nothing else. But then Laurie's thoughts strayed to Tim Miller—to the fact that he was spread out on her orange couch and that Alyson had appointed herself as his guardian. The problem was that Alyson didn't have anything to do yet in town—not anything structured. Her high school in Detroit had allowed her to graduate a month early so she could make this move to Colorado, but that meant she didn't even have studies to occupy her. Perhaps if Laurie went back to the house right now, she and her daughter could find something to do together. That was one of the main reasons Laurie had chosen a small-town practice. It would give her more time with her daughter.

"Seeing as there aren't any more patients—" Laurie began, but Bess interrupted her.

"When there aren't any patients around is a good time to go over the books. Unfortunately the clinic's finances are not all that they could be."

"I suppose this is your way of telling me Dr. Garrett didn't know how to handle money."

Bess stiffened. "I'm not saying that at all. I'm just suggesting that as long as you're here you should go over the bills with me. You should see exactly what you're up against."

Laurie understood the unspoken meaning: Bess thought she could discourage her by showing her the clinic's finances. Maybe Bess hoped Laurie would throw up her hands in despair and go off to find a more lucrative practice somewhere else.

Nothing doing. Laurie had taken this job with the full knowledge that it did not pay spectacularly well. But she'd believed that Grant was the place where she could finally make a real home, and she wasn't about to give up on that dream.

"Let's get to it then," she told Bess Thompson. "Bring on the books."

THE KID FINALLY WENT upstairs and gave Tim a reprieve. She'd been hovering for the past hour or so, asking if he wanted a drink of water or an aspirin or the newspaper to read or a blanket. And what about breakfast? She could make him pancakes or scrambled eggs and toast. Or how about waffles?

Tim, just to get some peace, had finally said yes to the scrambled eggs and toast. Alyson had brought him a carefully arranged plate, and his simple thank-you had seemed to please her inordinately. He figured her intentions were good, but all he wanted was a little peace and quiet to consider his predicament.

Now he lay on the orange sofa, cursing his back for betraying him. Most of the time he could go along not paying any attention to that old injury, and he was just fine. It was his bad luck to have this happen now.

He didn't like the thought of Laurie Russell's taking over the clinic today just because he was incapacitated. If he thought he could manage it, he'd get up and limp his way over there. But he wasn't stupid. He knew the quickest cure for him was to stay here flat on his back. Out of the action.

Laurie Russell was handling their first bona fide patient. And meanwhile he was stuck on a couch so bright and ludicrous he ought to be wearing sunglasses to protect his eyes.

He heard Alyson coming down the stairs and knew he wasn't to have much of a reprieve, after all. She came tiptoeing into the room as if she thought he'd gone to sleep.

"Are you okay, Tim?" she whispered.

"I'm fine," he repeated for the countless time that morning. And why the heck was she whispering?

She came closer and asked in a more normal voice, "Are you comfortable? Do you need an extra pillow or anything?"

"I'm fine," he said again. That didn't make her leave, though. She started wandering around.

"This house is kind of pathetic, don't you think?"

No, he hadn't given it any thought. "It's just an old house," he said.

She came to perch on the other sofa across from him. "This place is my mother's idea of the perfect home. Drafty rooms, creaky floors, cracks in the ceiling. If it was up to me, I'd choose something a lot different."

A pause. Tim knew what he was supposed to say next. He resisted, but Alyson looked so hopeful he finally gave in.

"What kind of place would you choose?"

"I'd live next to the ocean somewhere," was her prompt answer. "One of those Cape Cod-type houses. Not too big, not too small."

"Hmm…Cape Cod," Tim said unenthusiastically. The conversation languished, but then Alyson startled him.

"I wanted to ask you something," she said, glancing away from him. "Mainly…if you could just tell me…if someone—a girl—wanted to get a guy interested, how would she do it?"

Lord, the kid wanted advice from him. "I think that's the kind of thing you should ask your mother," he said gruffly.

"Not likely. Mom has only one word to say when it comes to the opposite sex, and that is 'don't.' Don't count on a man. Don't trust a man. Don't let a man into your heart."

It didn't seem like the smartest idea, finding out details of Laurie Russell's private life. Then again, Tim was something of a captive audience.

Alyson went on, still looking away from him. "You see, my dad walked out on us before I was born. And after that…well, okay, there hasn't been anyone who'd stick around. But it doesn't make it easy to talk to her about…certain things."

"I'm no expert myself," Tim said.

"But you're a *guy*. And if you could just tell me— Oh, hell, forget it."

Something about the misery in the kid's voice got to him. Right now she looked a lot younger than seventeen.

"Is it anyone in particular?" he asked casually.

She gave a shrug that didn't quite come off. "There's a guy I saw yesterday... I haven't even talked to him yet. But that's the whole point, you know? If I could just *get* him to talk to me..." Her voice trailed away uncertainly.

Tim thought about it. "All I can tell you is—be cool."

Alyson nodded. "Be cool," she repeated.

"That's right."

"Okay," she said, but then she shook her head. "No, it's not okay. What does it actually mean—be cool?"

Not only did the kid want advice, she wanted specifics. "Look at it this way," he said. "Just be yourself. Be relaxed. And don't be too ready to please anyone. Especially not a guy. If he gets a chance to talk to you, it's his privilege—not yours."

Alyson nodded, but she still appeared uncertain. She got up from the sofa and started to leave the room. Then she turned back.

"This blouse—is it cool?" she asked.

Now the kid wanted him to be a fashion consultant. "You look fine," he said.

"You keep saying things are *fine*. That's getting to be a pretty meaningless word."

By now Tim was starting to feel sorry for anyone who happened to be a parent. "Being cool is not about what you wear," he said. "Being cool is an attitude."

"Sure," Alyson muttered, and went back upstairs. At least Tim had finally succeeded at something—he'd managed to drive the kid away.

So much for advice to the teenage generation.

CHAPTER FIVE

IT TURNED OUT to be the middle of the afternoon before Laurie could get away from Bess's grim tour of the clinic's books. She let herself into the house and found Tim Miller right where he was supposed to be—on her couch. He was also fast asleep.

Laurie stood in the doorway to the living room, gazing at him. He was frowning in his sleep and snoring just the slightest bit. She saw his foot twitch as if he might be "wrassling" a bull in his dreams. She wanted to retreat. To be looking at him like this, without his knowing, seemed to give her an unfair advantage. But there was nothing defenseless about him. He was all too handsome as he lay stretched out there. All too male.

At last Laurie did start to back away. The floor creaked under her feet. Tim moved restlessly and opened his eyes. Those incredible blue eyes...

"Hello," Laurie said awkwardly. "I didn't mean to wake you."

"I didn't mean to fall asleep." Apparently his mood hadn't improved any.

She stepped into the room. "Where's Alyson?"

"Out walking. I think she finally decided she's not cut out to be a nurse." He did seem relieved about that.

She checked the heating pad. It was turned off and there was no evidence of the ice pack. "You were supposed to alternate heat and cold."

"None of that makes any difference with my back. It's gonna run its course—one way or another."

She felt annoyed. "It's pretty elementary stuff, I'll admit, heating pads and ice. But sometimes it helps."

"Not with me," he grumbled.

Laurie reminded herself that doctors made the worst patients. Why take it personally? She fished a bottle from her skirt pocket, shook out a pill and handed it to Tim with the glass of water from the coffee table. "Muscle relaxants," she said, "ordered up fresh from Grant's state-of-the-art drugstore."

Tim, apparently, chose to ignore the irony in her voice. "Don't need 'em," he said.

"How could I forget? You're into being the strong tough male who doesn't mind a little pain. Make that a lot of pain."

"It doesn't hurt that much," he muttered.

"Tim," she said, "what do *you* tell a patient who won't take a medicine that's perfectly reasonable and that'll help him get better?"

He gave her a baleful glance, but ended up swallowing the pill. Laurie sat down on the shabby sofa across from him and leaned her head back. She felt a tiredness creep over her and knew it was a combination of circumstances—all the arrangements for moving, the long drive from Detroit, not being able to get a good night's sleep since. But being tired was nothing new to her, not after a residency where logging a hundred hours a week was the usual.

"Rough day at the office?" Tim said gravely.

"Actually, yes," she admitted. "I've had twenty-hour days at the hospital that ended up feeling easier than this one. Bess made certain I knew about every single financial difficulty the practice has had in the past forty years. Then the patients... The first one was Shirley Patterson, who's convinced she can't trust her husband with a female doctor. And three or four others called to talk to Bess and check me out. Bess had the audacity to say that, yes, I was a pretty young thing."

"It's a small town," Tim reminded her. "A lot like the one where I grew up, as a matter of fact. And besides, you are, you know, young and pretty."

"New Mexico," she said, purposefully ignoring his remark. "That's where you're from, isn't it?"

She saw a certain look cross his face, a reticence, a closing in. Yet he spoke easily enough. "Stillwell, New Mexico," he said. "My hometown. Nothin' to do but get into trouble, and I sure managed that. Of course, I spent some time in Texas and Arizona along the way."

"I'm sure you caused trouble there, too."

"As much as I could."

Laurie straightened. When it came to Tim Miller she felt an undeniable curiosity. At the moment she couldn't resist it. "What made you decide to become a doctor?" she asked. "And this time don't tell me about following in your father's footsteps or your brother's, because I won't believe it."

"You think I have some deep underlying motivation?"

The mockery in his voice didn't faze her. "Yes," she said simply, "I do."

Tim didn't answer for a long moment, and when he frowned he seemed to be undergoing some battle with himself. At last he glanced at Laurie again.

"I'll tell you something," he said quietly, "that I've only told one other person in my life. I wanted to be a doctor ever since I was a kid. At first it had a whole lot to do with being like my dad. I looked up to him. I thought he was the smartest person around. But afterward...it started to seem important to be exactly the opposite of him. The opposite of my brother, too. And that meant giving up the dream I'd had since I was a boy. Both Gabe and my father were doctors, so I had to try being something else. Anything else."

All of a sudden Laurie didn't feel tired anymore. She'd listened intently to every word Tim said and knew there was still a whole lot he *wasn't* saying. And once again, that annoying curiosity got the better of her.

"Who's the other person?" she asked.

"What?" He sounded distracted, as if his own thoughts had already moved on.

"You said there was only one other person you'd told. And I just wondered...who it was." She felt foolish for asking, but as usual around Tim Miller, she ended up doing unexpected things.

He smiled slightly. "My sister-in-law, Hallie. She's the one I told. That was back *before* she became my sister-in-law. When she was just the prettiest thing in town."

"Oh." Laurie felt a new unaccountable sensation—a flicker of jealousy? She had the horrible suspicion it showed on her face. "Well, nothing wrong with keeping things in the family," she said inanely.

"My brother, Gabe, didn't seem to think so. He didn't like me proposin' to Hallie, right along the same time *he* proposed."

Laurie stared at Tim. "You wanted to marry her? You were in love..."

His smile broadened. "Only a little bit in love, I guess. That's the best way to do it—never fall all the way."

Laurie stood. "This has all been highly entertaining, but I'm sure we both have better things to do—"

"Not me, Doc. I'm kind of stuck here for the time being."

She felt more foolish than ever. For a minute or two she'd actually forgotten about Tim's back problem. Such was the man's presence that he could sprawl there on her couch and still seem to command the entire room.

"Do you need anything else?" she asked in her most professional voice.

"That pill is already doin' its job. Or maybe it's just that your couch is so comfortable."

"I told you I bought it for a good reason. How about something to eat?"

"No, thanks."

She gave him a sharp look. "You're hungry, aren't you?"

"I don't like bein' waited on, Doc Russell."

She went to the kitchen where she quickly prepared two turkey-breast sandwiches. She set both of them on a plate, added some potato chips and took them out to the living room.

Tim eyed the plate. "All that's for me?"

"Are you complaining?" she asked dryly. She set the plate down on the coffee table. As she straightened, Tim reached out and caught hold of her hand. Her first instinct was to pull away, but oddly she didn't obey it. She merely ended up standing there, her fingers captured in his warm grasp.

"Tim—"

"I just wanted to say…thanks. For the sandwiches. And the use of the couch."

She observed him closely. "Maybe that muscle relaxant really is doing its job. You sound almost too mellow."

"That's me. Mellow." The devil-may-care attitude was back. He tugged her gently, ever so gently, enough to make her off balance. She ended up sitting on the very edge of the couch beside him, her hand still cradled in his.

"Tim, what are you do—"

"I told you. I'm thanking you."

She looked right into his eyes, and for a second or two she couldn't seem to remember what she'd wanted to say.

"Tim…"

His own eyes lingered on her, and she could tell what he was thinking about as plainly as if he'd said it. His gaze seemed to trace the outline of her lips, a look that was the next thing to a touch.

"Dammit," she said. She slid away from him. "Next time you say thank-you, you don't need to go so…overboard."

Disappointment flickered across his face. "We were just gettin' started, Doc Russell."

"No, Tim" she murmured. "We weren't starting anything."

ALYSON KNEW she'd made a colossal ass of herself with Tim this morning. All the stupid things she'd told him—how she wanted a house someday on Cape Cod. Worst of all, though, she'd told him about the blond guy, Kevin Nichols. Maybe she hadn't mentioned Kevin by name, but she'd admitted wanting to get his attention. She'd made herself sound like such an idiot asking for pointers from Tim. He'd probably think she'd never even been on a date.

In Detroit, though, she'd had a few boyfriends—technically at least. She'd dated one guy for almost six months, even though nothing much had come of it. She hadn't been in love, not even close. There had been a lot of kissing, a few fumbled gropings. Innocent stuff, but it probably would have made Mom go ballistic if she'd ever known about it. Alyson had just made sure her mother didn't know.

Now she wandered aimlessly along Main Street staring into the dusty windows of the storefronts. This whole town felt like it had been hibernating for the winter and was barely starting to wake up. At one souvenir store the windows had actually been washed, and she caught sight of her reflection: ordinary face, ordinary brown hair that hung too long and limp. The blouse she wore had to be all wrong, too. It was too sweet, a flower print with lace at the collar. She'd bought it a few months ago on a shopping expedition with her mother, and at the time it had seemed like something special. For once she and Mom had splurged, accumulating three shopping bags full and then eating lunch together at a nice restaurant. Days like that hadn't happened very often, not with Mom always at the hospital. Even though they'd had a good time, Mom had looked exhausted that afternoon, and she'd fallen asleep as soon as they'd arrived back home at their apartment.

For quite a while Alyson had privately questioned her mother's devotion to her career. It didn't seem like really living—grinding away hour after hour at a big depressing hospital, surrounded by sick people. But the move to this nothing little town didn't seem like living, either. So far, only two things of interest had happened. Tim Miller had ended up in the middle of their living room, and she'd seen a blond guy she very much wanted to see again.

Alyson crossed the street and walked back down the other side. She wished she didn't feel so confused. Tim Miller made her feel a way she couldn't explain. He *was* just about the most gorgeous hunk she'd ever known, but he was also…old. Her mother had been right about that. As far as the blond guy, Kevin Nichols, Alyson knew he was out of her league. Guys like that could afford to pick and choose.

Alyson glanced up and saw she was passing the diner. From inside, the waitress waved to her. She gave a quick embarrassed wave in return and hurried on. The woman probably thought Alyson spent all her time wandering up and down this street. Unfortunately she was right. But where else was there to go? What else was there to *do*?

She began crossing to the other side of the street again and that was when she saw him—the blond guy. He'd just come out of one of the stores dragging a ladder with him. He propped the ladder against the brick wall and climbed it until he could reach a faded sign that read Nichols Jeep Tours.

Alyson wanted to run and duck for cover, but she remembered Tim's advice: be cool. Her mouth suddenly dry, she forced herself to cross the rest of the way. She also forced herself to walk slowly along until she came even with the ladder. She glanced up as casually as she dared. Kevin Nichols glanced down at her.

"Hi," he said.

For some reason no words would come out of her mouth. She just stood there and gazed up at him. Even from this angle, he looked good—the dark blond hair falling almost to his shoulders, the T-shirt stretching across his muscled back. Alyson tried to remember what else Tim had told her. Something about being relaxed and not trying to please anyone. But Alyson didn't know how to translate that into anything useful, anything concrete. All she could do was stare up at Kevin Nichols, behaving like an idiot all over again.

He came down the ladder. "What do you think of the sign?" he asked conversationally.

At last Alyson found her voice. "Uh...I like it. Nichols Jeep Tours," she mumbled.

"It's no good," he said. "It needs to be flashier, something that grabs attention."

That was exactly how Alyson felt about herself. "Is that what you do—you give Jeep tours?" she asked.

"Once the tourist season hits, I have almost more business than I can handle. There are trails all over these mountains and I know every one of them."

"It sounds really interesting," Alyson told him,

wondering why she couldn't think of anything intelligent to say. She searched her mind. "If you have enough business, you don't really need a new sign, do you?" *Brilliant, Alyson. Just brilliant.*

"I don't like to stand still. I'm expanding, should even be able to hire a few employees this year. Don't you think the sign should reflect that?"

"I guess. I mean...sure." There was a pause. Kevin Nichols stepped out into the street and looked at his sign from there. He almost seemed to have forgotten Alyson.

"I just moved to town," she said.

"No kidding. Good for you."

"It doesn't seem like there's a whole lot to do around here," she said after another pause.

"You're just not looking, then. These mountains are full of things to do. They're something special."

"Really?" Another scintillating contribution.

"Really," he said. "I know a lot of people think this town is a drag, but I've never been one of them. I've seen my friends leave for Denver or out of state, and they all have the wrong idea. You just have to get into the mountains. After that, you never want to leave."

Alyson was caught by the tone of his voice. He made the Rockies sound like something alive, something exciting.

"Well," Alyson said, her own voice coming out in a little bit of a croak. But she went on, impelled by some new boldness. "Maybe you could take me on a tour sometime...show me the mountains."

"Sure. Tell your parents about me. I give family

discounts." He went back to his ladder and climbed it again.

Alyson stood there, her skin flaming in humiliation. He'd mentioned parents. He'd mentioned families. You only brought up things like that when you thought you were talking to a kid. She was almost eighteen! What was wrong with her that both Tim and Kevin Nichols treated her as if she hadn't passed puberty yet?

She didn't even bother to say goodbye. She just went on down the street, very careful not to look back at him. But once more she caught sight of her reflection in a window and saw that too-sweet blouse with its lace collar and its flower print.

She was never going to wear this blouse again.

Tim was beginning to feel like a prisoner without any hope of parole. It was only the start of his second day on the orange couch, but it felt more like a year. The problem was, he'd spent his whole life immersed in physical activities. Ranching off and on, training horses for a while there, being a general roustabout at any number of occupations. It had always been something where he'd had to dig in, use every muscle, test his body to the limits. He'd liked doing that. Even when he'd finally given in to his boyhood dream and opted for medicine, he'd relished the physical nature of much of the job. But here he was now, flat on his back, motionless except for the occasional trek to the bathroom, and there wasn't a thing he could do about it. Simple monotonous rest was the only thing that had ever unkinked his back. There were times when you couldn't fight your own body.

He frowned at the accoutrements building up on the coffee table: his toothbrush in a glass, a stack of books and magazines, the telephone extension, the remote control to Laurie's TV set. Yesterday he'd even succumbed to watching golf on TV. Who knew what he'd give in to today.

He heard her coming down the stairs—Laurie. He felt that quickening of pleasurable anticipation only she could evoke in him. And here she was, coming briskly into the living room, looking more beautiful than ever. More desirable than ever, if he was going to be honest. It had something to do with the hint of unruliness in her dark hair, as if it would go its own way even after she brushed it. Not to mention the dark brown of her eyes, a brown so deep you wanted to linger and learn a whole lot more about it. There was also the stubbornness that never quite seemed to leave her features, and the slim curves revealed by the soft material of her shirt. Cataloging Laurie Russell's attributes was one of the hazards of his current situation. He didn't have a whole lot else to occupy his mind.

"Good morning," she said, and then the inevitable question. "Where's Alyson?"

"Gone already," he informed her.

"But it's so early. I had plans for the two of us—" Laurie caught herself, glancing away as if she didn't want Tim to see her disappointment.

"Maybe Alyson's out making friends," he said. He wondered what the proper social etiquette was in this situation. A seventeen-year-old girl tells you she's interested in getting some guy's attention. Do you turn around and tell the girl's mother as much? It took

Tim only a few seconds to decide it wouldn't be such a good idea. He didn't want to be in the middle of any problems between Laurie and her daughter.

"I know she misses her friends in Detroit," Laurie murmured. "I know there are a lot of things she misses. But this move just seemed the right thing to do…"

For the first time he heard a trace of uncertainty in her voice about coming to Grant. "Second thoughts, Doc Russell?" he asked.

She looked at him full on, and he saw it—the flash of competitiveness. "Not on your life, Dr. Miller. I'm going to make this job my own."

"Busy day ahead?" he asked. He could see her trying to appear unconcerned.

"No appointments this morning, but I'm not surprised anymore. People are still uncertain how to handle this…situation."

"The too-many-doctors situation," he elaborated.

"I intend to speak to the members of the town council again. This morning would be as good a time as any."

"Right," Tim said. "See if you can get those folks organized. I hear Jason Cramer is still ticked off at everybody else on the council, and nobody can convince him to come back."

She gave Tim a look of exasperation. "How do *you* know so much? You've just been lying here."

He gestured toward the phone on the coffee table. "Don't forget, I have my connections. Bess keeps me informed about what's going on around town."

"Wonderful," she muttered. "Well, I'll get your breakfast." She headed off to the kitchen. This was the part he disliked the most, having somebody wait on him. It made him feel more like an invalid than ever. But again he didn't seem to have any choice.

A short while later Laurie brought in a tray—a cup of fresh coffee, toast, a bowl of cereal with a glass of milk to the side.

"Thanks," Tim said unenthusiastically.

"Maybe Alyson's right and what you really want is waffles."

"There's nothing wrong with the food," he said. "It's just that I've never obliged a woman to look after me. I've always shifted for myself."

She set down the tray, not seeming impressed by this revelation. "I'm sure you've kept women occupied in plenty of other ways," she said, and then flushed. "I didn't mean that the way it sounded," she added hurriedly.

Tim watched the appealing color spread over her skin. "Doc Russell, I haven't had a lady friend in quite some while."

"Like I believe that. Not that it's any of my concern."

"If you sit down, I'll tell you about it." He patted the couch beside him. The thing was such a monster, there was plenty of room.

"No thanks," she said. "I really have to be going."

He nodded. "All those patients waiting." But then he took hold of her hand just as he had yesterday and drew her down beside him. She perched awkwardly on the edge of the couch.

"Dammit, Tim—"

"I just want to set you straight," he murmured.

"You seem to have the wrong idea about me. It's been a long time since I've been...close to anyone." Maybe he was saying more than he should. But he liked the feel of Laurie's hand in his. And he liked her nearness. He liked it a lot.

"So you're going to tell me there haven't been many women," she said skeptically.

"There've been women," he admitted. "But not anybody special."

"What about your sister-in-law—Hallie?" She seemed to regret the words as soon as she said them, her fingers moving restlessly in his. But he held on to her. His feelings about Hallie were a little complicated. He didn't know quite how to go into them.

"Hallie wasn't meant for me," he said at last. "She was meant for Gabe."

Laurie looked dissatisfied. "Like I say, it's no concern of mine."

He tried to think of a way to keep her here beside him a few more minutes. "Doc Russell, maybe you're going to tell me there haven't been many men."

"I'm not going to tell you anything."

"I'm a good listener," he said.

"What you are is bored. You're sick and tired of being on this couch and you're looking for any diversion."

"So...there've been lots of men?"

"A few. That's all."

His gaze traveled over the curve of her cheek. Suddenly he didn't want to know about anyone else in her life. He'd started this conversation almost as a game—yes, even as a diversion, as she'd accused. But now he felt something else, something darker and deeper running in a current between them.

"Don't think about it," he murmured.

"About what?"

"Whatever's making you sad right now."

"Sad? I'm not sad in the least..."

But he had seen it, the shadow in her eyes, as if she'd remembered something. He wanted to erase that shadow for her, but what made him think he had the power?

"I'd kiss you," he said, "if I could reach you."

She stared at him. "Tim, do you ever stop—"

"Care to help me out?"

She just went on staring at him. Her lips parted slightly, as if she meant to tell him exactly what he could do about his kiss. But she ended up not saying anything after all. If possible, her eyes darkened. Her breath seemed to rise and fall unsteadily. And then, ever so slowly, she bent her head toward his. A silky strand of her hair brushed his cheek. Her lips came so close to his he could feel her breath. He could tell she used a minty toothpaste, and he smiled at the thought.

It had been the wrong thing to do, that smile. Laurie pulled back instantly. "I can't believe it," she said. "I can't believe I almost— Tim, just eat your damn breakfast!" She jumped up from the couch and left him. And all he knew was an unexpected unwelcome sense of loss.

CHAPTER SIX

FOUR HOURS after she'd almost kissed Tim Miller, Laurie was still worked up about it. No matter what she did, she couldn't seem to get the incident into proper perspective. This morning she'd tried to stay busy by trekking around to meet with different members of the town council. But she'd only reaffirmed the fact that the council, at this particular time, could not seem to agree on anything—least of all on how to solve the two-doctor situation. Which left Laurie contemplating the other doctor in town and how she'd so very nearly brought her lips to his....

"For crying out loud," she muttered as she stood in the middle of Corinne's Classics, Grant's one somewhat upscale clothing boutique. The saleswoman immediately came up to her.

"I beg your pardon?" she asked.

"Just arguing with myself," Laurie said, her attempt at humor not quite coming off. The saleswoman gave her a considering look, and Laurie could just imagine the rumor that would start flying around town: lady doctor caught talking to herself in local store. That would do wonders for her already precarious position. She blamed Tim Miller. She wouldn't be talking to herself if it wasn't for him.

"Actually," she told the saleswoman, "I'm looking for a birthday present for my daughter. She'll be turning eighteen very soon, and I need just the right thing.''

The saleswoman became the soul of efficiency. ''We've just had in a new shipment of camisole dresses. They're the rage with girls her age.'' She led Laurie over to a rack of pretty but flimsy dresses. Laurie surveyed them doubtfully.

''I'll think about it,'' she said. ''I'm just not sure this is her style.''

''We do keep up with the fashions here,'' the saleswoman said a bit stiffly before going off to wait on another customer. Oh, wonderful. Laurie could envision another rumor—snobbish lady doctor implies that Grant is behind the times.

Laurie left, thanking the saleswoman, who nodded coolly. Laurie didn't think it was her imagination; wherever she went in Grant, the townspeople seemed to treat her with a combination of skepticism and curiosity. Maybe it would just take them a little time to get used to her. Somehow the thought didn't cheer her up, and she flashed again on the image of Tim Miller sprawled on her couch. Then the image of herself, leaning toward him....

She'd been a fool to give in to his charm that way. She'd seen the amusement in his eyes. Yet, despite that, she'd wanted to kiss him. She'd wanted to quite badly. And standing here on Main Street, she still wanted to.

''Stop,'' Laurie whispered. Damn. This habit of talking to herself about Tim seemed to be getting worse. If only she had something else to occupy her mind. She glanced down at the beeper attached to her belt, willing it to go off and inform her that patients were lining up to see her at the clinic. But Bess Thompson hadn't beeped Laurie all morning. There was no reason to think she'd start doing so now.

Laurie walked down the street as if motion alone would give her a sense of purpose. Was this how Alyson felt, on the long rambles she seemed to be taking? Perhaps she believed if she kept moving, eventually she'd reach a solution to whatever bothered her. And now the too-familiar refrain haunted Laurie: if only her daughter would confide in her...

An elderly man was walking along the sidewalk toward her. He gave Laurie an appraising look as he drew even with her. "So," he said. "You're Dr. Laurie Russell." He held out his hand. "I'm Jonathan Garrett. I've been wondering when I'd meet up with you."

The elusive Doc Garrett himself. Laurie shook his hand and gave him an appraising look of her own. He was a rather untidy man in baggy pants and a jacket with frayed elbows, yet he was somehow very attractive. That he was almost completely bald and a bit rotund did nothing to detract from that.

"Dr. Garrett," she said, "I've been hoping to talk to you, but you're a hard person to locate."

He waved a hand dismissively. "I know, I know, everyone says I'm spending all my time in Digby doing who knows what."

Laurie remained diplomatically silent about the Estelle rumors. "If I could just set up a time to meet with you, I'm sure we could straighten out some misunderstandings."

"You think if we talk, you'll convince me to retract

my offer to Tim Miller and you can take over my practice?''

It was a straightforward question, maybe even brusque, but it didn't seem to diminish Dr. Garrett's agreeable manner. Maybe it was because he spoke without rancor. He gave the impression that his thoughts really *were* in Digby with the scandalous Estelle.

"I just want to make sure everyone's side is heard," Laurie began.

"Forget the b.s., Dr. Russell. You want the job, and it ticks you off that I've already offered it to Tim."

Straightforward, indeed. "That sums it up," she admitted. "I accepted the council's offer in good faith and—"

"Hell, if we're going to talk about the town council, I can't do it on an empty stomach. I'm on my way to lunch." He continued walking down the street. Laurie stayed where she was for a moment, then turned and caught up with him.

"Dr. Garrett, are you always this direct, or is it just me?"

He surprised her with a chuckle. "Dr. Russell, I've alienated half this town over the years. And the other half still can't decide about me."

"Not according to what *I* hear," she said. "Apparently no one can accept the fact that you're retiring."

"Welcome to Grant. They bitch and complain about you until they find out you're leaving. Then they bitch and complain about whoever's coming after." The doctor disappeared into the diner. Laurie didn't wait for an invitation; she was right on his heels. He went to a booth toward the back, giving the impression he'd headed for that very same booth countless times in the past. Laurie slid into the seat across from him just as the waitress came over.

"We're all out of sesame-seed buns, Doc."

"Just bring me the lousy hamburger, Susan."

The waitress stood poised beside Laurie with her pad and pencil, no apparent expression of interest on her face. That was a relief; for once, someone in Grant didn't seem to care about Laurie one way or another.

"I'll have the chef's salad," Laurie said.

"Suit yourself," the waitress answered cryptically, making Laurie wonder if she'd made a mistake. She glanced at Dr. Garrett, who seemed to understand her unspoken question.

"Anything you order is at your own risk," he told her.

"Hah," said the waitress. "Tell that to Joe."

"I've complained to Joe about his cooking plenty of times. He knows where I stand."

The waitress started to leave, then spoke to Laurie again. "That kid of yours is a little glum, if you ask me. Cute, but glum."

So much for disinterest. Laurie watched the woman saunter away and wondered how much time her daughter had spent in this place—a down-at-the-heels diner. Alyson obviously needed some diversions, and soon.

"Don't mind Susan," said the doc. "I never do."

Laurie creased a paper napkin, then set it down.

"Dr. Garrett, I sure wish you could explain how this town ended up with two doctors for your practice. Everybody seems to know everybody else's business. So how on earth—"

"The point is, Dr. Russell, not everybody knows *my* business. They may think they know all about me and Estelle, but...anyway, that's another story. When I decided to hire my replacement, I figured it wasn't Phil Cline's affair or anybody else's damn affair. Enough said."

Laurie tapped her fingers on the table. There was a whole lot more she wanted to say, but the food arrived with amazing promptness. The chef's salad looked only a little wilted, but otherwise suitable for consumption. Dr. Garrett's hamburger arrived on a plain bun, pickles on the side.

The doc went a few rounds with a half-empty catsup bottle.

"I'll tell you something about Tim Miller," he said. "He's so talented he could've had any job he wanted. He even received an offer from the Jacobs Institute."

"Really," Laurie murmured. The Jacobs Institute was one of the most prestigious research organizations in the country. Tim *had* to be talented if they'd considered him.

"Okay, I'm impressed," she said reluctantly. "But if Tim is in that league, what's he doing here?"

"He belongs here," the doc said emphatically. No longer did he give the impression that his thoughts were elsewhere. He seemed completely serious and completely intent. "There's a lot of good that can be

done in a small-town practice, and Tim's the one to
do it. I never had children of my own, Dr. Russell,
and I guess you could say I've always imagined myself with a son like Tim. I want him to carry on for
me. Him and no one else. The town council never
should've gone behind my back like they did. It's just
too bad you got caught up in the mess. But you can
see why Tim's the one who has to stay.''

The force of his words silenced Laurie for a moment. How could you argue with someone who saw
his practice as a legacy and who wanted to leave it
to the man he considered almost his own son?

But Laurie had good reasons for staying, too.
"Look," she finally said, "I packed up my entire life
to come here. Maybe Grant isn't perfect, but something tells me it's the place my daughter and I can
finally put down roots. I won't give that up."

Dr. Garrett already seemed to be focusing on his
own thoughts again. "Suit yourself, Dr. Russell. I figure Tim can handle you. I'm going to eat up and get
out of here. Digby is sounding mighty good right
about now."

Laurie pushed her salad away. She'd been holding
out the hope that Dr. Garrett would somehow be reasonable and use his authority in town to settle things.
But clearly he was going to retreat from the fracas.

"If Tim can handle me, I can handle *him*," she
muttered, staring out the window. And that was when
she saw her daughter standing across the street. Laurie
slid out of the booth and walked toward the front of
the diner. She was just about to open the door and
call a greeting when she realized that Alyson was

speaking to someone—a young man. She seemed to be gazing at him earnestly as she talked.

The waitress, Susan, came up beside Laurie and gazed out the window too.

"What do you know," she said. "That daughter of yours seems to be latching on to Kevin Nichols. But if I were you, I'd try to keep her away from him. That one's bad news."

A SHORT WHILE LATER, Laurie arrived back home. It had taken all her willpower not to go across the street from the diner and introduce herself to Kevin Nichols. She'd wanted to let him know that Alyson had a mother watching out for her. But Laurie's instincts had warned her what a mistake that would be—humiliating her daughter in public. So she'd stayed where she was, watching as Alyson finished talking to the young man and then wandered off on her own. Alyson, always on the move these days, trying to escape from...what? Perhaps the knowledge that she'd never had a real father? After all this time, was that what troubled her?

Laurie stood on the porch of the house, feeling the stir of an old long-buried guilt. Over the years she'd been so careful about explaining things to Alyson, telling her that her father's abandonment was never a reflection on *her*. Why, she hadn't even been born when he'd left. But there were certain facts that Laurie had glossed over to protect her daughter. In a strictly technical sense she hadn't been entirely truthful with Alyson. Had there been any other choice, though? She'd always put Alyson's well-being first—nothing else mattered.

Sighing, Laurie let herself into the house. Her first stop was the living room, where she expected to confront Tim. But the orange couch was empty. What made Tim think he was in any condition to get up?

"Tim," she called as she went down the hall. "Tim, where the heck are you?"

"In here," came his disgruntled voice from behind the bathroom door. "I'm taking a bath, all right? Thought it was allowed."

She stood outside the door. "I didn't mean you should try it on your own. You should have waited until I was around."

"You were going to help me into the tub, that it?"

"Yes."

"Laurie, if you don't mind, I'll take the damn bath on my own."

She stood outside the door another minute or two, then retreated into the living room again. One of the pillows on the couch still bore the imprint of Tim's head, and the blanket looked as if it had been tossed impatiently to one side. It was going to be quite a job keeping Tim down as long as he needed to be. She straightened a few of the items on the coffee table but had no idea what to do next. In Detroit every minute of every day had been accounted for. She'd been so rushed at the hospital she'd scarcely had time to think. She'd longed for the day when she'd have her own practice and a little breathing space. Well, now she had both—almost. And her life suddenly seemed much too open-ended and uncertain.

There was one thing she could do. She could have a decent lunch after having had only those few bites of chef's salad. She went to the kitchen and opened a can of black-bean chili. While it was heating on the stove, she went down the hall and paused in front of the bathroom door.

"Okay in there?" she asked.

"Fine," Tim grumbled.

"I'm having chili for lunch."

"Enjoy."

"Tim, I'm asking if you'd like some."

"No, thanks. It took me long enough to get into this tub. I'm staying."

She gazed at the closed door. "I hope you were careful."

"I'm still in one piece," he said.

There didn't seem to be any other choice than to go back to the kitchen and eat her chili. Afterward she washed her bowl and then sat at the table. Surely there had to be something she could do to get her life on track, some way to rout Dr. Timothy Miller. She began formulating a vague idea about drawing up a petition...but who would she petition? The town council, in its current stage of bickering chaos? The citizens of Grant, who regarded her with obvious distrust? Dr. Garrett, who had already anointed Tim his heir?

"Laurie!" Tim bellowed from down the hall. She was at the bathroom door seconds later.

"I'm right here," she said. Silence greeted this announcement. "Tim, are you all right?"

"I'm stuck," he said at last, sounding more disgruntled than ever. "I can't get out of the damn tub."

"I'm coming in. Don't worry, I won't look."

"Doc Russell, you could take a dozen photos right now, for all I care. I just want to get out of here."

She turned the knob and it wouldn't budge. "Tim, I don't believe it. Not only did you try to take a bath on your own, but you locked the door?"

"What did you expect? I'm in a house full of females." He sounded beleaguered.

She leaned down and examined the knob. Fortunately someone had replaced the hardware not too long ago; the cheap modern type was always easier to jimmy. "Okay, I'll be right back," she said. After a visit to the coat closet, she had a wire hanger in hand. She unbent it and jabbed it through the small hole in the center of the knob. She heard the lock click free and then opened the door just a crack.

"I'm coming in," she warned.

"Resourceful, aren't you," he muttered.

"You could, you know, drape a washcloth over yourself or something."

"Laurie, let's just get this over with."

She didn't know why she was hesitating. In her line of work she'd seen countless males in various stages of undress. She'd managed it just fine. At last she stepped all the way into the warm steamy bathroom.

Immediately she saw the problem. The tub had never been replaced by the cheap modern variety. It was vintage, with claw feet and high curved sides. In his condition, Tim would most certainly find it difficult to climb out on his own.

He sat there, glaring at her. Without any volition of her own, her gaze seemed to linger on his chest, where russet hair curled damply.

"I'll have you out of there in no time," she said. "I'm going to support you from behind, and then you can use this." She grabbed a towel and held it up.

"Do you really think I'm worried about modesty?"

Why did her heart have to beat so uncomfortably? With anyone else she could have behaved in a completely professional manner. Keeping her eyes on neutral objects only—the sink, the medicine chest, the old maple washstand—she came around behind the tub.

"All right," she said, "I'm going to be holding on to you and I want you just to slide upward." She bent down, brought her arms around his chest. This meant her cheek was pressed right next to his, but finally the doctor in her seemed to be taking over. She concentrated only on the task to be accomplished. Tim anchored his hands along the top of the bathtub for support, and oh, so carefully she eased him upward. She felt him strain and took more of his weight upon herself. They worked together and soon had him in a sort of crouching stand. And then Laurie, despite all her promises, did take one quick look. She couldn't help herself. She caught just a glimpse of a well-shaped masculine posterior before she hastily threw the towel over him. After that it was back to business again. She held on to Tim as he lifted first one leg and then the other out of the tub. She could tell from his grimace that the effort cost him.

"It was too soon for a bath," she said.

"I was starting to go stir-crazy." He'd wrapped the towel around himself, but he still needed to lean heavily on Laurie. She walked him gingerly down the hall and into the living room. A few more steps, and he sank onto the couch once more. Laurie, still holding on to him, ended up collapsing there with him. Every detail she'd refused to notice before suddenly tantalized her senses—Tim's skin underneath her fingers smelling freshly of soap, the warmth of his body seeming to radiate into hers, the strong outline of his muscles. Laurie started to pull away from him, but now *his* arms held her fast.

"Thanks," he said, gazing at her. "Seems you have to keep getting me out of fixes."

"All in a day's work," she answered. Her voice wobbled a little. If she wanted to think straight, she had to stop this. Had to stop it right now. But she stayed where she was, her body pressed to Tim's.

"You looked, didn't you?" he murmured.

She felt the color burn in her face. "I did not..." she began indignantly, only to realize it was a shameful lie. "Oh, all right," she said grouchily. "I looked at your butt, that was all. And only for a second or two."

He smiled. And then he brought his head down to hers and he kissed her.

Laurie felt as if she'd been waiting for this kiss, wanting it, *needing* it, for a very long time. How could it be, when she'd known Tim Miller only a few days? Reaching up, she tangled her fingers in his hair, deepened the contact between them. She probed her tongue against his mouth, felt him smile again. Did

Tim always smile when he kissed? At this moment it seemed right somehow. She felt as if she were melting into the warmth of his body, into the lean strength of him. And now, as her heart pulsed, it seemed in answer to some secret irresistible command of his.

It was Tim who ended the kiss, far before she was ready to have it end. But apparently he wanted to study her. He held her face in both his hands, his gaze traveling over her features. His expression was too intense, too perceptive.

"Who hurt you?" he asked softly.

"I don't know what you mean."

"Why do you keep trying to pretend with me?"

"I don't know what you want," she said in a low voice. "For all I know, you really are just going stir-crazy, and I'm the only available entertainment."

"Someone put that look in your eyes," he murmured. "That look as if you'll never trust another man—"

She put her fingers over his lips. "Don't...please. Tim, just don't."

He seemed about to say something else. But then, his eyes deepening to midnight blue, he brought her face near his and kissed her again. This was all she craved right now, the unthinking delight of being in Tim Miller's arms, his mouth on hers—

The sound of the front door creaking open came like a shot to Laurie. She scrambled off the couch, staring at Tim in dismay. As he lay there with only a towel for cover, he looked far far too masculine. Operating on adrenaline, Laurie tossed the blanket over him and then sprang to the opposite sofa. She sat down in a heap, trying futilely to smooth her hair.

Alyson came walking into the room. She looked first at Tim, then at Laurie, then back at Tim. An unreadable expression crossed her face.

"Hey," she said in a flippant voice. "Go right ahead—don't mind me." And then she turned and went upstairs.

CHAPTER SEVEN

LAURIE WAITED for what she considered an appropriate interval and then followed Alyson upstairs. She left Tim there on the couch, the blanket draped over him, his face troubled. Yet he couldn't be feeling *half* of what Laurie was. The last thing she needed was for Alyson to think...well, whatever Alyson was thinking.

She knocked on the door to her daughter's bedroom, then opened it. Alyson was bringing clothes from the closet and spreading them out on her bed.

"What are you doing?" Laurie asked uneasily.

"I'm...organizing, Mom. I really wish you wouldn't barge in here like that."

Alyson sounded almost reasonable. But the way she avoided Laurie's gaze was telling enough.

"Alyson," Laurie began, "whatever you think you saw—"

"Could we just drop it, Mom?" Alyson said in a long-suffering tone. "I really don't care what you and Tim Miller do. In fact, I'd rather not think about it at all."

"I don't want you getting the wrong idea."

"Really. Let's drop it." Sometimes Alyson could sound like a jaded adult. She continued dragging skirts and dresses and blouses out of her closet, dumping them on the bed. "I'm busy," she said significantly.

"I can see that. I just thought we could talk a little. And maybe I could help you organize your wardrobe."

"No thanks," Alyson said, her tone very polite now. Laurie felt a surge of irritation. This was a new habit Alyson had taken up, trying to dismiss her with a sort of cool civility. But Laurie refused to be dismissed. She sat down in the chintz armchair Alyson had loved ever since she was a child.

"At last we have more time to spend together," she said. "And I do want to talk, just to see how things are going with you."

"They're dandy." The edge of sarcasm had crept back into Alyson's voice. She held up a pair of pants and inspected them critically.

Laurie searched for the right words. "I was hoping maybe you'd start to make some friends in town. In fact, I saw you today...talking to someone. A boy."

Alyson lowered the pants and gave Laurie a stricken look. "You've been spying on me?"

Laurie straightened. "Of course not. I was in the diner with Dr. Garrett and I just happened to see you."

"Like I really believe that." Alyson's voice trembled with anger. This was going all wrong, but Laurie couldn't afford to back down.

"Alyson," she said calmly, "I think you know me well enough to realize I'd never spy on you."

"Is there a law against talking to a guy? I'm not supposed to talk to anyone of the opposite *sex*?"

Laurie fought down another surge of irritation.

"Kevin Nichols is too old for you. And he has a rep—"

"You know his *name* already?" Now Alyson's look was one of disbelief.

Laurie cursed herself for uttering the boy's name—a strategic error. "I didn't go snooping around for information. Someone volunteered it. And I'm going to be frank with you, Alyson. Apparently this Nichols guy doesn't have the best reputation in town." That was putting it mildly. The waitress at the diner had all too obligingly offered tales of Kevin Nichols's exploits with the opposite sex.

"So now you listen to gossip," Alyson said, her voice rigid. "I thought you always told me to give people the benefit of the doubt. Don't judge too quickly and all that."

Laurie reminded herself that she was going to stay calm. "I would still tell you exactly the same thing. But not judging too quickly means keeping an open mind both ways."

"I was only talking to him!" Alyson exclaimed. "And do you think, do you honestly think a guy like that would even look at a girl like me?"

Laurie heard the despair in her daughter's voice. She stood and went over to her. "Sweetheart, you're beautiful. You don't have anything to worry about. Any boy would be lucky to—"

"Save it, Mom," Alyson said flatly. "I know the drill."

Laurie had been reaching out her hand, but now it fell to her side. She felt an ache in her heart, the ache of knowing she couldn't soothe all her daughter's hurts. She knew she could tell Alyson over and over what a lovely girl she was, what a special unique person, but Alyson wouldn't believe it. Not from her own mother. Not anymore.

Alyson went on, "I was talking to Kevin because I wanted to ask him for a job. He said he'd think about it. He said he might actually hire me."

Laurie stared at her daughter. "A job? Doing what?"

Alyson picked up a blouse, then threw it aside as if it displeased her. "Kevin has his own business. He gives Jeep tours in the mountains. The tourist season is going to start very soon and he needs someone to manage the office."

Laurie shook her head. "Alyson, you don't need a job. We've already discussed it. We're going to have a nice enjoyable summer together, and then you'll be going away to college."

"*You* discussed it," Alyson said. "You made all the plans. I kept trying to tell you I wasn't sure about college, but you never listened."

Laurie felt a sense of unreality. She remembered so clearly Alyson's enthusiasm for their plans and dreams. How could she have mistaken that? It was only the past few months that Alyson had started to draw away. Yet, even as she'd grown quiet and morose, she'd never once said anything about not going to college.

"Honey, you've talked about doing premedicine. You've talked about becoming a doctor."

"Just like you, right?" Alyson's tone was caustic. "Yeah, sure, I talked about that a long time ago. Back when I wanted to be a little clone of you. Now maybe I just want to be myself. Is that too much to ask?"

"I've always encouraged you to be yourself."

"No, Mom. Everything's always centered around you. *Your* dreams, *your* goals. And I was just supposed to be the cheerleading squad."

The sense of unreality cushioned Laurie, and for a moment or two she didn't feel the pain inflicted by Alyson's words. This couldn't be her daughter speaking, she told herself. It was all a mistake. She reached out her hand again.

"Alyson, you're the most important thing in the world to me. Don't you know that? Nothing else compares—"

"Knock it off." Alyson's voice shook with anger, as if resentments she'd been harboring for years now threatened to spill out. "Your career has always been the most important thing. Everything else has come second. Everything! Why else do you think no guy ever sticks around? It's just too hard, always coming second."

"Alyson," Laurie whispered. At last she felt the pain, twisting inside her.

And Alyson seemed to realize she'd gone too far. Looking stricken, she gazed at Laurie. "Mom…" she said hesitantly. But then, as if catching herself, she turned away. "I really would like to finish up in here. On my *own*."

With all her heart Laurie wanted to draw her daughter close, hold her as she had so often before. But this Alyson was a stranger, someone Laurie barely knew.

Without saying anything more, Laurie walked out of the room and closed the door behind her.

NEXT MORNING, Laurie actually had some doctoring to do. Not much doctoring, but at least it was something. One woman arrived at the clinic with her fourteen-year-old son, who had a sprained ankle, and another brought in her baby for treatment of an ear infection. Everything was going well until the last woman remarked that she'd never consulted a female doctor before. It became obvious that she'd only brought her baby in because she hadn't seen any other choice. It certainly hadn't been because she was ready to give Laurie a vote of confidence. Laurie wondered how many other townspeople were delaying medical treatment because they'd never seen a female doctor.

"This is ridiculous," Laurie told Bess for the tenth time. "In this day and age there are women who are all over the place!"

"Not in Grant," Bess said. "Like it or not, you're the first. How's Tim doing?"

"Tim is just…Tim. That is, he's fine. He's recuperating as best as can be expected." Laurie knew her face was turning red. She thought about the bathtub incident and kissing Tim Miller on the couch. And afterward, that terrible conversation with Alyson. Lord, yesterday had been one mistake after another. Laurie told herself that today had to be better. Maybe if she kept telling herself that often enough, she'd believe it.

She flipped open the appointment book and began to scan the pages. "Look at this," she said. "You didn't tell me that business was picking up. Two people coming in tomorrow and another on Monday."

Bess gave an unladylike snort. "Let me tell you a little something. Chad Holland has never been sick a day in his life, and he couldn't tell me exactly why he wanted to consult with you. The best he could come up with was an achy toe. Chad's always looking for a way to make his wife jealous. And Scott Lowery had a checkup only three months ago. Dr. Garrett gave him a clean bill of health. But Scott has some excuse about a bad shoulder. As for Keith Vance...well, he didn't even bother to come up with an excuse. He just came right out and said he wants to meet the pretty new doctor in town."

"You must be joking. You're trying to tell me these three men only made appointments to...to..."

"They want to check you out," Bess supplied.

Laurie slammed the appointment book shut. "That's ridiculous!"

"You keep saying that," Bess reminded her. "But if you want to live in a small town, you'd better get used to its ways—no matter how difficult they are at times."

The door of the clinic opened, and in came a gentleman Laurie was glad to see.

"Mr. Cline!" she exclaimed. "I've been hoping you'd get back to town. Maybe we can finally straighten out this mess about two doctors."

Phil Cline was the most dignified member of the town council. When Laurie had flown out to Colorado for her interview, she'd been impressed by his genteel yet authoritative manner. It was Phil Cline, more than anyone else, who'd convinced Laurie that Grant was the place for her. But he was one of the two council members who had been on vacation this week. Thank God he'd finally returned.

"Dr. Russell," he said, "how good to see you

again. I *am* sorry you've had to suffer through this mix-up. Certainly we will straighten it out.''

These were exactly the words Laurie needed to hear, proclaimed in his confident tone. He was approximately the same age as Dr. Garrett, but the two men could not have been more dissimilar. Phil Cline wore a somewhat awful leisure suit in pale blue with contrast stitching, but it was immaculate, certainly compared to Doc Garrett's haphazard appearance.

He took his time giving a courtly greeting to Bess, while she gave only a perfunctory response. The nurse didn't seem to like the man, but Laurie couldn't worry about that. She ushered Phil Cline into her office and had him sit down across from her desk. The office was still cluttered with Doc Garrett's outdated medical texts, but Laurie was in the midst of packing them up and substituting her own books. She realized it was difficult to tell at a glance whether someone was moving in or moving out.

"Dr. Russell," Phil Cline began, "I'm very sorry I wasn't here when you arrived to take up your duties. My absence was, however, unavoidable. You see, my wife's sister won a trip to Hawaii, and we were privileged to accompany her." Phil Cline paused to give a satisfied smile. "Jonathan Garrett, it turns out, is not the only person who can go jaunting about in tropical climes. And Hawaii is far preferable to the *Caribbean.* Don't you agree, Dr. Russell?"

"Actually I've never been to either one, but—"

"Do take my advice, and when you have the opportunity go to Hawaii. I can recommend some very adequate hotels."

"How kind of you," Laurie said. "Now, if we

could just discuss this mix-up of ours. Grant can't support two doctors, as I'm sure you're aware.''

"It was all over town that we'd flown in our own candidate to interview for the job," Phil Cline stated. "If Jonathan hadn't been spending all his time in the Caribbean and then in Digby, he would have heard about it. He would not have brought in his own candidate."

Laurie didn't think it was that simple. She had the feeling Doc Garrett would have brought Tim in no matter what the circumstances. But that didn't mean Tim had to stay.

"Surely you can get the council together," Laurie said, "and draft a resolution—or whatever it is that town councils do. Anything so it's official that I'm the doctor here."

"Dr. Russell, of course I will do everything in my power to resolve the situation as soon as possible. It's truly lamentable that you've had to suffer this indignity..." Phil Cline went on at some length, offering vague reassurances. And that was the part that started to bother Laurie—the vagueness. From what she could tell, he wasn't proposing any concrete solution. He seemed to become the most animated when referring to Doc Garrett.

"...and I assure you, Dr. Russell, Jonathan Garrett will not get away with this. It is unfortunately one more in a series of insults he has inflicted on me and I will not allow it. Absolutely not."

That was all Laurie needed—to find out that Doc Garrett and Phil Cline were engaged in some type of personal vendetta.

"Mr. Cline, you *will* be calling a meeting of the town council, won't you?"

"Just as soon as I am able to convene a quorum, Dr. Russell. Rest assured..."

She ushered him out of the clinic. And as she watched him go down the street in his blue leisure suit, she had a sinking sensation that today wasn't going to be better than yesterday, after all.

TIM WAS APPROACHING the end of day three on the orange couch. He felt like scratching the numbers on the wall, anything to mark the passage of time. Maybe under other circumstances he would've been able to relax more. But sharing a house with Laurie and Alyson Russell did not make for relaxation. Ever since Alyson had interrupted Tim and Laurie on the couch yesterday, mother and daughter had been so formal around each other you could almost see the tension in the air between them.

Laurie had been pretty formal around Tim, too. This morning she'd checked on him, brought him food and then left him alone as soon as she could. And that gave Tim too much time to think about how it had been yesterday afternoon holding her in his arms. Experiencing feelings he had no business experiencing.

"Lord," he said. He held out the remote and clicked off the mindless chatter of the TV. But silence didn't make things any better. He kept thinking about Laurie, kept remembering the feel of her body against his. He tried reminding himself of how it had always been with him and women. Never get too close, never stay too long. No expectations, no promises on either side. He couldn't say exactly when that pattern had started in his life. He just knew it worked for him. And if, once upon a time, he'd looked at a woman named Hallie Claremont and started to imagine what the long-term could be...well, he'd found out it wasn't for him. Hallie had chosen his brother, just as it should be. And Tim had gone back to believing in no promises.

He heard the front door of the house open. Laurie came into the room and gave him a cursory glance.

"Alyson's not here," he said before she could ask.

"Did she say where she was going?"

"Something about a job interview."

"I see." Laurie sounded grim.

"Shows some initiative, doesn't it? The fact that she's out looking for a job."

Now Laurie gave him what could only be called a withering look. "You don't know anything about it, Tim."

He didn't *want* to know anything about it. Alyson had avoided him most of the day and he'd had no complaint about that. But then, a few hours ago she'd come into the room and asked him if she looked "cool." He'd told her she looked fine. That hadn't gone over very well.

"Can I get you anything?" Laurie asked with forced politeness.

"No, thanks. Just tell me how it went at the clinic today. I have a vested interest in the place, too, you know."

Laurie's eyebrows drew together. "I'm sure Bess will keep you informed."

He gazed at her, at the lovely determined contours of her face, the sensuous curve of her lips.

"Stop," she said in a low fierce voice. "Don't look at me like that."

Silently he willed her to come over and sit beside him on the couch. After a long moment, though, she wrenched her gaze from his.

"Dammit, Tim, just…stop. We're not going to have a repeat of the…the bathtub incident."

He smiled. "That's what it is now—an incident?"

"Whatever you want to call it, it's not going to happen again."

He gave a reluctant nod. "I figured as much. But you can't blame a guy for tryin', can you?"

She gave him a sharp glance. "Do you ever take anything seriously?" she asked.

"I promise to keep my distance," he said. "It's not like I'm goin' anywhere fast." He made a gesture to include the sum total of his domain: the orange couch.

Laurie's gaze traveled over him in a purely professional manner. "How do you feel? Any better?"

"Getting there."

"You wouldn't be in this fix if you took care of yourself in the first place. You should be doing exercises to strengthen your back."

"Right," he said sarcastically. "I'll just change into sweats and start pumping some iron."

"I didn't mean you should start exercising this very minute," she said.

"So I'll wait till I'm better. Then it's a six-month trial membership at any one of Grant's fashionable gyms."

She looked skeptical, but then she slipped off her shoes and sat down on the rug. She stretched her legs in front of her and bent forward until her hands rested lightly at her ankles. Her hair fell forward, hiding her face.

"Forget Grant's imaginary gyms. First you have to limber up," she said, her voice a bit muffled. "Do something besides ride horses and bulls..."

Watching Laurie demonstrate stretches only confirmed what Tim already knew. She was beautiful. She was desirable. She wore the kind of clothes he liked on a woman—tailored, simple, nothing fussy—but they were always made of some soft silky fabric that seemed to move with her body. Everything she did seemed possessed of an unconscious grace.

She began to straighten up, but she kept her head bent as if she didn't want him to see her expression—which was enough to tell him that something was wrong. A moment later, however, she raised her head and stared at him almost defiantly. He saw the shimmer of tears in his eyes.

"Oh, damn," she muttered in apparent disgust. "Sometimes relaxing isn't such a good idea, after all."

"Unchokes the emotions, does it?" He attempted an easy tone. That was how he'd always tried to keep it with women—easy, on the surface. And he wanted to go on keeping it that way. Maybe he was a captive audience on this couch, but he was giving Laurie a chance to compose herself, a chance to say something light and superficial in return.

She didn't oblige him. She remained silent for a long while and then she spoke almost unwillingly. "I worked so hard to become a doctor. It's the only thing I've ever wanted to do with my life. But I thought I was doing it for both of us—for Alyson and me. I told myself it was a career where I could have some stability, give *her* the things she needed.'' She laughed bleakly. ''Of course, that was before I knew how much debt I'd rack up in med school. Or how many hours I'd work for pennies as a resident.''

''Think I saw some of those pennies myself,'' he murmured, but this attempt to lighten the mood also failed.

''The hardships always seemed worth it,'' Laurie said. ''It just felt so…right. No matter what sacrifices Alyson and I made. Because I was convinced of one thing. I was *born* to be a doctor.'' Now he heard the intensity in her voice, and it was something he understood.

''I've been there, too,'' he said, even though the words came reluctantly. ''Feeling like I was born to it. No matter how much time I wasted fighting the truth, I couldn't escape it in the end. I was meant to be a doctor.''

It seemed Laurie still didn't want to share war stories. She shook her head impatiently. ''It's one thing to be convinced of your own dreams. But when you find out that maybe you've given too much for them—when your daughter feels like she's come in second—'' Laurie stopped abruptly, and now Tim was starting to get the picture all too well. He didn't say anything, but apparently he didn't have to.

Laurie went on, speaking almost as if to herself, ''It's Alyson's theory that men don't stick around me because they get tired of coming in second. Her father left before she was born.... It's true that even then I wanted a medical career. Who knows, maybe the double dose scared him away. A baby *and* a doctor in his future. As for the other men...well, there've been a few. And they left all right." Her voice had gone brittle.

Tim couldn't take lying still anymore. He started inching his way into a sitting position.

"What do you think you're doing?" Laurie asked.

"I don't know," he grumbled, leaning awkwardly against the cushions.

"I didn't tell you any of this so you could pity me," Laurie said. "I told you because...I don't know why I told you."

"At least I'm one person who knows how much work it takes becoming a doctor," he said gruffly. "How much dedication. Obsession, even."

"Tim, be honest with me about one thing. All during medical school and residency, did you ever try to have a personal life? I mean a real personal life. Something that requires a dedication all its own."

He could recall plenty of short-term relationships. Except "relationship" was too exalted a term for anything he'd had. But it had been like that even before he'd entered medical school. Even when he'd just been bumming around from job to job, he'd never let himself get too serious about a woman. Not until Hallie, anyway.

"Maybe I'm not the best person to ask about this type of thing," he said.

"You know what, Tim? I *tried* to have a personal life. All along I tried. I thought I was putting my daughter first and I thought I could make a go of it with a man. I can stand failing at the last part, but if I find out I've failed with Alyson…how can I possibly handle that?''

He heard the sorrow in her voice, the fear. He knew plenty about failing when it came to himself, but he didn't know how to answer Laurie.

CHAPTER EIGHT

MOBILITY. AS FAR AS Tim was concerned, that was not something to be taken for granted. After three days on the orange couch, he was grateful to be up and about. Okay, so his back was stiff and sore—mighty sore—but at least he could stay upright now while putting one foot in front of the other. He made his way into the kitchen and experienced the unalloyed pleasure of pouring a cup of coffee. Not a cup brought to him by Laurie or Alyson, but one he served himself.

He eased himself into one of the kitchen chairs. Not so bad. Of course, he knew what Laurie would say if she could see him right now. She'd read him the riot act, tell him it was way too soon for him to get off that couch. And then, if Tim was lucky, she'd demonstrate another of her stretching exercises.

The image from yesterday afternoon lingered with him: Laurie, sitting on the rug, leaning forward gracefully, every move she made tantalizing him. And then the sudden tears that made her dark brown eyes more beautiful and luminous than ever.

Tim rubbed at a kink in his shoulder and told himself to relax. The sound of water dripping in the sink brought him a welcome diversion. That faucet had probably been leaking for years—Doc Garrett never would've bothered to fix it. About time somebody fixed it, though. Tim got up, then remembered his tools were outside in the truck. He started navigating his way through the house and opened the front door just as Alyson came dashing over the threshold. She almost bowled him over.

"Sorry!" she exclaimed, and then, "Wait a minute. What are you doing up?"

"Exercising," he said, continuing on. The porch steps gave him a little trouble, but he managed them. He made his way out to his truck. Alyson followed on his heels.

"You're not supposed to be doing anything," she said. "You'll get better a lot faster if you just stay on the couch."

He rummaged in the truck bed for his toolbox. "You and your mom have the same party line," he told her. Judging by Alyson's reaction, it was the wrong thing to say.

"I don't go around spouting the same things my mother does. I'm not *like* her."

Sometimes being with a teenager was like stepping through a minefield. "Whatever," he said. He started to lift the toolbox, then stopped. Common sense told him just how much he could and couldn't do.

"I'll take it," Alyson said. She hauled the toolbox out of the pickup and carried it toward the house. A few minutes later she'd deposited it on the kitchen counter. But if Tim thought he was going to have a reprieve after that, he was mistaken. The kid hovered as he searched for the right tools. She seemed worked up about something and at last it burst out of her.

"I got the job! I actually got it, Tim. What do you think about that?"

He found his Phillips screwdriver and his crescent wrench. "Congratulations. But you never did say what job you were applying for."

"It's an office job. Working for *him*. Kevin Nichols."

"Like I said, congratulations." Tim didn't know any Kevin Nichols. He opened the cupboard doors below the sink and tried to figure out how he was going to get down on his hands and knees so he could shut off the water. His back didn't like the idea.

"I guess I have you to thank for it," Alyson said. "I mean, you told me what to do and everything."

Tim didn't remember giving her any advice about job hunting. "Do me a favor, will you? Reach under there and turn off the hot water."

Alyson knelt by the cupboard and stuck her head under the sink. "Hmm...hot's on the right...counterclockwise or clockwise... Done," she said. Tim used a small flat screwdriver to pop the cap off the faucet. Alyson emerged from under the sink and continued to hover.

"It really did help," she said. "What you told me about being cool. At first I couldn't figure it out, but then...well, I just started acting like the job didn't mean all that much to me. And I acted like Kevin didn't mean anything, either. And he gave me the job!"

"I get it," Tim said. "This is the guy you were talking about the other day."

"Yes," Alyson said impatiently. "Kevin. I think it was pretty resourceful of me, asking him for a job.

This way I get to be around him every day. See him every day. Can you imagine? Anyway, I have you to thank. Because you told me about being cool. After that everything seemed to fall into place.''

Tim didn't like the sound of this. He'd made a few offhand comments to the kid and now she acted as if he was responsible for a major life change. He unscrewed the faucet cover.

''Of course,'' Alyson said, ''Mom's going to hit the roof when she finds out. Especially a job with *him*.''

Tim made no reply. The last thing he wanted was to get involved in some controversy between Laurie and her daughter. He worked his crescent wrench around the exposed faucet nut and hoped that Alyson would get tired of talking to him.

No such luck. She leaned against the counter and went right on chattering. ''Mom's already been hearing gossip about Kevin and she actually seems to believe it. But you know what I think? If someone's gossiping about you in this town, at least it shows you're alive. And you're somebody interesting.''

A little more work with the crescent, and the faucet unit popped out. Tim turned it around in his fingers and saw the corroded O-ring at the base. That was the problem right there.

''I figured maybe you could help me,'' Alyson was saying. ''You could tell Mom about my job and how you helped me get it. She'd probably listen to you and then we could all avoid a big scene.''

''Whoa,'' Tim said, the faucet no longer holding his attention. ''You're moving a little fast here, aren't you? I didn't help you get this job, Alyson. I didn't

have anything to do with it. And any problems with
your mother—you'll have to resolve those on your
own. I'm not involved."

"I thought you *were* involved," Alyson said scathingly. "I mean, you're *doing* it with my mom, aren't
you?"

Tim didn't say anything for a long moment. Alyson
stood there, arms crossed, gazing at him with a look
that said she was half scared, half pleased with what
she'd just said. She seemed to want to know just how
far she could push the limits. Tim once again felt
sorry for anybody who was a parent.

Finally he spoke, his voice calm. "You're way out
of line, Alyson. Not that it's any of your business,
but...there's nothing going on between your mother
and me. Not the way you're thinking, anyway."

She looked skeptical. "I'm not stupid. Give me a
little credit at least."

"If you have problems to resolve with your mother,
you should talk to her."

"Mom's *last* boyfriend wasn't like you. He decided right off that he'd found a ready-made family.
I was supposed to be the perfect daughter and Mom
was going to be the perfect wife. According to him,
anyway."

Tim wished that all he had to think about right now
was a leaky faucet. "I doubt that your mother would
like you getting into any of this with me."

"You mean she hasn't told you about Peter yet?"

"Look, kid," Tim said repressively. "Enough."

"You're dying to hear about him, aren't you?"
Clearly Alyson was enjoying herself. "I'll tell you
something funny. Peter seemed like *he* was going to

be perfect for us—the perfect husband and dad. Always doing little things for Mom, bringing her presents. And acting like he really wished I was his daughter. Peter had both of us suckered pretty good.'' A new tone crept into Alyson's voice, a sort of bitterness. She looked so young, but that tone in her voice sounded old.

"Alyson—'' Tim tried again, but already she was going on in a rush.

"You know what Peter's problem was? He fell in love with the idea of having a family. It sounded really great to him. He knew how to do holidays and birthdays and anniversaries. But when it came down to the ordinary day-to-day stuff, he couldn't hack it. And if there were ever any hassles, he couldn't handle those, either. He asked Mom to marry him, but then he backed out right before the wedding.''

Tim picked up the faucet parts again, but they didn't seem to hold his interest anymore. "How long ago did this guy walk out on you and your mom?'' he asked at last.

"Six months ago,'' Alyson said with a forced carelessness. "That's one of the big reasons Mom decided to move out here to Colorado. It was about as faraway from Detroit as she could get.''

"Tough break,'' Tim said almost to himself.

"It's like I told you. Peter had an idea of what the perfect family should be like, and in the end Mom and I didn't fit. So he was outta there.''

"Maybe it was good riddance,'' Tim said.

"Maybe.'' The carelessness was still there. "And maybe it's good *you* won't get involved. Forget I asked you to help me out.'' Alyson gave him a scornful glance. He could tell he was being lumped with all the unsatisfactory guys who couldn't commit to a real family. Tim didn't like the feeling. But he knew it fit him to a T—with one important exception. He'd never make promises he couldn't keep. He'd never worm his way into a family and then back out when things didn't go his way. He'd stay on the outside. Always the outside.

He wasn't congratulating himself. It was just the way it had to be.

LATE IN THE AFTERNOON Laurie dragged herself home from the clinic, no energy left. She knew she was suffering more from a weariness of spirit than physical tiredness. It still didn't make sense, though. At the hospital in Detroit she'd kept going hour after long hour. In her off time she'd collapse, but that was understandable, given her punishing workload. Here in Grant, however, all that had occupied her so far were a few appointments with reluctant patients. Why, then, did she feel so drained? Why was she allowing herself to become discouraged?

Reaching the porch, Laurie stopped and gazed at the mountains surrounding the town. The Rockies, taking on a rose-purple hue in the mellowed sun of the afternoon. It was because of the mountains that she'd decided to move here. They had made her feel awed and comforted at once. When she'd first set eyes on those peaks, she'd believed that nothing really terrible could happen in a place where they stood guard. Of course, she hadn't known then about Tim Miller, about the way he'd be threatening her job. Or about the way he'd threaten her composure every time he looked at her.

She hadn't known, either, that her problems with Alyson would only intensify in Colorado. She hadn't realized that her much-loved daughter would be capable of casting her glances filled with such obvious disdain, such obvious rejection.

Now Laurie knew why she felt so tired. These days she always carried with her the fear that she had failed her daughter in some important way. Laurie had been only nineteen when Alyson was born, and she'd never felt more alone in her life. But she'd also never felt more exultant than when she'd held her daughter for the first time. At that moment she'd silently promised Alyson that the two of them would face every obstacle together. And, cradling baby Alyson, Laurie had told herself that she could do it all—be the best mother in the world and achieve her dream of becoming a doctor. Had she been guided by nothing more than youthful arrogance? Had she shortchanged Alyson in all the years since?

Laurie didn't know the answers. She just knew that somehow, no matter what it took, she had to bridge the growing distance between her and her daughter. She'd never been one to give up before—not on anything. She couldn't give up now.

Dragging her gaze from the mountains, she opened the door and went into the house. Immediately she was greeted by the delicious aroma of basil and tomato. What was going on? Alyson, despite her recent complaints about fast food, didn't like to cook. Had she decided to change her ways? With Alyson, anything was possible.

Laurie crossed the hall, telling herself she was going to head straight for the kitchen. She refused to glance into the living room, refused to see Tim Miller sprawled on her couch. She wouldn't allow herself to feel that ridiculous attraction toward him.

She almost succeeded. She started to walk right by the double doors that led into the living room. She kept her eyes straight ahead. But then, at the very last minute, she looked, after all. And Tim was nowhere to be seen. She hated to think about the possibility that he might be taking another bath.

She went briskly down the hall and found that the bathroom door was ajar. No Tim Miller in the tub, thank goodness. But he *was* in the kitchen, stirring rather too energetically at a pot on the stove. His sleeves were rolled halfway up his arms, he had a dish towel tucked in the waist of his jeans—and, with his red hair tumbled over his forehead, he looked more handsome than ever.

"Hey, there," he said over his shoulder as he continued to stir. "Marinara sauce."

"That explains everything," she said. She stepped closer, and saw telltale splats of sauce on the wall beside the stove. "You'd better turn the heat down." Good advice in more ways than one, she supposed. The steamy warmth of the kitchen seemed to envelop her, and she felt a warmth deep within, too. *Cool it,* she told herself. *Just cool it.*

She reached over and turned down the burner herself. "You probably already realize I'm going to say this—but what the heck are you doing up? Not only up, but...cooking." She glanced around the kitchen and saw the pans and dishes scattered about, the greens cascading out the drainer, the prosciutto and the cannelloni strewn on the counter. "Where," she asked, "did you come up with such exotic food in *this* little town?"

"Darlin', this may be the middle of nowhere, but we know how to eat. Hell—take the sauce, will you?"

Laurie found herself stirring the marinara while Tim tossed the cannelloni into another big pot, this one somewhat battered. Doc Garrett had left behind all sorts of odds and ends, including cooking utensils of dubious vintage.

"Tim," Laurie said, "mind telling me what's going on? You just don't seem the domestic type."

"There is such a thing as stir-crazy," he muttered. "You know you're in trouble when a visit to the grocery store is the highlight of the day."

Laurie noticed the sink, where one of the faucets lay in pieces. "You really *have* been busy."

Tim followed the direction of her gaze. "Oh, yeah...that. I'm in the middle of repairs."

Tim seemed in the middle of a lot of things. He appropriated yet another burner. Into a big saucepan went the prosciutto, a dollop of butter, several stalks of chard and a generous dose of shallots. More savory smells pervaded the kitchen.

"Are you following a recipe?" Laurie asked doubtfully.

"Didn't I tell you? I was a short-order cook once."

"I get it. Short-order cannelloni."

"You just have to be inventive, that's all." Tim appropriated the last burner on the stove, starting a cream sauce with a splash of milk and a smattering

of flour. He had a look of intent concentration on his face.

"You really go all the way, don't you?" she murmured. "By the by, the pasta's bubbling over." She turned down *that* burner just in time.

Somehow nothing self-destructed on the stove. Before Laurie knew it, she was helping tuck the prosciutto and the chard into each cannelloni. The cream sauce, only a bit lumpy, was spooned in, too, and over all went the generous marinara—not to mention freshly grated Parmesan. Laurie watched the masterpiece disappear into the oven.

Tim wiped his hands on the dish towel at his waist. "That's it," he said, and grinned at Laurie. "Good thing you came along when you did."

She realized that she'd forgotten to be tired. The frenetic activity of the last several minutes had filled her with energy. And now, staring into Tim's eyes, she felt something else—a stir of longing perhaps? Or was she just hungry? He gazed back at her. And suddenly he wasn't smiling anymore.

"*Excuse* me," came Alyson's voice from the doorway. Laurie started, swiveling toward her daughter.

"Alyson," she said, her bright tone sounding forced, "I was hoping you hadn't…gone anywhere yet."

"Really," her daughter said in that new disdainful tone of hers.

"I was hoping we could do something together tonight."

Alyson raised her eyebrows ever so slightly. "Figure it out, Mom. From what I see, Dr. Tim's preparing a romantic dinner for two."

Irritation flickered across Tim's face. "It's dinner for all three of us. I just needed something to do."

"Sure," Alyson said.

"I thought maybe we could go to the movies," Laurie suggested.

"The *three* of us?"

Laurie felt her own irritation rise, but she refused to show it. "The two of us," she said levelly.

Tim spoke again, his own voice carefully neutral. "Come to think of it, I'll leave the two of you alone."

"Don't go," Alyson said quickly as if she couldn't bear the thought of being left with her mother. "I'm on my way out, anyway. I think I'll just go to the movies by myself." She paused. "I'm celebrating. I got the job. The one with Kevin Nichols."

Ever since Alyson had first mentioned this job, Laurie had gambled that it wouldn't pan out. Except for baby-sitting stints, Alyson had never been obliged to take a job; Laurie had wanted her daughter to focus on her studies. She'd hoped that Alyson's lack of experience would discourage Kevin Nichols from hiring her. Apparently she'd been wrong. She glanced at Tim, but his face was impassive. She turned back to her daughter.

"Alyson," she said as reasonably as possible, "what's the point of taking a job for only a few months? You'll be going away to college in the fall. It's fine—you can forget premed, but you'll have other interests…"

"You really don't listen, do you, Mom? *You're* the one who thinks college is the solution for everything. I think it could be incredibly limiting. I plan to explore other options."

Laurie felt that sense of unreality again. Didn't Alyson realize how few options she'd have without a college degree?

"You don't need this job," Laurie said flatly. "I don't want you to take it."

"Wait a minute. Are you *forbidding* me?"

"I wouldn't put it that way."

"Stop being such a hypocrite," Alyson said in a cold hard voice. "You're always trying to make things sound different than they are. To make them sound better. Just be straight with me."

Laurie studied the young woman before her and tried to remind herself that this was Alyson...her child. Her little girl. But the Alyson confronting her was almost a stranger.

"All right," Laurie said quietly. "I'll be straight with you. I don't want you to take the job. I certainly don't want you working for this Nichols. If I could, I *would* forbid you. But you're almost eighteen years old. And I know that, short of locking you in the house, I can't prevent you. All I can do is try to appeal to your good sense. And you know what, Alyson? It scares me knowing that you're not going to listen to me. Knowing that you've already made up your mind."

Alyson gave a humorless little smile. "You have it in you, after all. Some honesty."

Every word Alyson spoke cut Laurie like a knife. And to make things worse Tim was listening—even though he had the look of someone who couldn't figure out what he was doing here.

"I've always tried to be honest with you," Laurie told her daughter.

Alyson shook her head. "No. Ever since you were nineteen years old and you had a husband who walked out, you've tried to create some fake little world where there isn't room for anybody but you and me. And your career of course. Always your career." Alyson took a deep breath; she was shaking.

"Alyson, please—"

"I have to get out of here. I'm going to the movies—on my own. And I am taking the job with Kevin. I start work tomorrow. You're right—there's nothing you can do about it." She stormed out of the kitchen. A few seconds later Laurie heard the front door slam shut.

She felt hollow inside, more empty than she could ever remember. She sank into a chair at the kitchen table and cradled her head in her hands.

"Teenagers can be hell," Tim said.

"You don't know," she whispered. "You just don't know..."

"Right now, Laurie, you're going to tell yourself that your kid needs some independence, even if she's being cruel about it. And you're going to leave it at that. You're not going to tear yourself up." His voice was matter-of-fact. Slowly Laurie raised her head.

"It's not that easy," she said. "You don't know all the circumstances."

"I know you care about your daughter. And I also know you need a break from her. Seems to me Italian food is the answer." He went to the oven and looked in. "Just about ready," he announced. "Damned if I'm not good at this stuff."

She knew what he was doing. He was trying to make everything seem ordinary, trying to give her some time to collect herself. She appreciated his efforts. It was weak of her to depend on Tim right now, but she didn't know what else to do. All the mistakes of the past eighteen years seemed to be rearing up and accusing her. And so, in defense, she clung to the ordinariness that Tim offered her.

Minutes later he served up two plates of cannelloni. There was a baguette to go along with the meal, and a bottle of rosé that Doc Garrett had left forgotten in a cupboard. Tim did the honors, pouring a glass each. The wine warmed Laurie's throat as it went down. She told herself that if she could just concentrate on these simple things—good wine, good food, Tim sharing them with her—she would be all right. She'd be able to tell herself that her daughter was only rebelling. She'd be able to ignore the accusations inside her head.

She took one of the napkins Tim had managed to unearth from a drawer. It was made of a pretty peach-colored cloth. "Imagine Doc Garrett having something like this around," she said.

"The doc's parade of lady friends left traces behind," Tim said. "Since his last divorce, no woman has had the staying power. You'll just find these clues now and then, signs that somebody tried to snag him."

"Estelle from Digby seems to be keeping his interest."

"That she does," Tim said.

Laurie folded and refolded the napkin. "This is the kind of thing my parents would have. Cloth napkins at dinner. Not to mention the coordinating tablecloth. And only the most elegant salt-and-pepper shakers...'' Suddenly nothing seemed ordinary, after all. The accusations wouldn't leave her alone. "My parents were both very formal people, but I always knew how much they loved me. And that was why it was so difficult when...when I knew I'd disappointed them. Nineteen years old, and I could tell I'd destroyed all their hopes for me..." She pushed her chair back and stood. "I'm sorry. It's all very delicious, but I just can't...I can't do this." Hardly watching where she was going, she went down the hall and into the living room. There the orange couch confronted her with an accusation all its own.

Tim had followed her. He came up behind her and placed his hands on her shoulders. "Okay, so talking about your parents—that wasn't the best topic in the world. We'll find something else, Laurie."

"You don't understand," she said, her voice wooden. "A long time ago I did something wrong. I lied to Alyson. I lied to my daughter. And now I'm paying for it."

CHAPTER NINE

LAURIE FOUND almost a sense of relief in saying the words out loud. Tim stayed where he was, his hands still on her shoulders. He didn't move, didn't flinch, didn't behave as if she'd said something shocking. And maybe that was what gave her the courage to tell *all* the truth.

"I was nineteen," she said, her voice low, "and I thought I was in love. He was older than me—twenty-four. I thought he loved me, too. Then I told him I was pregnant, and it changed everything. He couldn't handle it, the idea of having a child. So he left. He walked out the door and never once tried to contact me afterward. A hundred times I wanted to tell him to go to hell, but he never gave me the chance."

She felt Tim's hands tighten, but he didn't know all of it yet.

"There I was, nineteen and pregnant and not even a prospect of a husband. I put off telling my parents as long as I possibly could—I just couldn't bear the thought of breaking their hearts. Well, finally I did have to tell them. And it devastated them, just like I thought it would. It didn't stop them from loving me, but I could tell how much it hurt. My mother ended up begging me...to pretend. She wanted us to tell everyone that Jack and I had gotten married, but the baby coming had been too much for him. A whirl-wind marriage, a whirlwind divorce, that was what we'd say." Laurie stopped.

She had to finish it. "I resisted at first. I didn't want to start my baby's life with a lie. But my mother and then my father, too…at last I gave in. I was a coward, and I did what they wanted. Alyson grew up believing I'd been married to her father, however briefly. You heard what she said—she thinks I had a husband who left me. She doesn't know it was a boyfriend who couldn't commit at all."

There, she'd confessed it, the whole sorry mess. But her sense of relief had been fleeting. Now all she felt was the weight of her own guilt. She would have given anything to go back in time, make things right—be brave enough to stand up to her well-meaning but misguided parents.

Tim took charge again. He guided her to the couch and prodded her gently until she had to sit down. It took him a minute or two to ease into a sitting position beside her, and she remembered his injury.

"You should rest your back," she said dully. "And I should…I don't know what I should do."

"You should stop beating yourself up," Tim said, his voice gruff. "Everybody makes mistakes. If you knew about some of mine… Well, anyway, let yourself off the hook."

"You still don't understand. I've been hiding from the truth! For years I've told myself not to even think about it—the lie I told my own daughter. I've buried it, but now I'm paying for it, Tim. Alyson senses the falsehood, even if she doesn't know what it is. That's what she called it, didn't she? The fake world I'd tried to build for her..." To her dismay, Laurie felt tears smarting in her eyes. "Oh, no, not again," she muttered.

Tim took her hand, held it firmly. He still had the look of someone involved in an unwanted situation, but he seemed determined to see it through. "Hey," he said. "Let me tell you a couple of things. First off, you weren't much older than Alyson is now. And you were just doing what your parents wanted."

"That doesn't excuse me," she said. "I take full responsibility for what I did. And Alyson knows something is wrong. Why else would she be making all those barbed comments lately about not having a father?" Laurie tried to pull her hand away, but he wouldn't let go.

"Second," he said inexorably, "what your kid's doing now isn't a payback for past sins. She's just trying to be independent. It's something all teenagers do. Lord knows I've learned that much."

She wished his holding her hand didn't seem necessary all of a sudden. "Maybe all teenagers do that," she said, "but that still doesn't excuse me, does it?"

"You wanted what was best for your kid. Maybe you were just trying to protect her."

"Yes," Laurie murmured. "I certainly wanted that. Deep down I guess I shared my parents' fear. That being illegitimate would harm Alyson..." She hated saying the word—the sound itself was unforgiving. *My daughter, my dearly loved daughter, is illegitimate.*

Laurie made herself speak again. "It's no use, Tim. Any way you look at it, I lied to Alyson. And I've allowed the lie to continue for all these years. That has to be why she's pulling away from me. I don't know how to set things right. After all this time...I just don't know."

Tim looked impatient now. "Don't you think she has to take a little responsibility for what she does? She said some things to you that *she* ought to regret. I do know teenagers, Laurie. They'll drive you crazy no matter how much you love 'em." He shook his head.

"Tim, I appreciate the effort, I really do. I know you're trying to make me feel better..."

"Not workin', is it?" he asked wryly.

"No," she admitted.

"Let's try something else." He got up, moving stiffly because of his back, and went to a corner shelf where an ancient record player was gathering dust— another relic left behind by Doc Garrett. Tim shuffled through a stack of records, chose one and slipped it out of its cover. A few seconds later, a ballad floated scratchily into the air. It was a love song that Laurie recognized from the 1950s, unabashedly romantic and sentimental. Tim came back to her, captured her hand once more and pulled her up beside him. Before she knew it, he was holding her close and they were dancing slowly to the music.

"This is ridiculous," she said.

"Don't say anything. Just lose yourself."

She seemed all too ready to lose herself in Tim's arms. She could feel his strength, the lean powerful lines of his body. Before she could stop herself, she rested her head against his shoulder, closed her eyes. Maybe she *could* lose herself, forget, just for a minute, what a mess of things she'd made with her daughter. She gave a sigh and Tim drew her closer. The music seemed to envelop them in their own private world. If only she could stay here for a very long while, safe in Tim's arms...

Perhaps it wasn't *that* safe. Because gradually Laurie began to feel a stirring of other sensations. She became aware of how her body seemed to fit against Tim's. The light caress of his hand on her back sent a new warmth through her. She lifted her head and his cheek brushed hers. When she turned her face, ever so slightly, she knew that he understood the invitation. He kissed her.

No, there was nothing safe about being in Tim Miller's arms. Not when his arms pulled her closer, not when an aching need flared inside her at every touch. She opened her lips breathlessly to him, heard his low groan just before he deepened their kiss. They no longer moved together in time to the music. For a moment they stood completely still, locked in this embrace. By unspoken accord, they stepped toward the couch. And then they sank down onto it, still holding each other.

Some shred of rationality warned Laurie to stop right now. This was no solution to her problems—it would only make things worse. But she wasn't listening to reason. All she knew was the flame that coursed through her, a flame brought to life by Tim. Her fingers tangled in his hair and she arched toward him. She heard the intake of his breath.

"Ah, Laurie, what you do to me..." He kissed her yet again, but she wanted even more from him. His caresses were so very gentle at first, tantalizing her, tempting her almost beyond control.

"Tim," she whispered against his mouth. "Tim…"

He seemed to understand exactly what she was asking. He tugged her shirt out of her waistband, encountering next the flimsy material of her camisole. But then, at last, his fingers touched her bare skin. Unheeding of anything but his nearness, she slid down to lie full length against the cushions, bringing Tim with her. He bent over her—stopped suddenly, gave a grimace of pain.

Instantly reality returned. She struggled upward, trying to anchor Tim. "Oh, no! Your back—"

"It's okay. Don't stop…" He tried to draw her close again, but all the warmth inside her had vanished abruptly, leaving cold stark recognition of her own folly. She scooted away from Tim, her shirttails dragging. He was still bent awkwardly, and she helped him settle into a more manageable position. His features seemed to relax a little.

"Better?" she asked tersely.

"More comfortable…yes. But better…no." For a second or two, the look in his eyes fanned the flame in her again. But at last, desire banked, she stood, hugging herself.

"We almost made love," she said. "If it hadn't been for your back…we would have made love."

He studied her intently, as if the very force of his gaze would draw her down beside him once more. She took another step away. That orange couch seemed to both mock her and accuse her.

"Don't you realize?" she asked. "I was just…I was trying to forget. I was *using* you, Tim."

"Darlin'," he said, his voice husky. "Go ahead. Use me."

She saw that wicked humor glimmering in his eyes and couldn't believe what she'd almost done. She almost *had* made love to Tim right there on the orange couch.

She could never let it happen again. She had no room in her life for Tim Miller. He had to go.

ALYSON SHOWED UP for work at exactly eight o'clock in the morning. She stood outside Nichols Jeep Tours and rattled the doorknob. The place was locked. She peered through the dusty windows, but she couldn't see anybody inside. She'd been so wound up about starting her job today, and Kevin wasn't even here yet.

She glanced down the street. No one seemed to be around this early. The town reminded Alyson of an old dog sleeping till noon because there wasn't anything else to do. But *she* was wide awake, her nerves jangled. This job seemed like such an important new beginning. She wanted to get on with it.

After coming home from the movies last night, she'd stood outside the door to her mother's room for a long moment. She'd wanted to knock, to go in and tell Mom that everything she'd said was an awful mistake. She'd even raised her hand and placed it against the scarred wood of the door. But then, without knocking, she'd gone into her own room and shut the door. She'd tried to sleep, but lain awake all night.

Now she walked back and forth in front of Nichols Jeep Tours, shivering in the morning air. The things she'd said to her mother had left a bad taste in her mouth. She remembered the wounded look in Mom's eyes, and even now she had a crazy impulse to run home, and fling her arms around her mother, say that none of it was true.

She couldn't do that of course. Because everything she'd said *was* true. She couldn't take it back. Mom didn't want a real daughter. She wanted a younger obedient replica of herself. That was always what she'd wanted. Alyson just hadn't been able to see it until recently. But that didn't make remembering any easier...remembering the awful hurt look in her mother's eyes.

She walked a little farther down the street as if to escape the weight of her thoughts. When she turned back again, she saw that Kevin was opening the door of his office. She hurried toward him.

"Hi," she said breathlessly, then reminded herself of Tim's advice. She had to be cool.

Kevin gave her a careless glance. "Hi there. I didn't expect you so early."

"You said eight o'clock."

He shrugged, then yawned. He didn't cover his mouth with his hand the way most people did. He didn't make any excuses for the yawn. And he managed to look good even when he did it. You couldn't say that about too many people, Alyson thought.

He opened the door and went inside first. After a hesitation Alyson followed. When she'd come for her job interview, she'd taken note of every detail of the place: the counter on which were propped a few small photographs of the mountain, the two desks and file cabinet crammed toward the back, the high walls with their dark wainscoting. She figured this building was decades old, and it certainly needed some sprucing up. Maybe Kevin would let her buy some nature posters to put on the walls, something that would really emphasize the Rockies. She couldn't help thinking it was a little strange the way he was so concerned about having a bigger sign outside, but didn't seem to care about the inside of his business. Well, she could help there. He'd be glad he hired her when he heard all the ideas she had.

Now he gave another yawn as he drifted behind the counter.

"Late night?" Alyson asked, doing her best to sound cool.

"Yeah, I guess you could say that." He gave her a glance that was just a little patronizing, as if he thought she was too young to hear about what he did nights.

Her face burned. She didn't want to think about Kevin Nichols out with some girl living up to his wild reputation. But more than anything, she hated looking so young for her age. This morning she'd gone frantically through her wardrobe again, searching for something decent to wear. She'd tried dressing up, but all her blouses and skirts looked too sweet and innocent. She'd settled on jeans and a pullover sweater, but this outfit didn't seem to make any difference to Kevin. He still looked at her as if she was only a kid, not someone almost eighteen.

"I'll show you the ropes," he said. "Here's the coffeemaker. I like mine black. I'd sure appreciate it if you had it ready for me when I walked in." For the first time he smiled at her. Alyson realized she'd be willing to do a lot for that smile.

"I guess you'd better get me a key, then," she said.

"I have a spare." He fiddled with his key ring, slid off a key and handed it to her. Their fingers bumped. Kevin didn't seem to find the contact significant in any way. He just pulled a beat-up ledger book from the shelf beneath the counter. "Here's where you'll record all the transactions. The cash box is here, too. You should clean out the file cabinet when you get a chance. Take whichever desk you want." He was already starting to sound bored with giving her instructions.

"I think I can figure things out," Alyson said quickly. "I just thought...well, the way you talked, I thought you had somebody else working here, too."

"I did, but she quit. You're it for now. When the season picks up, I'll be hiring more people. A few more drivers, maybe another office person."

Alyson nodded. "Sounds great."

"I'll definitely be expanding. This season should be a good one." He drifted back toward the door. "Look, I'm going over to the diner for breakfast. If anybody needs me, that's where I'll be."

"Sure."

His glance skittered over her again without any apparent interest. Then he was gone, leaving Alyson in charge.

She felt a curious letdown. She'd imagined that once she was his employee, he *would* look at her differently. Foolish as it was, she'd expected some magical transformation the minute she walked over the threshold of Nichols Jeep Tours.

At least he trusted her to manage the place while he was gone. She found a broom in back and swept the floor. She dusted off the counter and the desks with a tissue. She would have made coffee, too, but the coffee can was empty. Meanwhile, she picked the desk she wanted for her own and settled behind it. She pulled open the drawers, found a stapler that was jammed and a pen that had run out of ink. She supposed she'd better talk to Kevin about office supplies, as well as money for a fresh supply of coffee.

The morning passed slowly. Alyson kept expecting Kevin to come walking back through the door and so she tried to look busy—even though there was nothing to do. But Kevin never did come back. The clock inched toward eleven, then eleven-thirty.

She figured that since she was in charge, she could take her lunch hour whenever she wanted. She locked the door behind her and headed for the diner. She felt nervous, wondering if she'd find Kevin there. But that was silly of course—no one would linger over breakfast that long.

He wasn't there. Alyson felt both relief and disappointment. She wanted to see him, but it would definitely be more relaxing to have her lunch on her own.

She slid into one of the booths and the middle-aged waitress brought her a menu. By now Alyson knew the waitress's name was Susan, and she only stuck around in Grant because there were worse places to raise her six-year-old son.

"Hi," Alyson said as she took the menu.

"Hi yourself. So…first day on the job with wonder boy."

Alyson regretted being friendly to the woman. She

opened the menu and tried to concentrate on it, even though she already knew it by heart.

Susan didn't give up. "Did he tell you his big plans for the business? How he's going to make an overnight success of himself?"

"This tourist season will be a good one," Alyson said defensively.

"Already has you trained, doesn't he. Amazing how he can look into the future and see something like that."

Alyson set down her menu. "What do you have against him?"

Susan gave a shrug. "Let's just say that Kevin Nichols is the kind of guy who makes me *very* glad I'm married to my predictable faithful husband. So...aren't you even curious about what happened to Kevin's last girl Friday?"

"No." Alyson stared at the menu and wondered whether to have the pancakes or the meat-loaf special. That was one thing about this place—you could have breakfast or lunch or dinner any time of day you chose.

"I'll tell you what happened to her," Susan said irrepressibly. "She went to bed with Kevin and then the little snot dumped her. He has a habit of doing that—dumping the girls he's bedded. You'd better watch out for him. I told you—he's bad news."

Alyson felt a strange sick feeling inside. She tried to tell herself that it was just looking at this menu that made her lose her appetite. "I don't care what Kevin Nichols does," she muttered.

"Hah. I've seen the way you look at him. Anybody

can see it. You'd better watch yourself, I'm telling you."

Alyson slapped the menu shut. She didn't think about what she said next. It just came spilling out of her, and she heard it almost as if someone else was talking.

"I don't need Kevin Nichols. I already have somebody else. Tim. Tim Miller."

Susan gave her a hard look. "You have to be joking. That man is old enough to be your—"

"What does age have to do with anything? Tim is…he's wonderful. He's a dream. It's all happened pretty fast, but sometimes you just know. You know when you've found someone special." She couldn't seem to stop herself. It was like listening to a tape recording speed out of control. "Anyway," she rattled on, "why would I even look at someone like Kevin Nichols when I have Tim? It just wouldn't make any sense."

"Yeah, right," Susan muttered. "I wonder what your mother has to say about this."

"She doesn't have anything to do with it." Alyson heard her voice wobble, but still she couldn't stop. "My mother doesn't have anything to do with it at all. Tim and I, we're going to be together no matter what anybody says!"

CHAPTER TEN

BY EARLY AFTERNOON, Tim had enough of going stir-crazy. He'd tried to do the sensible thing. He'd tried to lie here on the damn couch resting his back. And then he just couldn't do it anymore. He needed motion, activity. He needed anything besides lying here remembering last evening and how it had felt to take Laurie in his arms. How it had felt to have her draw away from him.

He got off the damn couch, made his way to the kitchen, grabbed the faucet he'd dismembered yesterday. Then he headed out to his truck. He drove down to the hardware store on Main Street, climbed out of the truck and went inside.

A salesclerk approached. The guy had a beard he wore rather self-importantly; he kept stroking it. "Can I help you?" he asked. "Dr. Miller, isn't it?" Then he gave Tim what could only be termed a funny look. Tim paid no attention. He handed over the faucet parts.

"Think I need a replacement. Or maybe just a new O-ring."

"Hmm..." The man examined the pieces as if studying artifacts. "I'd replace the whole thing, myself. Might take some doing, though. Stay right here." He disappeared into a storeroom.

Tim glanced around at the boxes of nails and tacks and bolts. He didn't like being left alone with his own thoughts. That was why he'd gotten out of the house in the first place.

The truth was, he couldn't stop thinking about last night. More specifically, he couldn't stop thinking about Laurie. Lovely desirable stubborn Laurie. She'd made that confession to him, and he hadn't known what to do with it. He hadn't wanted it, that was for sure. According to her, she'd committed a terrible crime in letting Alyson think she'd been married all those years ago. When Tim compared that to some of the paths *he'd* taken earlier in his life, some of his more rebellious moments…when he did that, Laurie's sin seemed pretty insignificant.

Then again, he had to admit he wasn't an expert on parenting. Maybe you were supposed to be absolutely truthful with kids or you'd warp them for life. How the hell did he know? He'd just heard the way Laurie blamed herself, seen the misery in her face, and the next thing he knew he'd pulled her into his arms.

He cursed, walking past a row of saws and belt sanders. Every instinct he had told him he was getting in too deep with Laurie Russell. Way too deep. Through circumstances beyond his control, he found himself planted right in the middle of her chaotic life. So how did he unplant himself? Good question.

The clerk came back out of the storeroom. "Success," he said. "I didn't think we carried this make of faucet anymore, but here it is. You'll be able to replace the whole thing good as new."

"Fine," Tim said without much interest, pulling out his wallet.

"Doing some repairs on the old place, I take it," the man commented, stroking his beard.

"Something like that."

"Must be interesting, the three of you stashed in that house together."

Tim gave the man a repressive glance. "How much do I owe you?"

The clerk rang up the sale at the cash register. "Two ninety-six. I'm giving you a bargain, seeing as it's an out-of-date item."

Tim handed over three dollars and waited for his four cents change. The man seemed a bit slow about handing it over.

"We could all take a lesson from you," he said in a confidential tone. "Have to admit you worked mighty fast. She's a pretty little thing, isn't she?"

Tim stared at the man. "What are you talking about?" he asked quietly.

The man started to look a little uncomfortable. "Hey, nobody's blaming you. Living in the same house and all, who wouldn't grab the opportunity?"

That was the problem with this town—too much speculation. "Leave Laurie Russell out of it," Tim said.

"Who's talking about the mother? The way I hear it, you and the daughter... That's where you're getting the action."

Tim went still. And then he fixed the man with another stare—the Miller stare. He'd learned it from his older brother. It was something that had come in pretty useful at rowdy bars and other dubious locales. It had the required effect now.

The man's gaze skittered away. Quickly he took the four pennies out of the cash register and dropped them in Tim's hand. "Glad we could be of service," he said.

Tim wasn't done with him. "Where did you hear a sick story like that?" he said, his voice still quiet.

The man stroked his beard uneasily. "You know, just something floating around. If I'd thought it would bother you..."

"It bothers me all right."

The man paused. He glanced at Tim, glanced away again. "Forget I said a thing. *I'll* forget I ever heard it."

Tim left the store and climbed into his truck. He tossed the new faucet onto the seat beside him, finding that he'd lost his taste for home repairs. One thing for certain—he'd like to know who'd started the rumor about him. Lord, as if he'd ever have anything to do with a seventeen-year-old kid. It was sick. And if he ever found out who was responsible for the story, that person would be sorry. Very sorry.

A FEW HOURS LATER, Tim showed up at the clinic. So maybe his back was still giving him grief, but he'd decided to ignore it. He'd fixed the faucet. He'd fixed himself a sandwich. And then he'd realized it was time to fix his life. He'd come to Grant, Colorado, to be the town doctor. It was time to start filling that role, bad back or not. Laurie Russell or no Laurie Russell, for that matter.

"You shouldn't be here," Laurie said now, studying him with cool disapproval.

"You're not doing yourself any favors, you know, Tim," Bess added. "Ignore the problem and it'll just get worse."

Tim began shrugging into a white doctor's coat, only to grimace.

"Hurts, doesn't it?" Laurie asked without sympathy.

"I'm a little stiff, that's all."

"Maybe you're a little pigheaded." Laurie came close to help him work his arm into a sleeve. He caught her light yet provocative scent—something subtle and spicy. He looked at her. She looked back. And then she turned quickly away and began to flip through the appointment book as if it had some secret to tell her.

Tim kept on looking at her until Bess gave a discreet cough. He tried to remember why he was here, and observed that the sleeves of his white coat were too short. The rest of the thing was too baggy.

"Bet it fit Doc Garrett," he said.

"If you want to order new ones, just tell me where I'll get the money to pay for them," Bess said.

"We can't be in that bad a shape."

"Pretty bad," she said.

Laurie flipped a blank page of the appointment book. "Patients will start coming in," she said, her voice almost ringing with conviction. "They'll get over all the nonsense that's keeping them away. They'll be here."

Tim wondered if she knew how much nonsense was flying around this town. The story about him and her daughter, for one. Not that it was worth repeating. Laurie already had enough worries because of her kid; she didn't need any more. He became aware that he was watching her again when Bess gave another discreet cough.

"Tickle in your throat, Bess?" Tim asked.

"If I did have one," she replied, "I don't suppose I'd have anything to worry about. Not with so many doctors in town." She gave Laurie a disparaging glance as if to imply who was the extra doctor.

Meanwhile Laurie gave Tim her own disparaging glance. He wondered what she regretted most—telling him about that deception of hers or almost making love with him on the couch. Probably both.

The door of the clinic opened and a man came in. He appeared to be in his fifties and his manner was hesitant. Either that, or he didn't like doctors' offices. The minute he was in the door, he gave the impression he was going to turn around and walk right out again.

"Hello, Franklin," Bess said. "You weren't scheduled to come in until next week."

"I know," he said. "Just thought I'd stop by— No, forget it. I'll just come back."

Laurie stepped forward. "If there's something we can do for you now, we'll be more than happy," she said reassuringly. She offered her hand. "I'm Dr. Russell, by the way."

"Franklin Patterson." He shook hands with her, although he continued to give the impression he'd rather be anywhere else.

"Ah, yes," Laurie said. "I believe your wife came in to see me a few days ago."

"That she did." Franklin Patterson continued glancing toward the door. Now Tim stepped forward.

"Hi," he said. "I'm Dr. Miller. What can we do for you?"

The man looked from Laurie to Tim and then back again. Tim felt for the guy. It must be lousy when you didn't like going to the doctor, and then found *two* doctors vying for your attention.

"I was supposed to have a physical," Franklin said finally. "Shirley wanted me to go to Cortez, but..."

"It might be more convenient for you to have it here," Laurie said. "But that's up to you of course."

Tim had to hand it to her. She'd struck just the right note with Franklin—helpful but no pressure. At least the guy had stopped looking as if he was about to bolt.

"It does seem kind of a nuisance driving all the way to Cortez," Franklin admitted. Then Bess intervened.

"For goodness' sake, Franklin J. Patterson, make up your mind. You want your physical or don't you? We can work you in today—right this minute. It's not like we have any other takers."

Tim saw Laurie wince at the nurse's blunt pronouncement. But surprisingly, Franklin didn't seem put off.

"That dang physical's been hanging over me," he muttered. "I guess I do just want it over with."

Laurie gave an efficient nod. "Very well, Mr. Patterson. Bess will show you into an examination room and I'll be right there."

Franklin made an uncomfortable gesture toward Tim. "Actually...you're both doctors, aren't you?

One as good as the other?'' The message was clear. He wanted Tim, not Laurie. And now Tim saw a shuttered expression come over Laurie's face. No overt disappointment, no show of displeasure, just a careful absence of emotion. He supposed she was too professional for anything else.

"Mr. Patterson," Tim said, "I think you should know that Dr. Russell comes with very high recommendations. You couldn't do better..."

Laurie frowned at Tim, and now her expression said quite emphatically that she would fight her own battles. She turned back to Franklin.

"You know, I believe you *would* be more at ease with Dr. Miller. Bess will show you to the examining room and then Dr. Miller will be right in."

Tim had to hand it to her again. She'd spoken with just the right amount of brisk understanding. Franklin seemed relieved.

"Thanks, Dr. Russell," he said before disappearing down the hall with Bess.

Laurie looked at Tim. "You don't know anything about my recommendations," she said.

"I imagine they're pretty good."

She merely shrugged. "Your patient is waiting, Dr. Miller."

Bess had handled the preliminaries. When Tim entered the examination room, he saw Franklin Patterson already perched on the table wearing a paper robe. It occurred to Tim that those robes always made patients look forlorn and out of place.

"You'll be out of here in no time, Franklin," he said. The man didn't seem convinced. Tim scanned the patient chart. Bess had already taken the man's blood pressure and the reading was acceptable. Franklin had had his appendix out six years ago, suffered from periodic hay fever and had been treated for bunions. No medical history could have been more prosaic. "Nothing earth-shattering here," Tim said. "Routine physical, that's all?"

"Yeah, routine," Franklin said morosely. "The thing is, they're making some of us at the plant take a physical. Insurance purposes, they tell us."

"Says here you work for Pine Ridge Clothing."

"That's right." Franklin still sounded unhappy. Tim knew that the clothing company, situated out on the highway where the mountains opened up into farmland, was Grant's leading employer. Its existence was the main reason the town hadn't folded entirely. It was a small manufacturer of "natural" sportswear, whatever that meant, and it used the cachet of "made in the Rockies" to sell its wares.

Tim sensed there was something Franklin wanted to get off his chest, but didn't quite know how. "Everything okay at work?" he asked casually.

"They say it's just a routine physical," Franklin replied, "but how do I know what they're up to? Maybe they're just looking for an excuse to get rid of us longtimers. New management came in last fall. Things haven't been the same since."

Tim studied his patient. He had thinning hair and a long pale face, which at the moment was creased with worry. He didn't seem the type of man who'd pursued a lot of options in his life.

"Any health concerns?" Tim asked, his tone still casual. "Anything that might make you concerned about this physical? You know, anything beyond the fact you'd like to tell management to take a running leap off a cliff?''

Franklin almost cracked a smile. ''Nothing beyond the fact that I'm too young to retire and too old to give a damn.''

''Let's get this over with, then. Chances are I'll be giving you a clean bill of health.''

''Sounds good to me, Doc.'' It was the familiar nickname everybody had given to Jonathan Garrett these past forty years—Doc. Tim didn't know how he felt about inheriting it. The nickname seemed to fit him no better than Doc Garrett's coat.

Conducting a physical examination presented no great challenge. Tim followed steps he'd taken countless times before. He tested Franklin's reflexes and watched the man's bony leg jerk forward. Ears, nose and throat—check. Now Tim placed his stethoscope to Franklin's back. ''Take a deep breath,'' he said. ''Another. That's good.'' Heart and lungs—check. Tim couldn't help picturing the Jacobs Institute in Chicago, where he'd been interviewed only a few months before. All you had to do was walk through the door of that place, and you had the sense you were embarking on something important, something that mattered. Chances were, you wouldn't be asking some guy to open his mouth and say, ''Aaahh.''

Maybe a physical wasn't the most exciting work in the world, but Tim was as thorough as possible. ''Mr. Patterson,'' he said finally, ''looks like you're pretty darn healthy to me. Bess will take some blood for the usual workup, and I'd also like you to think about starting some aerobic exercise. Walking's the best way to begin. You can build up gradually to jogging.''

"Jogging. Sounds like you're going somewhere, doesn't it?''

Franklin left with a decided spring to his step. He seemed to have latched onto the idea of an exercise program. Maybe he just needed something to help him forget his problems down at the sportswear company. Was that the key to life in Grant? Tim wondered as he returned to the waiting room. Latching onto something to help you forget you were in a dead-end town?

"No need to look so glum," Bess said tartly. "I'll start to think you're less than thrilled to be here.''

"Bess, we need some excitement in this place.'' He glanced around the empty room. It showed Bess's touch: the walls were painted dandelion yellow, the chairs were the comfortable padded variety, and there was a children's corner, complete with dollhouse, building blocks and oversize storybooks. None of that changed one basic fact—the room was deserted. No patients, no children. "This has to be a joke," Tim said.

"People in town just don't know what to do," Bess answered. "Having two doctors makes it all too much of a decision. Before they didn't have any choice—it was Dr. Garrett or nobody. But now...''

"Where's Laurie?" Tim asked.

"She got a phone call," Bess said. "It perked her right up, so it must have been good news. And then she hightailed it out of here.''

"She didn't say where she was going?''

"I didn't ask. Unlike most folks in this town, I believe in minding my own business."

"Wish I knew what was going on," Tim said.

"Don't tell me *you're* getting nosy," Bess chided. "Or maybe it's Dr. Russell that has you so interested."

Tim glanced around discontentedly one more time. "Since you're so discerning, you've probably noticed that Dr. Laurie Russell doesn't much approve of me."

"She doesn't approve, that's certain. But she's attracted all right, just like you are. When the two of you are around each other, you send out enough electricity to run a small generator. It's a bit wearing, I'll tell you. All the more reason not to have two doctors in this town."

Tim figured he needed to steer Bess onto a new subject. "I got a letter from Gabe and Hallie yesterday," he said. "They sent along more pictures of the kids." He fished them out of his back pocket.

Bess was immediately interested, just as he'd known she'd be. She spread the snapshots in a fan before her. "Oh, look at that darling Lia...and Sara's grown so big! They're both adorable, aren't they?"

"Yeah, that they are," Tim said gruffly, observing the photos of his two young nieces. Hallie had adopted Lia from Guatemala before she'd even met Gabe. Then, after Hallie and Gabe had married, they'd produced a little sister for Lia. Now Lia was on the brink of twelve, a star pupil, as well as a devoted horsewoman; Sarah, five years younger, worshiped her big sister and tried to imitate everything she did. It made for quite some family.

Bess was watching him too closely. "You know,"

she murmured, "it's not impossible. You could end up with a wife and a couple of children someday."

Tim shook his head. "It's not for me."

"How do you know?"

"Just one of those things, I guess."

Bess wouldn't let up. "Just because your own father botched the job of being a parent, that doesn't mean you would."

Tim gathered up the photos. Maybe bringing them out hadn't been such a good idea. "It's a lot more complicated than that," he told Bess.

"Like hell it is," she said inelegantly. "Here's the truth of it. Your dad was a rotten parent, so you decided to retreat from family life altogether. Falling in love with your soon-to-be sister-in-law, Hallie, was just a convenient way to *really* make sure you'd avoid having a family. After all, as long as you're carrying a torch for her, you can't have a real relationship, can you? Pretty convenient, I'd say."

Tim scowled at Bess. "What the devil makes you think I was ever in love with—"

Bess waved a dismissive hand. "Oh, I'll wager you were never genuinely stuck on Hallie. You knew right from the start she was meant for Gabe. But she makes a good excuse not to get involved with anyone else. Now, let me guess. I imagine the subject of your sister-in-law has come up more than once when you're talking to Laurie Russell. 'Sorry, Dr. Laurie, don't expect too much from me because my heart was taken long ago.'"

Sometimes Bess really got on Tim's nerves. He returned the photographs to his pocket. "Don't you have anything better to do than analyze my private life?'' he growled.

''It's just that I can't stand to see you waste your potential. Don't you realize, Tim? Everybody has someone they're meant to love. And I mean really love. One special person…'' Suddenly tears sprang to Bess's eyes. She grabbed a tissue and swiveled away from Tim.

Tim couldn't figure out why he had this effect on females lately. First Laurie Russell seemed to cry when she was around him, and now Bess.

He took hold of her elbow and guided her to one of those padded chairs, then sat beside her. She began to cry in earnest, holding the tissue to her face. Competent no-nonsense Bess Thompson—in tears. It wasn't something he liked to see.

''Okay, you'd better tell me what's wrong,'' he said, handing her an entire box of tissues. She clutched it to her.

''It's nothing,'' she said, her voice wavering.

''Right—nothing. That's why you're sobbing your heart out.''

''I know I'm making a damn fool of myself,'' she said crankily. ''But…oh, Tim. I actually do love the wretched old geezer!''

He stared at her. ''What?''

The tears had slowed to a trickle. ''Don't tell me you haven't figured it out by now.''

''Afraid to say I haven't.''

She blotted her eyes. ''I'm in love with Jonathan Garrett. Have been for years. Tell me I'm crazy. Tell me I'm throwing my life away. You'd be right on

both counts. But I can't seem to do anything about
it."

He tried to take it in. Maybe he was dense, but
he'd never even suspected. Bess had always seemed
too sensible to fall for someone like Doc Garrett, a
man who went through women the way some people
went through lightbulbs. The doc made sure he never
settled too long with any one woman. Tim knew the
type. He was a little like that himself.

"Bess," he said, "this is…a bummer."

"Tell me about it. The way he's carrying on with
Estelle…oh, I could slap his silly bald head."

"Does he know how you feel?"

"Never!" Then her voice wavered again. "But the
old coot really is something, Tim. He does come
through when you need him. If only you'd known
what it was like after my divorce—you can imagine,
with this town. Everybody had a different theory
about why I broke up with my husband. Some people
even thought *I* was the one who had the affair. But
Jonathan—he told me just to ignore everything they
said. He'd already gone through two divorces himself
and nothing seemed to faze him. He knew exactly
what I needed, Tim. Not sympathy. Just…com-
panionship. We became friends. That's how it was.
We worked together and we were friends…" Her
voice trailed off, and she buried her face in another
tissue.

She had it bad, Tim knew that much. Doc Garrett
probably didn't have a clue. He was just having a
good time with Estelle over in Digby. Tim sat there,
trying to think of something to say and knowing there
wasn't anything. He wasn't an expert on love and

broken hearts. Bess was right about one thing—he'd made certain to stay away from real love. It was a habit he'd perfected. And it was a habit he didn't know how to break.

CHAPTER ELEVEN

LAURIE STRAINED as she pushed the orange couch inch by inch across the floor. She kept telling herself she was making progress, but at last she had to stop, panting, for a rest.

"You should let me do it," Tim said.

"Forget it. You'd hurt your back and you'd be laid up all over again. Is that what you want?"

He didn't answer, just watched her with a disgruntled expression. She wished he would go away and let her do this on her own. His presence unsettled her. She was too aware of everything about him. Tim Miller was the kind of man who took over a room, seemingly without effort. All he had to do was stand there, as he was doing now.

Laurie forced her gaze away from him, and focused on the couch. Both she and Tim had agreed it should be moved into the den off the living room. That way Tim would have more privacy. It seemed he needed the couch. Last night he'd tried sleeping on the lumpy old bed down the hall, only to end up retreating to the orange couch in a good deal of pain. Apparently it was the only thing that soothed his back.

Now, gazing at the couch, Laurie was reminded of certain events. The bathtub incident. Not to mention the almost-making-love incident the other evening.

"When are you going to tell me about it?" Tim asked.

She started guiltily and felt her skin flush. "What...?" she asked distractedly.

"Bess says you got a phone call at the clinic yesterday, and then you ran out of there like you'd had the best news in the world. I've kept my mouth shut for the better part of twenty-four hours, but now my curiosity's gettin' to me."

"You know what happened to the cat that got too curious," she said.

He grinned slowly. "Yeah. In my version it ended up satisfied. So, Doc Russell, what gives?"

Somebody ought to censor that smile of Tim Miller's. Laurie felt a swirl of warmth inside just looking at him. She glanced away resolutely.

"If you have to know...Phil Cline called to tell me he'd finally gathered the town council for a meeting and I was welcome to join it."

"So," Tim said, "you met with the venerable council. Let me guess—they voted to keep you as resident physician. Then they voted to boot me out. And you felt so bad about it you delayed telling me."

"The blasted meeting never got to a vote. They started arguing about protocol, and this time Harold Lattimer was the one who walked out in a tiff. It was awful. It was humiliating. Nothing got resolved! Are you happy?"

He made an unsuccessful effort to look solemn. "You didn't have to hide what happened, Laurie."

His words stung. "Maybe that's me," she said. "Maybe I have a habit of hiding the truth."

Now he really did look serious. "I didn't mean it

that way. I wasn't accusing you. Why would I? But something tells me you spend a whole lot of time accusing yourself.''

She sank down onto the couch. He was right—she couldn't stop blaming herself.

"Don't you realize?" she asked. "It's as if I took one wrong turn eighteen years ago and I haven't found my way back since.''

"Laurie...I've taken a few wrong turns myself. More than a few. But there's only one thing you can do to find your way back, and that's forgive yourself.''

She wanted to believe him. With all her heart, she wanted to. But these past few days Alyson had drawn farther and farther away. Her young face turned stony whenever she saw Laurie. She was spending even less time at home than before. She'd taken that job with Kevin Nichols, but even during her off hours she found one excuse after another to get out of the house—as if she couldn't bear the thought of being around her mother a second longer than necessary.

Tim sat beside Laurie on the couch. He gazed at her for a long moment as if debating something. With gentle but irresistible persuasion, he turned her face toward him. And then he brought his lips to hers.

She knew she ought not to allow his kiss. She had no place in her life for a man like him—a man who wasn't the settling-down type. She ought to pull away before it was too late. But then she realized the truth. It was already too late. Tim Miller did something to her. When he touched her she seemed to forget everything else. With a sigh she gave herself up to him...

A knock came at the front door. Neither Laurie nor Tim paid any attention. Tim just went on kissing her.

"Don't stop," she whispered against his mouth.

"I'm not..."

The knock came again, more insistent this time. Laurie slowly untangled herself from Tim, emerging out of a warm sensual haze. And then, as reality finally intruded, she scrambled to her feet. She stared at the couch in dismay.

"Every time we're around that...that *thing,* something happens!"

"Tell me about it," Tim murmured. His eyes had darkened to a smoky blue and his gaze lingered on her.

The knocking continued. Smoothing her hair and hoping that Tim's kiss didn't show in her eyes, Laurie went to open the door. There stood Bess, her own silvery hair swept into an elegant yet tidy chignon.

"Why, hello," Laurie said, with an attempt at normalcy. "Do you need us over at the clinic?"

"Not likely," Bess said.

A social call from Bess was not usual, but Laurie did her best to go with it. "Won't you come in?" she asked.

Bess stepped inside. She peered into the living room, where Tim now stood beside the orange couch.

"Hi there," he said genially.

Bess studied Tim, then Laurie. She raised her eyebrows in just the slightest speculation. It was enough to galvanize Laurie into action. Forget social calls— it was time to do something productive.

"Bess," she said, "how about giving me a hand? I'm trying to move the couch into the den."

"If I did it, we'd be finished in no time," Tim grumbled.

"No," Laurie said.

"You'd think a *doctor* would have the sense to let his back mend," Bess contributed. "You'd think he wouldn't let his pride get in the way."

"Amen to that," Laurie said. Bess, however, did not seem to welcome any camaraderie. Her manner still professional, she went to one end of the couch and started pushing.

Laurie joined her. With two of them working at it, they made real progress. Tim went ahead toward the den. He surveyed the width of the doorway. "It's going to be a tight fit," he warned.

"Oh, no," Laurie said. "Don't tell me we're going to have to tip it again."

Fortunately, however, this doorway was just wide enough. Laurie and Bess maneuvered the couch through and at last the job was done. Admittedly things were a bit cramped. More of Doc Garrett's junk was piled here: crates of books, a broken lamp, two guitar cases propped in the corner, stacks of cardboard file boxes.

Bess looked around. "The man is a disaster," she stated. It took Laurie a minute to realize that Bess was talking about Doc Garrett. That was a surprise— every other time Laurie had heard Bess mention the doc, it had been with a tinge of reverence.

"Thanks for your help," Laurie said. Bess wasn't paying any attention. She crossed to one of the crates, took out a book and read the spine.

"Really," she muttered. "What did he think he was doing with a volume of poetry?"

"You know Doc," Tim said. "He collects everything."

"I'm sure he's never *read* any poetry." Bess tossed the book down almost contemptuously. Then she was all business. "Much as I enjoy moving furniture, I didn't come over here for that," she said. "I thought I should tell both of you about something I've heard." She paused. "I'm not quite sure the best way to put this."

"Spit it out," Tim said.

"Very well. There's a nasty story going around town, Tim. A story about you and Alyson. That the two of you are...involved. And it seems that Alyson herself is the one who started it."

THE LIVING ROOM appeared too large and empty without the orange couch. And to Laurie, Alyson looked small and vulnerable sitting there in the middle of Doc Garrett's shabby little sofa. Her daughter also looked defiant.

"Why did you do it?" Laurie asked. "If you could just tell me that much. Dammit, why would you spread such a harmful story?"

"I'd kind of like the answer to that myself," Tim said. His voice was quiet and even, but Alyson flicked an uncertain glance at him.

"You're both blowing this whole thing out of proportion," Alyson said.

"No, I don't think we are." Laurie struggled with too many emotions right now—anger that her daughter could have been so careless and unthinking, love for Alyson no matter what she did, panic that she'd never again know what was going through her daughter's mind.

"Just tell me," she repeated. "Why did you do it?"

"I don't know!" Alyson burst out. "And I didn't say all those things everybody *says* I did. I never said I had sex with him—"

Tim winced. "Not even the hardware clerk was *that* graphic."

Laurie stared at him. "You sound as if you've heard about this before."

"I did get an unfortunate dose of it the other day. I can tell you this much—that damn hardware clerk won't be repeating it."

Laurie folded her arms, suddenly feeling cold inside. "You heard this and you didn't tell me?"

"I refused to give it any credence," Tim said brusquely. "I wasn't going to dignify it by taking it seriously."

Laurie shook her head. "*I* take it seriously."

"You say that like you almost think there's some truth to it." His voice had gone flat and hard. Laurie gazed at him, saw the carefully impassive lines of his face. And after what he'd told her about his past, she suspected why he looked that way. Tim Miller, no doubt, had known too many people in his life ready to think the worst of him.

"Of course I don't give it any credence," she said firmly. She was being completely honest about that. Instinctively she trusted Tim's honor.

"Excuse me," Alyson said. "*I* could have told you the story isn't true. You could believe *me*."

"Hard to do right now," Tim said grimly, "considering you're the one who started the story. But we'd like to understand what's going on here."

Alyson examined her thumbnail. "You told me to be cool," she mumbled. "You said if I wanted a guy's attention, I should act like it didn't really matter to me."

Tim looked beleaguered. "How the hell do you get from that to—"

"You were giving advice to my daughter?" Laurie interrupted. "*Romantic* advice?"

He ran a hand through his hair. "It wasn't like that. The kid asked me. I said the first thing that came to mind."

Alyson got to her feet. "Glad to see it was so important to you," she said, her tone mildly sarcastic. "'The kid' bugs you with a question, so you tell her any old thing. I get it."

"It's no use trying to make yourself the victim here," Laurie intervened. "What you did was wrong—very wrong. What on earth were you thinking, Alyson? I still don't understand why you did it!"

"Join the crowd," Alyson said, her voice oddly restrained. "Because I don't really know why I did it, either. Maybe I just…maybe I wanted everybody to stop treating me like a child. If it's any consolation, Mom, Kevin treats me like one, too. Anyway, I know what I said was stupid and I'd take it back if I could. Excuse me, but I need to leave now."

"Alyson, we're not finished yet, not by a long shot."

"I really do need to leave, Mom." Moving with a certain dignity, Alyson made her way to the front door and went out, shutting the door behind her. Laurie started to go after her, but Tim put a restraining hand on her arm.

"There's nothing more we can do right now," he said. "She's playing the wounded heroine. I think it's safe to say, though, she won't tell any more cockeyed stories."

"That's not good enough," Laurie said in frustration. "She has to talk to me. I *have* to know what's going on with her."

"She pretty much told us, didn't she? She wants this guy's attention. It's the old trick—make it seem like you're involved with somebody else. Make the somebody else an older man, and I guess you're really in business."

Laurie couldn't stand still. She began to pace, as if that would somehow calm her worry and anger. "Now I really feel wonderful," she muttered. "My daughter is starting terrible rumors so she can catch the eye of some...some little twit who just wants to see how many conquests he can make."

"Maybe the rumors about him aren't true, either."

Alyson had suggested as much. She'd accused Laurie of listening to gossip. But when it was your very own daughter involved, you couldn't afford to take any chances. Maybe you had to believe the rumors until they were proved wrong.

Laurie stopped to consider Tim. "You're taking all this rather well," she said. "You don't seem nearly as upset as you could be."

He sat down on the sofa, his lanky frame taking it over. "I'm not happy about it," he said. "In fact, I'm pretty teed off at your daughter. But I grew up in a small town, remember? I've seen how these things work. For a while something's big news, then another story comes along to take its place. We just have to ride this out—it'll be over soon enough."

Laurie's frustration only seemed to grow. "We can't just ride this out. We have to do something— set people straight…"

"What do you suggest, Doc Russell? Alert the media? Or maybe call a meeting of the town council?"

Laurie resumed pacing. "Don't you worry how this will affect your reputation?"

"Reputation… Never had much of one to begin with. Of course, before this, nobody ever accused me of consorting with a seventeen-year-old. Lord."

"There *is* one solution," Laurie said. She came to a stop in front of him. "Let's face it. If we stopped sharing the house, the rumors would stop."

He gazed at her steadily. "In other words, you want me to move out."

"Alyson and I could be the ones to move out."

"Where would you go?"

Trust him to ask the most direct question. "The tourist season is almost here," she said. "The bed-and-breakfasts will start opening."

"And you can really afford that."

She frowned at him. "No, not really. But I'd manage somehow."

"Let me guess," he said. "Now I'm supposed to do the noble thing and offer to pack my bags."

"Look, I know you can't afford it any more than I can, but—"

"Actually I probably can," he said. "I had some ranch land that I sold to put myself through medical school. It was a good piece of property—I still have some of the money left from that sale."

She gazed at him. He lounged there on that sagging old sofa, looking for all the world like a devil-may-care cowboy—denim shirt, worn jeans, scuffed boots. Yet as always, Tim was full of surprises. To hear him tell it, not only had he held every job imaginable in the past, he'd also been a landowner.

"So," she said, "you could afford to leave." She ought to be relieved at the thought. Instead, all she felt was a strange emptiness.

He straightened. "Yeah, I could afford it. I could walk out of here, find myself another place. But you know what, Laurie? That would really be giving credence to the story. It's like admitting there was something going on, after all."

"I don't like the idea of that any more than you do," she admitted. "But what else can we do?"

"Like I told you, we can just ride out the rumor. The folks of Grant will soon find something else to chew on."

"I suppose you're right." She sighed. "I also suppose you need my orange couch—because it's therapeutic," she added hastily. "For your back."

He gazed at her seriously. "Sure turns out the darn thing's comfortable. But that's not the reason I'm staying, Laurie."

"I know, I know. You're staying because you don't want to give the rumor any credence."

"That's not the real reason, either." He looked unsettled. "The reason I'm staying is because…hell, I don't know, it's almost like I feel I'm standing guard somehow."

She frowned. "What are you talking about?"

Now he looked truly perturbed. "Don't ask me to explain it any better than that. I just feel like...with you and Alyson, I'm standing guard."

"You think you have to look out for me?" she asked disbelievingly.

"Something like that."

"Why?"

"Beats me," he said. "I didn't say there was any logic to it. You've made it pretty clear you can take care of yourself. So why the hell... It's just how I feel. Damned inconvenient, too."

She'd never once had a man say he wanted to look out for her. It was something new and she didn't know quite how to react. But she looked at Tim and she had the sudden conviction that if she ever *did* need a man to stand guard, he'd be the one she'd want. Trick back or no, Tim Miller radiated physical strength. But it was more than that. It was the strength she sensed inside him. Surely that was something a woman could rely on....

He stood. "Look, forget I said anything. You're right—it doesn't make any sense. You can take care of yourself, you've made that much clear. And I don't make a habit of butting in on other people's lives...ever."

She didn't know why she felt a sense of loss. Just because one minute Tim Miller offered to look out for her and the next he said it was a mistake? That was no reason for her to feel such a letdown.

"Of course you don't butt in," she said. "A convenient way of saying you don't get involved."

He made a restless gesture. "I'll admit I've never

wanted the responsibility of a family—but suddenly I'm right in the middle of one, complete with a teenager who's spreading stories about me."

"I apologize for Alyson," Laurie said stiffly. "It was terrible what she did. And very unfair to you. But you're not in the middle, Tim. This is *my* family, not yours."

He gazed at her, his blue eyes serious and intent. "I understand better than you think," he said. "Because we're two of a kind, Laurie. We've spent a whole lifetime doing the same thing. Making sure we didn't need anyone else...anyone at all."

ALYSON WENT TO WORK early the next morning. She'd slipped out of the house well before there'd been any possibility of confronting either her mother or Tim. Now she turned her key in the lock and let herself into Nichols Jeep Tours. From her few days on the job, she knew it would be a long time before Kevin would show. That meant she'd have the place to herself.

She went to the counter and started the coffeemaker. Even though the pot would probably be hours old by the time Kevin appeared, she wanted to be ready. She didn't want to leave any detail undone, didn't want to give him any excuse to think she was a rotten employee. She'd even bought a fresh can of coffee out of her own meager supply of money. Every week her mother gave her an allowance. They didn't call it an allowance of course. Ever since Alyson could remember, Mom had almost made it seem like the two of them were financial partners. They never had much money, but they shared. And Mom had always trusted her to handle money well. In that sense she had never treated Alyson like a child.

Alyson stared at the coffee dripping into the pot, and she felt something horrible inside, something she couldn't really explain. But she remembered the expression on her mother's face yesterday. Disapproval. Disgust, even. As if she couldn't believe Alyson had been capable of committing such a terrible crime. Telling such a lie.

Alyson tried to argue with herself. She hadn't really done anything that outrageous, had she? She'd only said those things to that waitress, Susan. She hadn't said anything to anybody else. It wasn't her fault that Susan had gone blabbing to practically everybody else in town and the story had grown in the process. Alyson hadn't intended for that to happen. She'd never intended anything at all. She hadn't *planned* any of it.

She wasn't doing a very good job of making herself feel better. She couldn't seem to forget that expression on her mother's face. Mom had looked at her a lot of ways before—with worry and concern and love. Anger sometimes, too. Exasperation. But the way she'd looked at Alyson yesterday had been something entirely new. It was as if, for the first time, her mother had wondered if she even *liked* her.

The horrible sensation she had was only getting worse. She knew guilt had a lot to do with it. She'd done something wrong and now she was paying for it. She had a pretty good idea that Tim Miller hated her after what she'd said. But how could anyone have actually believed it? She was ordinary and plain— how could anyone really think she'd gotten a man's attention? Maybe everybody was just laughing at her. What would Kevin think when he heard? He'd probably have a good laugh, too.

Alyson made a small sound of despair. She'd really messed things up, and she didn't see any way to get out of it. And what haunted her the most was the memory of that disappointed look on her mother's face. Sometimes she just wanted to get as far away from her mother as she could, but right now all she wanted to do was run home and fling herself into Mom's arms and beg her to make things the way they'd been before. The two of them, safe and together, no one else allowed inside their magic circle....

The door open behind her. Alyson turned and saw Kevin wander in, giving one of his unfettered yawns.

"You're early," she said, wondering immediately if it was the wrong thing to say. She didn't want to imply that Kevin was lazy or slack. The tourist season hadn't even started yet—he had a right to take it easy. She was awfully glad she'd started the coffee. It was ready now, and she poured him a mug and handed it over.

"Thanks." He smiled at her, and she thought she'd never seen anyone as gorgeous. Not even Tim Miller could compare. The morning light came through the windows and fell on Kevin, burnishing his blond hair. Alyson was glad she'd cleaned the windows. The light almost seemed to gleam on Kevin's tanned skin.

"I sure am tired," he said.

"Another late night?" She was proud of her careless tone. But this time when Kevin smiled, it was as if to himself.

"Yeah, I guess you could say that. Another late night."

Alyson wondered who he'd been with. Probably some beautiful girl with cleavage. But then Alyson didn't want to think about any girlfriend of Kevin's. She felt small and stupid and wished she could just disappear. She went to her desk and sat down. Unfortunately there wasn't any work to do. She'd already organized the file cabinet and dusted the place countless times. She didn't know how to make herself look busy. Maybe she ought to buy a ream of paper so she could pretend to use the old electric typewriter.

Kevin came over and sat on the edge of her desk, balancing his mug on his knee. "So, how was your night?" he asked.

"Uh...fine." No way would she admit to him that she hadn't had a date in months.

"Nothing exciting with the boyfriend?" he asked.

She raised her head quickly. "The boyfriend?"

"Kind of old for you, isn't he?"

She couldn't believe that Kevin was speaking about *Tim*. And he was looking at her differently than he had before. He was looking at her with...interest.

For a minute Alyson couldn't speak at all. She couldn't do anything but gaze back at him. For the first time—the very first time—he actually seemed to be seeing her. Not a kid. Not a child. Just someone who knew about late nights, too.

Deep inside, she knew that this was the time to tell him the whole thing had been a mistake, a lie. She ought to confess that there'd never been anything between Tim and her. But somehow she just couldn't get the words out of her mouth. She couldn't bear the thought of Kevin laughing at her.

"It's just...it's over," she mumbled. "What happened between me and Tim Miller—it's over." She listened to the sound of her own voice, and again it seemed as if she was hearing somebody else speak, somebody she didn't even know.

"The guy works fast," Kevin observed. "You just moved to town and already he dumped you. Too bad."

"It didn't happen that way," she said sharply. "I'm...I'm the one who ended it. I mean, he's too old."

"Yeah, it's pretty creepy when you think about it. A guy that age going after a teenager." He gave a shrug as if he was far too old for teenagers himself.

"I can take care of myself," Alyson said. "It's not like he was the first for me." She didn't know where the words were coming from. They just seemed to spill out of her mouth.

Kevin seemed amused. "Not the first," he echoed. "I'm supposed to believe you're a woman of experience?"

Any second now he *would* be laughing. "Forget it," she said. "It's none of your business, anyway, is it? I'm just here to do a job. That is, if there's ever going to be any work."

Kevin slid off the desk. He didn't seem offended by her snide remark. "There'll be plenty to do in a week or two when the tourists start hitting this area. You'll be sorry you ever complained." He gave her another glance, a measuring one this time. And she could tell he didn't know what to think about her, after all.

She knew it still wasn't too late. She could still tell him that she'd made up the story about Tim, that there was no truth to it. But Kevin's speculative half-interested glance kept her silent.

CHAPTER TWELVE

IT WAS ONLY twenty-four hours or so later that Tim nearly skidded his truck into a lamppost on the corner of Main and Vermont. He hadn't been driving particularly fast, nor had he swerved to avoid an oncoming car or a runaway dog. No, what had caused the near accident was a fluorescent blue poster in the front window of the Rocky Mountain Cleaners.

Tim climbed out of his pickup in that stiff-as-a-board manner he had begun to perfect since he'd thrown out his back and went over to get a closer look. The poster proclaimed exactly what Tim had thought:

VOTE FOR LAURIE RUSSELL,
TOWN DOCTOR.

Beneath the big bold lettering was a photograph of Laurie looking very pretty and very professional in her dress doctor whites, a stethoscope draped around her neck.

Tim, cursing the day he'd met Dr. Laurie Russell, went into the dry cleaners and ripped the poster from the window. He was prepared to argue this appropriation with any and all comers, but the place was empty.

He went back out and climbed into his truck. He'd barely gotten the old engine started when he noted another bright blue placard in the barber's window—and one in the five-and-ten and the bakery and the green grocer's and...

The damn things were plastered in all the windows up and down Main Street.

Tim slammed down the clutch and notched the truck into first gear. There was going to be hell to pay for this. And he knew just where to go collect it.

LAURIE HAD THOUGHT things couldn't get much worse between herself and the indomitable nurse Bess. She'd thought wrong.

"It's not that I don't like plants," Bess grumbled at Laurie. "Don't get me wrong. I dated a botanist when I was in college—and don't I vote for the Green Party in every election? It's just...they make me feel so darn guilty. Watching them die and all. Knowing it's my fault..."

"All right, Bess. Fine. Didn't I already say I'd take it back?" Laurie scooted the offending plant—a pretty geranium in a clay pot—farther off to the side of her desk behind the lamp. "I was only trying to spruce things up a little. Make myself feel at home. How was I supposed to know you detested plants?"

"You see," Bess said. "There you go. Someone expresses a simple preference for a plant-free environment and automatically people start assuming they're the kind of person who steps on flowers or who sprays No-Grow in their backyard. So I replaced the grass out back with that patio extension—but the circular drive covering the front is only there because the old Studebaker doesn't back up as well as it used to. I was as sorry as the next person to see all that grass dug up."

Bess walked over and frowned at the geranium. "They only give you your money back over at the nursery if you've kept the receipt. You did keep the receipt, Dr. Russell, didn't you?"

"Bess, don't worry. Of course I kept the receipt. What kind of fool throws away the receipt for such a controversial purchase as a geranium?"

Bess's expression said she didn't really appreciate Laurie's humor. In fact, she had the look of someone about to say something downright nasty in return, but then the familiar rumble of Tim's truck pulling up in front of the clinic distracted her.

"Dr. Tim will be on my side," Bess said. "I'm almost certain he'll agree with my point of view. No plants in the office."

Bess was already heading through the reception area, as if she thought the sooner she got Tim's support, the better. But when Tim banged open the front door, he had the look of someone who was too disgruntled to agree with anything.

"Mornin', Bess, Doc Russell," Tim said in a tone that was anything but cheery. He was holding something crumpled up in one hand, and without any explanation he smoothed it out carefully on the counter as if concerned with every crease.

"A real pretty picture of the doc here, Bess, don't you think so?"

Now Bess was standing beside Tim, perusing. "Hmm," she said. "I'm not saying it is a pretty picture...and I'm not saying it isn't. I like the slogan, though. Kinda' catchy. 'Vote For Laurie Russell, Town Doctor.'"

Laurie was up from behind her desk in a flash, giving the poster her own once-over. "Where the heck did you get this, Tim?"

"Now that's about how I thought she'd play it, Bess. The old innocent never-even-seen-this-before routine."

"Tim, if you think I had anything to do with this, you're mistaken. Why…just look at it. The whole thing's ridiculous!"

Just then the phone rang and Bess answered with her usual proficiency.

"Grant Family Practice. Why, hello, Phil. Uh-huh…yes…uh-huh… You don't say, Phil. Uh-huh… Well, I never… Fine… Bye-bye now, Phil."

Bess gave Laurie what could only be described as a smug grin. "That was Phil Cline. Seems the town council met last evening over at the diner—a sort of emergency dinner buffet. Anyhow, seems Rowena Maxwell had a rather vivid dream about running for president—but in this dream she had to take a leave of absence from the campaign trail to have her appendix removed. Anyway, to make a long story short, the town council loved the idea so much they had Beverly Davis get her husband to rush the posters through last night."

"Idea," Laurie said. "What idea?"

Bess's grin got a little wider. "Seems that you and Tim are going to have to let the people of Grant decide which one of you to keep. We're going to have an election!"

Laurie couldn't believe what she'd just heard.

"This is preposterous. Get Phil back on the line. I'll set him straight. No way am I going to stoop to such tactics for a position that was promised to me in the first—"

"That's just what Phil thought you'd say," Bess interrupted. "And that's why he was calling from a pay phone, and why he and the council rushed this through. Seems they thought it might just be better all around if you two didn't have a choice in the matter."

"I don't believe this!" Laurie looked accusingly at Tim.

"Hey," Tim said. "Don't point the finger at me. Rowena Maxwell's the one having dreams."

"I'm a doctor, not a politician," Laurie said indignantly. "I won't agree to it. I simply won't."

"Patients haven't been showing up at the clinic," Bess reminded her. "Nobody's known for certain who's the real town doctor, so they've stayed away. An election will change matters. It'll give people a clear-cut choice. Power to the people and all that."

Laurie wondered if this situation could get any more absurd. She glanced at Tim again. "*You* can't possibly be willing to agree."

His expression conveyed what he thought of the whole idea.

"At least we see eye to eye," Laurie said.

Bess only gave another grin. She, at least, seemed to be enjoying herself thoroughly. "I'm afraid neither one of you understands how this town works. The council may be slow at making up its mind, but once it does, watch out. You see, Dr. Russell and Dr. Miller, once those posters hit the streets, this election was already a done deal!''

THE NINE-YEAR-OLD sat very rigid and straight as Tim stitched the cut on her finger. He could tell she was trying hard to be brave, but her chin trembled. The little girl's mother wasn't much help. *Her* face had gone white and she looked as if she might faint at any moment.

"Have a seat, Mrs. Vance," Tim said easily. "This won't take too much longer, but you might as well make yourself comfortable." From his experience, this was the one thing people always wanted to hear—medical procedures would be over in a flash before you even knew what was happening.

"Amy," Tim said to the little girl, "my nieces tell me that computer games are the latest craze where they live. Is that your experience?"

Amy didn't look quite so frightened anymore. "We have a computer at school," she said dismissively. "It's okay, I guess. But my friends and me, we like skateboards better."

"Skateboarding," Tim said. "That was the thing when I was growing up."

"*You* know how to skateboard?" Amy didn't hide her skepticism.

"I was the champion on my block. Of course, it's been a long time since then, but still…"

Tim and Amy went on to discuss the relative merits of basketball versus football; Amy claimed to have a killer jump shot. Her face grew animated as she talked, and Tim continued to do his job.

"All done," he said after a bit, swiveling the light away.

"Already?" she asked.

"If you want more stitches, I'll be happy to oblige."

"No thanks."

"Next time be more careful when you try carving up a bar of soap."

"It was an experiment," Amy said loftily. She scrambled off the examining table and headed out the door, not even waiting for her mother. That was something else in Tim's experience—people wanted to get out of doctors' offices just as fast as they could.

Mrs. Vance stood and Tim saw that the color had come back into her face. "Thank you, Dr. Miller," she said. "You were wonderful with Amy. And you know something? When it comes election time, I'm giving you *my* vote." Then she left.

It was only day two of the so-called campaign, but Tim could tell where it was headed. A popularity contest between him and Laurie Russell. Some people were trying to decide whether or not he really was a jerk who'd mess with a seventeen-year-old girl. He'd even heard rumors that some people wanted to run him out of town, and that the only thing preventing it was Laurie Russell's staunch assertion he hadn't done anything wrong. Laurie had also insisted that Alyson make public efforts to set the record straight. Which had only made matters more tense between her and her daughter, but she hadn't backed down.

Laurie. She'd defended Tim, even though the two of them were now competing flat out for this job. Laurie, a woman of surprising loyalties and stubborn self-sufficiency. A beautiful woman, her dark eyes betraying a vulnerability she didn't want anyone to see.

Tim cursed under his breath. He had to stop thinking about Laurie Russell. She wasn't for him. She'd already made it very clear that she could take care of herself and that she didn't want it any other way. Besides, she had a daughter who'd already caused Tim no end of grief. She had a complicated life, and Tim had a lifetime of avoiding complications with women. Maybe the best thing he could do was get out of that house. He could bunk somewhere else— anywhere else. He could put some distance between himself and the lovely Dr. Laurie Russell. He could try forgetting the notion that he had to look out for her somehow.

Bess came into the examining room. "Going to stay in here all day, Tim? The waiting room actually has two people in it."

"Two people? At least one of them must be here to see Laurie," he said.

"Nope, not these two. They're asking for you. Said they don't like the idea of a lady doctor. Set in their ways, I guess."

Tim gave her a sour glance. "Where is Laurie, anyway?"

"She went out half an hour ago. Something about canvassing for votes. She wouldn't say much more."

This election stuff was already going crazy—and it was only two days old. "I wonder where she is," he murmured. "I wonder what she's up to."

"That's a campaign secret, I'm sure. Come to think of it, Tim, we ought to set up our own campaign headquarters. We could use some banners, some flags,

and we need a slogan. Definitely a slogan. Let's see…
How about 'Tim Miller, The Doctor With A Heart'?
That has a certain ring to it.''

He gave Bess a hard look, but she managed to keep
a perfectly bland expression. Just then the door to the
examining room swung open and Doc Garrett came
in. He was as rumpled and untidy and full of energy
as ever.

''What the devil is everybody doing back here?''
he asked. ''I need to speak to you, Tim-o. I leave
town for a few days, and when I come back everybody's talking about some damn-fool election. That's
not the way it's supposed to go.''

''How *is* it supposed to go, Jonathan?'' Bess said
icily. ''If you spend all your time in Digby, you can't
very well expect to have a say in matters.''

The examination room suddenly seemed a little
cramped to Tim. It was an uncomfortable burden,
knowing how Bess felt about the doc. Jonathan, however, didn't seem to have a clue.

''What's eating you, Bessie?'' he asked without
rancor.

She stiffened. ''Please don't call me that. I've told
you before I don't like it. Save your silly nicknames
for Estelle.''

''Don't tell me you're against her, too,'' the doc
said. ''I thought you'd be the last—''

''I have nothing personal against Estelle,'' she said
in a forbidding tone. ''And I'm sure the two of you
will be very happy.''

Doc Garrett gave Bess a puzzled glance. Meanwhile Tim rubbed the kink in his back.

"Think I'd better get out there and see to those patients," he said.

"Don't go," Bess said instantly, the underlying message clear: *I can't stand to be left alone with the man I love, not even for one minute.* Tim wished heartily that she'd never confided in him.

Doc, however, still seemed oblivious. He gave Bess another quizzical glance, but then he addressed Tim.

"Why'd you agree to some idiotic idea like this? Phil Cline's poking his nose where it doesn't belong. I have a mind to tell the old fathead what he can do with his damned election." Jonathan seemed to be getting awfully worked up; even his bald pate was turning red.

"Watch your blood pressure," Bess said none too kindly.

"To hell with my blood pressure. I'm telling you, it's not supposed to happen this way. I hired you to take over my practice, Tim, and that's the end of it."

Tim thought about that research position in Chicago—the position he'd given up so he could embroil himself in small-town intrigue. He wondered again what he'd been thinking.

"Perhaps an election is the only fair way to go," he said.

"Is it because they're spreading gossip about you? Is that why you gave in to them?"

Chicago was sounding mighty good all right. "I haven't given in yet. But this way both Laurie and I can have a fair shot," Tim said. "May the better man/ woman win and all that."

Old Doc Garrett didn't look convinced. "We'll see about that," he muttered. "We'll see." He glanced at Bess again. "Thought you'd be on my side," he told her.

"I want Tim to take over the practice every bit as much as you do. But if you really want things to go your way, you shouldn't be spending all your time in Digby."

"That doesn't have anything to do with it," Doc said. And with that he vanished from the room as abruptly as he'd appeared.

"Doesn't he have any sense?" Bess asked unhappily. "I'd be the last to gossip about Estelle, but she's no good for him. No good at all!"

"Yeah, well...about those patients," Tim said. Bess went into action, putting a fresh cover on the examining table and clearing the instrument tray. But that didn't stop her from talking.

"How do you compete with a woman like Estelle? All sparkle and dazzle...and I just know what Jonathan thinks about me. Boring dependable Bessie. Always there for him. Always in the background."

"No one could call you boring." Tim considered just slipping out the door of the room. Bess, however, went on talking in a rush as she restocked the cotton swabs.

"That's the problem right there. I've always been too dependable, too predictable. I'm glad you helped me to see it, Tim."

"Hold on," he said. "I didn't help you see anything."

"Yes, you did. Just now you said that no one could call me boring. But it's exactly the opposite, isn't it? No one's gossiped about *me* in years. Not since my divorce, anyway. That experience was so unsettling

I've bent over backward ever since to be the model citizen. Above reproach. What a fool I've been. Really—thank you for helping me realize it.''

Every time he got around females lately, they thought he was giving them advice. But it was what they *did* with his advice that scared him.

"Bess, you haven't been a fool. Now, about those patients—"

"Oh, I've been a fool all right. But that's about to change, Tim. Everything's about to change. I'm going to give this town a reason to spread stories about me. And Jonathan Garrett...well, *he's* going to sit up and take notice!''

CHAPTER THIRTEEN

DAY THREE of the campaign. Day three of the most ridiculous frustrating exasperating time Laurie had ever known. Her feet ached from walking. Her knuckles hurt from knocking on doors. Her jaw felt sore from forcing one smile after another. She couldn't believe she'd been reduced to this—pounding the street in search of votes to keep her job.

She climbed the porch steps and let herself into the house. The truth was, she hadn't seen any choice but to go door to door. Even if a few patients were finally showing up at the clinic, they all wanted to consult Dr. Timothy Miller. It seemed clear to her that she was entering the campaign as the underdog. But if the people of Grant wouldn't come to her, she would just have to go to them. And so she'd begun canvassing the town. Tomorrow she would start canvassing all over again.

She told herself not to think too far ahead. Coming into the living room, she gazed at the stretch of empty floor space. The orange couch was hidden away in the den—officially Tim's room now—but its existence continued to mock her. She wondered if Tim was still over at the clinic getting the chance to practice the art of medicine. That was all she'd ever wanted—the chance to practice medicine.

She began wandering through the rest of the house. "Alyson," she called, without much hope. But a few seconds later she heard her daughter answer grudgingly from the kitchen.

"Back here."

Laurie went into the kitchen and saw Alyson sitting at the table, her head bent over a cookbook. The cloth cover of the book was frayed, the yellowed pages marked with years-old splatters. Another relic left behind by Doc Garrett—or perhaps by one of his lady friends.

"Looks interesting," Laurie remarked as casually as possible. "Maybe we could fix some dinner together."

"Since when do you like to cook, Mom. Stop pretending we're going to turn into the cozy nuclear family."

Laurie felt the all-too-familiar tightening in her stomach, but she kept her voice neutral. "I know everything to do with moving here has gotten in the way, but we really do need to spend some time together."

Alyson ducked her head even lower. "Isn't it enough that you're totally humiliating me in this drippy town? A campaign to be town doctor...and what's your platform? You're promising everybody that your daughter isn't *really* having sex with your rival. That's a twist."

Laurie took a deep breath, then another. She told herself she wouldn't react. "Alyson," she said, "we're not going to let anyone—not even one single person in this town—believe your story about Tim Miller."

Alyson closed the book with a rustle of brittle pages. "I only ever opened my mouth to one person…okay, maybe two," she said guiltily. "How did it get so out of hand?"

"It just did, that's all. And we have to clear up the damage."

"I already went back and told Susan at the diner it's not true." Alyson sounded genuinely miserable. "That was bad enough. Do you have to go around telling *everybody*? I mean, I heard you on the phone last night. It was awful."

Last night Laurie had been speaking on the phone to the owner of the drugstore. In the middle of a discussion about supplies for the clinic, certain veiled comments had been made about her daughter and Tim. Laurie had not allowed them to pass.

"Alyson," she said now, "you did something very wrong, and we're all paying the consequences."

"I know it was wrong!" Alyson burst out. "I've already said I was sorry. Over and over I've said it."

"And maybe over and over we'll just have to set the town straight. We'll do whatever it takes." Laurie knew Alyson felt bad about what had happened. She also knew that Alyson had to go on facing the consequences. But right now all she really wanted was some of the old companionship with her daughter. "Look," she said, "let's not think about it any more today. We'll take a sabbatical from it—just for tonight. We'll cook dinner together. We'll make some plans for your birthday. Heck, we might even break out the popcorn, play a round of Parcheesi."

Alyson stared at her with a much too adult expression. "That kind of thing worked when I was ten or twelve. Whenever we had a problem, that's what we'd do. We'd make some popcorn and bring out the Parcheesi. It was a good way to hide."

"Not hiding, Alyson. Just being together."

"No," her daughter said flatly. "It's hiding. Pretending that the problems aren't real. You always do that, Mom. It would be great if it worked—pretend for one night that I didn't do something stupid and rotten. Pretend for one night that we're actually getting along when the truth is, we can hardly stand each other anymore."

"How can you say that?" Laurie asked. "Alyson, maybe I don't like what you did, but that doesn't change the way I feel about you. I love you."

"Not that. Not the maternal thing, please." Alyson stood, holding the cookbook against her as if for protection. "I wish you'd be real with me for once. Just once, Mom—be real."

"I *am* being real. I care about you more than anything or anyone in the world. And that's exactly why I want us to handle this situation together."

"What a team. We could go all over town announcing to the world that I didn't sleep with Tim Miller, after all. That I only lied so Kevin would pay attention to me." Alyson gave a harsh little laugh. "You know the funny thing, Mom? It worked. It actually worked. Kevin *has* started paying attention. He even asked me to go out with him. A real date. He's going to come pick me up tomorrow night and everything."

Laurie felt a growing sense of dismay. She'd been hoping all along that even though Alyson worked in

Kevin Nichols's office, he would ignore her—he'd just leave her alone.

"You have to tell him the truth," Laurie declared. "If he's only interested in you because he thinks you have experience, it shows exactly who he is."

"Don't worry," Alyson said. "He won't be interested for long. When he finds out it was all an embarrassing lie, he'll think I'm really stupid. He sure won't stick around because…just because I'm *me*."

"Oh, honey." Laurie stepped toward her daughter. "You're an incredibly pretty young woman. And you can attract someone who wants to be around you for all the right reasons. Give it a little time."

"Won't you *stop?* I don't feel very good about myself right now, and I have plenty of reasons to feel that way. I'd actually have more respect for you if you were honest and said you didn't feel too good about me, either!"

"I can't say that," Laurie answered helplessly. "I've already tried to explain. I don't like what you did, but I love you, Alyson. I love you very much."

Even as she said the words, she knew they weren't reaching her daughter. Alyson merely stood there, clutching that pathetic cookbook, her expression one of unrelenting misery. She'd already accused Laurie of trying to build a false world around the two of them. And now Laurie's own guilt accused her. She'd started her daughter's life off with a lie. Had pretending become a habit after that? Pretending that she and Alyson didn't really need anyone else, that they could solve all their problems on their own? Yet, no matter what Alyson said, Laurie wasn't pretending right now. She was facing the truth head on. She didn't know how to get through to her daughter, and it frightened her.

Laurie heard footsteps down the hall, the sound of Tim's cowboy boots on the wooden floor immediately recognizable. A few seconds later he appeared in the doorway. He glanced from mother to daughter.

"Guess I'm interrupting something," he said.

Alyson stared at him. "Do you hate me?" she demanded. "Please just tell me. Do you hate me for what I did?"

Tim got a pained expression, the look of a bachelor who wished he'd come home to a nice quiet house and a can of beer—nothing more. "No, Alyson. I was ticked off at you for a while, but I don't hate you."

She seemed to think this over, then gave a careful nod. "At least *you're* honest." Still moving with care, she set the cookbook down on the table. "I was actually going to do something stupid again," she said. "I was going to make something for Kevin and take it into the office tomorrow. I don't know, fudge brownies or something. Like that would really impress him. Dumb, huh?" She left the kitchen and went down the hall, and then Laurie heard the front door closing after her. It was a much too familiar sound these days.

The worst part for Laurie was feeling so powerless. She picked up the cookbook, flipped through the pages. "I've never owned one of these, you know? I never had the time. In spite of that—or because of it—Alyson seems to believe the way to a man's heart is through his stomach. I guess the joke's on me."

Tim came to her and extracted the cookbook from her hands. And then he gave her a hug, an unexpected

I-know-your-daughter's-driving-you-up-the-wall hug. For a moment Laurie allowed herself to take his comfort. She melted into the warmth of his arms, relishing his strength. It occurred to her that it would be very pleasant to know you could come home to a man like him each night and accept his comfort as a matter of course. Slowly she raised her face to gaze at him, almost lulled by a sense of security.

"Just because we're political opponents," he murmured, "doesn't mean we can't get friendly in our free time." She saw the lazy gleam of amusement in his eyes. That and his lighthearted words gave her a jolt back to reality. How could she have believed she'd find safety with devil-may-care Tim Miller, of all people?

She pulled away. "Let's not start," she said.

"Why not?" he asked solemnly.

"I'll tell you why not. Because Alyson just may be right—I spend too much time pretending. And if I let you hold me, Tim, that's pretending. You don't want to let anybody into your life and neither do I. So let's not do it. Let's not pretend." She hurried from the kitchen and went upstairs. She needed something—anything—to take her thoughts away from Tim. She saw the boxes of Doc Garrett's junk still cluttering the end of the hall. She could straighten the clutter or at least get it out of sight. That ought to do the job. Grabbing one of the boxes, she began climbing the small ladder that led to the attic. Unfortunately the trapdoor seemed to be stuck.

"Want some help with that?" Tim asked from the hallway below.

She ought to have known he wouldn't leave her in

peace. She balanced her box awkwardly with one hand and jiggled the trapdoor with the other.

"I'll have it in a second. Don't you have something else you'd rather do?"

"Nope. There's only so much campaigning a person can do in one day." He climbed the ladder until he was standing on the rung just underneath hers. Reaching up, he pushed at the trapdoor and it came open with only a brief protesting creak. Then he reached around to take the box from her.

"Your back," she warned.

"Yes," he said. "My back."

He was standing so close she could feel his breath on her cheek. She made a great effort not to turn toward him. "As your doctor," she said, "it's my recommendation that you *not* carry boxes." She advanced the rest of the way up into the attic, sneezing at all the dust.

"As *your* doctor," he said, "I recommend you not irritate your sinuses."

She paid no attention. Setting the box down, she surveyed the space. The rafters peaked above her, and late-afternoon sunlight filtered in through the grimy panes of a small medallion window. All around her was more clutter, strewn with cobwebs. "Doc Garrett is hopeless," she said. "Doesn't he ever throw anything out?"

Tim climbed the rest of the way, too. He knelt to poke inside the box that Laurie had brought with her. "Look at this," he said. "Patient files from fifty years ago. These must have belonged to his father. Jonathan Garrett, Sr., M.D."

"I didn't know his father was a physician, too."

"Garretts have a long heritage of doctoring. Jonathan's great-grandfather was a medical missionary who came out West back in the 1870s."

"I see," Laurie said. "No wonder Doc wants you to continue the practice. He doesn't have any children of his own, and he can't bear to see the tradition die out." She wished she hadn't had this insight. Going up against so much tradition in her fight for Dr. Garrett's practice made her feel like more of an underdog than ever.

Tim was still poking through the box. "This is exactly the type of stuff my own dad hordes," he said. "Patient files nobody wants anymore. Medical journals nobody reads."

There was something in Tim's voice when he spoke about his father, something murky and complex. Laurie's instincts warned her to leave it alone. But she didn't listen to them.

"When was the last time you saw him?" she asked.

"Years," Tim answered, his tone short. "Come on, I'll help you carry a few more of those boxes up here."

"Wait. Is he really such a horrible person?"

"He's my father, that's all. He doesn't much like me and I guess you could say the feeling is mutual. Don't get that worried look—I've learned to handle it by now."

Again Laurie knew she should let it go. And again she couldn't. "Tim, the problems I'm having with Alyson, they make me realize one thing. If there's any way at all to make things right with your dad, you ought to do it. Because the alternative is...it's just too painful.''

Tim continued to kneel beside that box of ancient files and outdated journals. He made a gesture as if he wanted to close it up again and push it off to the side. But then he spoke.

"You have to understand something, Laurie. Not all parents are like you. They don't all want everything to be wonderful with their kids. My dad...'' A long pause and then he went on. "My father just didn't know what to do after my mother died. She had cancer, and I guess he blamed himself for not being able to cure her. I know that Gabe and I blamed him, too. And after that...he blamed us. We gave him plenty of cause, I'll admit that. The two of us pushed it just about as far as you can go. But where Gabe was concerned, my father learned early to forgive. With me...I guess he still hasn't forgiven. That's all. I've accepted it and I've gone on.'' Tim spoke matter-of-factly, but even in the dimness of the attic Laurie could swear she saw the sadness in his eyes.

Unmindful of the dust, she sat down on the floor, drawing her legs up and wrapping her arm around her knees. "I don't believe you, Tim," she said. "You want more from your father. And why shouldn't you? But maybe you have to be the one to make the first move.''

"I've already tried," he said, and now his voice was harsh. "Laurie, I've tried countless times. When I turned my life around, part of me felt like I was doing it for him—so he'd be proud of me. But he couldn't even bother to show up when I graduated from medical school. And that was when I knew that nothing would ever change between us.''

"Tim...I'm sorry."

"Don't be. I've gone on with my life."

He could say anything he liked, but Laurie saw pain and regret in his eyes. She didn't think about what she did next. She merely scooted over to him and took his hands in hers.

"I'm sorry," she repeated. She wanted to offer him comfort—just as he had tried to comfort her a short while ago. But touching him provoked other emotions. She gazed down at their clasped hands, afraid now to look into his eyes.

He bent his head over hers. Slowly, ever so slowly, she raised her face to him once more. His lips brushed her cheek and that was all it took to make her tremble.

"Oh, damn," she said raggedly.

"Laurie—"

"Don't start." She'd already told him that today.

"Maybe we just have to admit what's happening." His voice was low, husky.

"I already know what's happening. We're rivals. In a couple of weeks one of us will win. And then—"

He stopped her with a kiss. His mouth was warm, so very warm. It was a long moment before she broke away from him, breathing unevenly.

"We can't do this," she whispered.

"I want you, Laurie. I've wanted you from the first time I saw you."

She closed her eyes as if that would give her some measure of control.

"I want you, too." The words seemed to spill out

of her. "But we can't, Tim. We just can't! We have no future together. One of us has to go..."

"We're together right now. I'm not asking for anything more." He kissed her again and she was truly lost. She couldn't think beyond this moment, either. Not when Tim held her and caressed her and called forth a need from deep inside her.

A tattered quilt was draped over a broken stool a few feet away. Tim pulled the quilt down, then lowered her gently onto it. She made one last desperate effort to stop.

"Your back, Tim—"

He silenced her with yet another kiss. She tangled her hands in his hair, opened her mouth to his. And now impatience seized both of them. She tugged his shirt free of his jeans and he tried to lift her blouse over her head.

"Doesn't this thing have any buttons?" Tim asked, and she heard the amusement in his voice. This time she couldn't resist it.

"My blouse—it's a shell."

"What in tarnation is a shell?"

"Just...a blouse like this. Only two pearl buttons...right at the nape."

He kissed her even as he found the buttons and fumbled with them. A few seconds later he slid the blouse off her. Together they worked the clasp of her bra, bumping each other in their haste. More buttons to remove Tim's shirt, but at last they lay together, skin against skin. His fingers moved over the swell of her breast.

"Laurie—" his voice was strained now "—you're the most beautiful woman I've ever seen...."

"Just hold me, Tim," she whispered. She had never felt like this with any man, as if every intimate touch must incite a new and deeper response. Warmth cascaded through her, turned to flame....

From two stories below came the sound of the front door opening and closing. Faint as the noise was, it was enough to make Laurie freeze.

"It's Alyson!" She sat upright so quickly her head very nearly collided with a coatrack.

"Easy," Tim murmured, sitting up beside her.

"How can you say that. My daughter—" Already Laurie could hear Alyson climbing the stairs to the second floor. And then she'd come down the hall and see the open trapdoor to the attic...

Laurie searched frantically for her bra, but couldn't find it anywhere. It was Tim who finally located it. She snatched it from his hand, yanked the straps over her shoulders and wasted valuable seconds struggling with the clasp. Then she pulled her blouse over her head, smoothed her hair and rather wildly patted the dust from her pants. During this entire procedure Tim merely sat there and gazed at her with a curious expression. She could see the amusement again sure as anything glimmering in his eyes.

How had she gotten herself in this position? Didn't she realize by now that Tim would retreat behind that humor and leave her feeling bereft? Why *hadn't* she realized that before it was too late?

She heard her daughter come along the hall. She also heard Alyson pause below the open trapdoor. It seemed a very meaningful pause. It probably lasted no more than a few seconds, but to Laurie it seemed an eternity. At last she heard the sound of her footsteps going into her room.

Damage control—that was what was needed now. She gave Tim a glance warning not to follow and then climbed down the ladder to the hall.

"Hi, Alyson," she called casually. "I'm just...Tim and I are just cleaning up some of Doc's junk."

Alyson appeared in the doorway of her bedroom. She looked Laurie up and down. "Nice try, Mom. Really nice try. But your blouse is on backward." With that, she disappeared into her room once more.

THE NEXT MORNING when Alyson let herself into the office, she could tell that Kevin had already been there. The coffeepot was going and his half-empty mug sat on the counter. He must have come in really early. She wished she'd known so she could have arrived before him. Making coffee was one of her few duties, and she always liked knowing she'd accomplished it. The rest of the day she just sat around a lot, trying to feel useful even if she didn't do anything.

Kevin must have gone out again. He usually ate breakfast over at the diner. Maybe by now the waitress had told him the humiliating truth—that Alyson and Tim Miller weren't an item. The two of them would have a good laugh over it. Then Kevin would come back across the street and tell Alyson he didn't want to go out with her tonight, after all.

Kevin's impending rejection was so vivid in her mind that she almost ran out the door of the office before it could happen. But she forced herself to stay. She washed Kevin's mug in the bathroom sink and dried it with a napkin. She'd purchased the napkins herself, along with a box of coffee filters. Kevin was a little vague when it came to discussing money. She wasn't even sure when payday would be, but she figured that was the least of her worries. Her life had become a major disaster ever since she'd arrived in Grant.

And if things weren't bad enough, yesterday her mother and Tim Miller had been *doing* it in the attic. Alyson's face burned at the thought. She didn't know if she could stand to be in that house much longer with the two of them. The way they were always looking at each other, as if lost in some private world all their own. It made Alyson feel like such an outsider. It made her feel lonely in a way she'd never known.

But that wasn't even the worst of it. What Alyson couldn't stomach was the pretense, the way her mother tried to act like nothing was happening. It was just part of the same old story—Mom trying to make everything perfect, doing her best to clean up messes, refusing to see that *nothing* was right anymore.

Too wired to sit still, Alyson went to stare out the back window of the office. And that was when she saw Kevin out in the small gravel lot behind the building. He was washing his Jeep. She watched as he dipped a sponge into a soapy bucket of water and then ran the sponge over a fender. He seemed completely engrossed in the task.

More than ever, she wanted to run away. Maybe she could leave a note on her desk, some excuse about not being able to work here anymore. After that, she could do her best to avoid him. If he wanted to laugh at her, it could be behind her back.

Kevin glanced up and saw her staring at him through the window. He gave her a jaunty wave with his sponge. It was too late to run now. She'd have to go out there and face him. Her insides clenching, she opened the back door and stepped outside.

"Hello," she said.

"Hi." He didn't seem interested in talking. Whenever Kevin got around his Jeep, it took up most of his attention. Maybe that would be annoying with somebody else, but Kevin's Jeep was his livelihood. He had to take it seriously.

She watched him for a few minutes. He didn't act like he'd heard anything over at the diner. Maybe Alyson would have a little bit of a reprieve before he found out what an idiot she was.

But he *would* find out sooner or later. She already knew this town well enough to know that. Nobody could keep any story under wraps for very long. It was just a matter of time.

Suddenly she knew she couldn't wait. If the worst was going to happen, she wanted it to be now. She couldn't take the suspense any longer.

"Kevin," she said.

"Yeah." He went right on sponging the Jeep.

"There's something I have to tell you. The fact is, Tim Miller and me—we never had anything going. It was only a...joke. No, a lie." She listened to herself with a horrified fascination. "A lie," she repeated, as if to make sure Kevin Nichols *really* knew what an ass she'd been.

"Figured as much," he said, lovingly washing a door panel.

"You figured... What?"

"Come on, I knew all along you didn't have anything to do with that guy."

"How did you know?" she asked weakly.

"You're not exactly a femme fatale, are you? Heck, you're still wet behind the ears. Anyone can see that."

Alyson bit her lip. She didn't know whether to feel relieved or even more horribly humiliated than before. "You don't have to go out with me tonight," she mumbled. "Not if you don't want to."

"Why wouldn't we go out?" Amazingly he dropped the sponge into the bucket and came over to her. "I didn't hurt your feelings, did I?"

"No, it's just that—"

"Of course we're going out." He smiled at her. Then he tilted her chin, his hand leaving a dab of suds there, and he kissed her. Alyson wanted to grab hold of him, because she had the funniest feeling she was going to keel over. But Kevin finished the kiss before she could do anything. He went back to his Jeep and started washing it again, a little smile still on his face.

It occurred to Alyson that sometimes miracles really did happen.

CHAPTER FOURTEEN

DAY NINE of the campaign. The Ulysses S. Grant High School marching band was out in full force, even though it was officially the summer break. It seemed the election had inspired all kinds of community spirit. As far as Tim could tell, the entire town had turned out to witness him and Laurie engage in a public debate.

This was another wacky idea dreamed up by the venerable town council. According to them, the folks of Grant couldn't properly make up their minds without a debate between the two candidates. And the council, no doubt, had seen the publicity potential: a great way to inaugurate the tourist season.

Now Tim sat in the bleachers of the school football field, high enough up that he was separate from the crowd. He watched the band go through its routine. The trombone sounded slightly off-key but appropriately enthusiastic. The weather had cooperated, the brilliant blue sky stretching overhead like a canopy held up by the mountain peaks. Laurie sat a short distance away from Tim, ostensibly going over her notes. If possible, she looked more beautiful than ever today, her dark hair fluttering in the breeze, the outline of her features clear and determined.

"Nervous?" he asked.

She gave him a cool glance. "Why should I be? I do this kind of thing every day now—make a total fool of myself in public."

"I notice you don't have any campaign buttons yet."

"Let me put it this way, Tim—stuff a sock in it." She went back to her notes.

Ever since the attic incident—not to be confused with the bathtub incident or various assorted orange-couch incidents—Laurie had been keeping a firm distance from Tim. She'd given him a big speech about how she had to set a better example for her daughter and could therefore indulge in no further incidents. Besides, she'd reminded him, there could be only one winner in this absurd election. One winner, and the loser would have to leave. Either way it fell, Laurie and Tim would no longer be a part of each other's lives.

There was only one problem. The more Laurie kept him at arm's length, the more he desired her—and the more he couldn't stop thinking about her. Living in the same house didn't help his predicament.

Temporary. The situation was only temporary. That should have made him feel good. When it came to women, he'd always tried for temporary. He'd purposely never thought about the future. So why was he thinking about it now?

He knew what Laurie would tell him. *We have no future.* The phrase seemed to echo in his head and he cursed softly.

Laurie swiveled toward him. "What was that?"

"Nothing you want to hear."

She cast him a speculative look. But then she

frowned down at the podium, which had been set up on the fifty-yard line. "I'd like to delay this silly debate as long as possible. At least up here I feel anonymous."

"Darlin', you'll never be anonymous in this town again. Not after the way you've been rustlin' up votes."

"A lot of good it's been doing me," she muttered. "It gives a whole new meaning to a physician's house calls. I knock on people's doors, and wives act as if I've personally come to steal their husbands away. They just can't get used to the idea of a female doctor."

"You'll convince them if anyone can."

"You're actually defending me?"

"You won't let me do anything else."

"Tim—"

"I know. I'm not supposed to start."

She tightened her fingers on her note cards. "Don't you understand? Because of Alyson, I *can't* make any more mistakes."

"You don't think she can handle her mother having a personal life?"

"I don't think she can handle anything about me right now," Laurie said bleakly. And he felt it again—the inconvenient need to take her into his arms, to soothe the shadows from her eyes.

"Is this about your daughter, Laurie…or is it about the guys who hurt you?" He kept his voice gentle.

"I don't want to talk about that." Her voice was firm.

"They did hurt you."

"Dammit, Tim—with Alyson's father, I was just

too young to know any better. And with Peter, the way he took off right before the wedding... I felt wounded pride more than anything else.''

He figured it had been more than that. Laurie Russell wasn't the kind of woman who promised to marry someone unless she was damned serious about it. So she'd been hurt and she'd closed herself off. Except for those few occasions when she'd let down her guard with him and revealed the passion she *couldn't* shut off.

''What did you say?'' Laurie asked. He realized he must have cursed again.

''Nothing,'' he said. ''Just that...there's something between us, Laurie, and it won't go away.''

She creased one of her note cards, smudging the penciled comments she'd made. ''What are you offering this time?'' she asked mockingly. ''Don't tell me you've decided to look for a wife and family, Tim. I thought Hallie was the only woman you could picture as your wife.''

She'd turned the tables on him, he couldn't deny it. He listened to the tuba struggling to keep up with the rest of the band. In Grant he supposed they were lucky to have a tuba at all.

''I knew Hallie wasn't mine for the having,'' he said reluctantly. ''I knew it all along. Bess tells me I've been avoiding a real relationship. Maybe she's right. Because I don't see myself with a wife and a family. No...I just don't see it.''

''Well, *I* don't see myself with a man. I tried going for it—I tried giving Alyson a father. It didn't work out. And now I have all I can do just making sure I don't lose my daughter.'' Laurie stood up, started gathering her purse. "We have to get down there and go through this ridiculous charade. So let's just do it."

He wanted her to linger with him here above the crowd. But it was true he had nothing to offer her. Family life wasn't for him any way he looked at it. He'd spent so much of his life going from one job to another, never staying in one place very long. Even though he'd changed as far as his career went, he knew a part of him would always be a wanderer. He'd never feel comfortable trying to settle down. He knew his place—on the outside, looking in.

Laurie started to leave, but then she sank down again. "Alyson's here," she said. "With *him.*"

Tim followed the direction of her gaze. Farther down and to the right Alyson sat in the bleachers with Kevin Nichols. Kevin had his arm draped around her shoulders. She leaned toward him and every time he spoke she seemed to listen in awe. Even from here Tim could see it.

"I would do anything," Laurie said fiercely, "to get that boy away from my daughter."

The way Tim understood it, during the past week Alyson and Kevin had been inseparable. They'd worked together during the day and gone out together every night. In short, Alyson seemed besotted.

Tim told himself he wasn't in the advice business. But he found himself speaking up, anyway.

"The more you try to keep her away from him, the more it will backfire."

"So I'm supposed to sit by and watch *that?*"

Now Kevin was nuzzling Alyson's ear. Tim winced.

"Okay, I'm not saying it's pleasant. What other choice do you have, though?"

"I don't know. But if you think I'm being unfair, Tim, I'm not. Yes, I know how inaccurate rumors can be. It's just that Kevin Nichols has the look of someone who fits his rumors. And that's what worries me."

Tim couldn't deny that Laurie had a right to be concerned. Nichols was the kind of guy you could spot a mile away—too confident of his own appeal, too calculating in everything he did. Even now, he seemed to be announcing to the world, *Here I am. I'm with a girl. She's crazy about me. What's new?*

Tim glanced at Laurie. She had leaned forward slightly and was looking at her daughter, as if the sheer force of her love would make Alyson turn around and come to her. Mother love—Laurie had it in spades, and it was obviously tearing her up inside. Maybe that was why Tim wanted to hold her right now. Maybe he wanted to protect her from the one person she loved most in all the world—her own daughter. That was irony for you.

"Let's go down," Tim said. The debate, no matter how absurd, might take Laurie's mind off her problems with Alyson. And it might take *his* mind off Laurie. He could hope, anyway.

A few minutes later Tim was seated to one side of the podium and Laurie to the other. The members of the town council fussed and took several more moments in settling down. Apparently there was some argument among them about seating order. At last the marching band had gone through its paces, and Phil Cline took the microphone at the podium. He rambled on for several moments about Grant's illustrious history as a once-upon-a-time mining boomtown and namesake of General Ulysses S. Grant. The audience started to fidget and Phil wound up his speech.

"Ladies and gentlemen, you know why we're here. In less than two weeks Grant faces a most important choice—the election of our very own town doctor. Without further ado, I give you Dr. Laurie Russell!"

A smattering of polite applause and then Laurie took the podium. She arranged her note cards in front of her. She did look nervous. When she happened to glance at Tim, he gave her an encouraging wink. He got the feeling she wasn't encouraged.

"Ladies and gentlemen," she began, her voice too faint. She leaned closer to the microphone. "Ladies and gentlemen, it is my great privilege and opportunity to stand before you today—" She stopped abruptly and placed her cards to one side. Then she started again. "If you want to know the truth, standing before you is the *last* thing I want to do today. I had a speech all prepared, I practiced it in front of the mirror...but the truth is, ladies and gentlemen, I'm not very good at speeches. What I really want is to be your doctor. I want to be available any time you have a question or a concern about your health. I want to make you better when you feel sick. I want to be there when your children are born and help them to grow up strong and happy. That's *all* I want. I'd far rather leave the campaigning to professional politicians. Thank you." She sat down and this time the applause was louder. For someone who didn't like to campaign, that had been one doozy of a speech.

Phil Cline took the podium again. "Ladies and gentlemen, I now give you Dr. Timothy Miller!"

Applause. The audience really seemed to be getting into the spirit of the thing. But Tim agreed with Laurie—there were a whole lot of other things he'd rather be doing right now. She'd been honest; he had to follow up with some honesty of his own.

"Folks," he began, "I can't tell you for sure why I'm here. Being a doctor is a dream come true for me, that part I know. But I'm not so certain why Jonathan Garrett thinks I'm the person for this particular job. I'll just have to leave it up to you to decide. Thanks."

This time the applause was uncertain. As Tim sat down, Phil Cline looked unhappy. He'd probably expected Tim and Laurie to praise the many wonderful qualities of Grant, Colorado. Instead, it was obvious they'd both disappointed him. He took hold of the mike.

"It is now Dr. Russell's turn for a rebuttal," he announced importantly.

Laurie stepped up again. "I would just like to say to Dr. Miller that he should have decided how he felt *before* he came to Grant. Thank you." She sat down.

Phil Cline was looking more and more unhappy. He adjusted the microphone a little more forcefully than necessary. "It is now Dr. Miller's turn for a rebuttal."

Tim stood up and leaned toward the mike. "I would like to submit respectfully to Dr. Russell that a person can try to make the best decision and still end up wondering what the heck he's doing."

Phil Cline didn't even bother to adjust the microphone this time. "Dr. Russell!"

Laurie edged Phil Cline aside. "With all due respect to Dr. Miller, I believe his problem is a reluctance to put down roots. What Dr. Miller should realize is that you can't have everything. You can't go after the career of your dreams and then just pick up and move on the way you always did before—"

Tim appropriated the mike from her. "Dr. Russell, I thought you wanted me to move on. I thought that was your fondest hope."

"Dr. Miller, *my* hopes don't have anything to do with it. For your own good, though, you really ought to consider where it is you're headed. I *want* this job. In spite of all the gossip, all the rumors, all the problems, I want to stay in Grant. I want to be town doctor, and I don't have any doubts about it. Can you say the same thing?"

They stared at each other, Laurie's glance never wavering. It was clear she'd issued a challenge and she wasn't about to back down.

"Sure I have doubts," Tim answered at last. "I grew up in a small town, and I can't say the memories are so good for me. So why did I come to *this* small town? It's bringing back a whole lot of memories I'd rather not have—that's all I can tell you."

With this utterance, it seemed that Tim had pushed Phil Cline beyond endurance. The man grabbed hold of the microphone.

"Ladies and gentlemen," he said loudly, "this concludes our debate. Please give our candidates a big hand. Hot dogs on the forty-yard line!"

Generous applause this time, but Tim suspected it

had more to do with the prospect of free food than anything else. The crowd milled toward the frankfurters, and he and Laurie were left to their own devices.

"I didn't realize," she said. "I thought you wanted this job as much as I did. And now I find out... I guess you really regret turning down that research fellowship, don't you? Doc Garrett told me about it, by the way."

Right now he was feeling any number of regrets. A lot of them had to do with Laurie, and not being able to take her in his arms and just say to hell with everything else. The breeze continued to weave its way through her dark silky hair, doing tantalizing things with her wayward curls.

"So why did you come to Grant, Tim? And why are you sticking around?"

He wished he knew. For the very first time in his life he'd been straight on the way to success, so why *had* he been sidetracked to this little town? He gazed into Laurie's eyes and he still didn't know the answer.

Doc Garrett interrupted the moment. He came up to the podium and took hold of Tim. "Please excuse us, Dr. Russell. My so-called protégé and I have some discussing to do." Jonathan didn't wait for an answer. He squired Tim off to the side and then scowled at him. "What were you thinking? You practically told these people you didn't want to practice medicine here. If you were going to get yourself involved in a damn-fool campaign, the least you could do is a little decent politicking!"

"Watch your blood pressure," Tim said.

"Okay, Tim...does this have to do with your dad? Is that what it's all about?"

Tim glanced discontentedly down the football field. The band was playing again, with more enthusiasm than expertise. Tourists with their cameras and their too-pristine summer outfits milled among the townspeople, and everyone was lining up for free hot dogs.

"This place reminds me of my father somehow," Tim said reluctantly. "It reminds me of failing and never measuring up."

"You've proved yourself," Doc argued. "You got your medical degree. You showed all of them what you could do—you even showed your dad. Why can't you just leave it behind?"

"Maybe somewhere else I could," Tim said in a low voice. "Maybe it's just this place. Small town...small expectations."

Doc Garrett looked as if he was getting ready to argue some more, but then his gaze was caught by something over Tim's shoulder. "Will you get a load of that," he said.

Tim looked, too. A short distance away Bess was laughing and chatting in a group of people, most of them men. She seemed different today. She sparkled. Tim couldn't think of any other word for it.

"What's with her?" Doc muttered.

"I'd say she's having a good time."

"Since when does Bess Thompson have a good time?"

"Since now, I guess," Tim observed.

"Scuttlebutt has it that Saturday she went out on the town with Ben Luna. And last night she was out with Max Worley. The guy's only fifty-five."

Tim remained noncommittal. "Does sound like she's getting around, doesn't it? Cradle robbing and all."

Doc gave him a sharp glance. "What do you know about this, Tim?"

Ever since he'd arrived in Grant, Tim had been trying to stay out of the middle of things. "Ask Bess yourself, Doc. I don't keep her social calendar."

"Everything's out of kilter," Jonathan said. "First you and now Bess. What gives?"

A good question. Tim's gaze strayed to Laurie. Some of the townspeople had come to talk to her and she was starting to look as animated as Bess. She seemed at home in this place, while he was still just an outsider looking in.

A sense of emptiness came over him, and he reminded himself that this was how he'd always wanted it. No real ties, no real home. That was his choice. But the emptiness didn't go away.

THE NEXT AFTERNOON, Tim declared a moratorium on the campaign. Forget public debates, forget door-to-door canvassing and, most of all, forget people coming up to you on the street and giving long convoluted explanations about why or why not they were going to vote for you. It was definitely time for a break. It was also Alyson's eighteenth birthday, and Tim had convinced both Laurie and her daughter to accompany him for a picnic celebration in the mountains.

Okay, admittedly the celebration wasn't going very well so far. Alyson had decided to play aloof and reserved. She sat with her back against the trunk of an aspen, hardly touching the egg-salad sandwiches

Laurie had made or the canned nuts Tim had contributed. Laurie made every effort to keep the conversational ball rolling with her daughter, but the stress was starting to show. After nibbling halfheartedly on a sandwich herself, she glanced around the forest glade where Tim had brought them.

"It's so peaceful here," she said wistfully. "The kind of place where you can forget about time passing. I'm glad we came."

There was, indeed, something special about the surroundings. A mountain stream trickled nearby, pine and aspen mingled, and then the forest opened up into a patch of columbine and other wildflowers. High above swept the tundra where no trees could grow, but where small alpine plants flourished—stonecrop, paintbrush, nailwort. During the few summers back in his teenage years Tim had spent with Doc Garrett, the old guy had taught him to appreciate the immense but subtle variety of the tundra. Doc loved these mountains and apparently he'd always hoped Tim would love them, too.

Laurie, however, was the one who seemed most appreciative. She leaned against her own tree trunk, eyelids drifting closed as she lifted her face to the cool mountain air. Tim couldn't take his eyes off her. She wore jeans today, the kind you could tell were her favorite pair because they'd started to fray and tear but she still hung on to them. And even though she wore a light jacket, Tim was all too aware of the graceful lines of her body. Too bad he couldn't just reach over to her...

But no, certainly not with the sullen presence of Laurie's daughter. Laurie continued to make it very clear she wanted to set a good example for Alyson. Tim wondered irritably if that was why he'd never tried parenting himself—he'd never been particularly adept at setting a good example. The more he thought about it, the more this parenting business seemed a whole lot of trouble. He wished it could have been just the two of them up here—him and Laurie.

As if sensing the direction of his thoughts, Laurie straightened and opened her eyes. "Alyson," she said brightly, "would you mind going to Tim's truck and bringing that extra blanket? It's getting a little cold."

Alyson appeared mutinous, but after a moment she stood and stalked toward the truck. Laurie went into action. She pulled the birthday cake from the big unwieldy picnic basket—another remnant left by one of Doc Garrett's lady friends—and started poking candles into the frosting.

"I should have done this earlier. Quick, Tim, the matches."

Half of the eighteen candles were lit by the time Alyson returned with the blanket. Her expression seemed unsure.

"Oh, Mom…"

"Hurry, Tim," Laurie urged as he lit the rest of the candles. She nodded in approval.

"Alyson, blow them out before the breeze does—and don't forget to make a wish."

Now Alyson looked pained, as if she couldn't believe her mother was subjecting her to this childish ritual. But Tim wondered if she didn't also look secretly pleased. She knelt beside the cake and managed to blow out the candles in one breath.

"Didn't you find something inside that blanket?" Laurie hinted.

Alyson hesitated, then shook out the blanket. A package fell from its folds.

"Mom, enough already. This is like present number six. You're really overdoing it this year."

Laurie grinned like a kid. Tim knew that early this morning she'd hidden presents for Alyson all over the house, just waiting for her daughter to stumble on them. Apparently this was something of a tradition for the Russell family. From what Tim had been able to tell, the presents hadn't been terribly expensive— it would be an understatement to say that Laurie was on a budget—but the gifts had been plentiful nonetheless: a comb-and-brush set, a couple of books, a bottle of perfume.

"Go ahead, open it," Laurie said now.

Alyson still seemed to be wavering between pleasure and world-weary cynicism. But at last she tore off the wrapping and opened the box. She lifted out a blouse and stared at it blankly.

"Oh," was all she said.

"Isn't it great?" Laurie asked anxiously. "Your favorite color."

Alyson crumpled the blouse in both hands. "Mom, I appreciate it, I really do," she said in a rigid voice, "but I wish you'd noticed. I just don't wear clothes like this anymore."

"Clothes like what?" Laurie asked. "Alyson, it's exactly the style you like."

"Lace and frills," Alyson said disdainfully. "That's just not *me* anymore. Why didn't you notice? Why can't you see what I'm really like?"

"Honey—"

"It's always the same, Mom. All you see is this picture in your head of what I'm supposed to be like. You don't see *me!*"

Laurie shook her head. "That's not true. I never tried to make you be a certain way—or wear a certain kind of clothes. You always picked your own style. I just tried to respect that."

"Can we leave now?" Alyson said in a brittle voice. "I have to get back to town. Kevin's picking me up."

"For goodness' sake, it's your birthday. This is a family time, Alyson."

"I went along with that. I did the picnic thing. I *could* have been spending the day with Kevin, but I did what you wanted. Now I'd just like to get out of here."

Tim decided that maybe a picnic hadn't been the greatest idea, after all. He glanced from mother to daughter, saw the strained expressions on both their faces. He ought to leave the two of them alone. So why did he stay where he was, an unwilling witness to their conflict?

"Alyson," Laurie said, "we're going to celebrate your birthday as a family."

Alyson shot an accusing glance at Tim. "*He's* not family."

"That's beside the point," Laurie said. "You can afford to spend one day with me. I don't want you going off and seeing Kevin."

"I already told him—"

"When we get back home, you can call him and tell him it's off."

"No," Alyson stated flatly. "I won't do it. Because you want me to stop seeing him altogether. You haven't even given him a chance."

"Alyson, he's too old for you—among other things."

"I'm going out with him tonight, no matter what you say." Alyson's voice had risen defiantly and Laurie's face hardened.

"You're not giving me any choice. I don't want you to see him. And not just for tonight. I don't want you going out with him at all."

Alyson drew in her breath sharply. "You won't let anything be real. You just can't take it, can you? I hate you! I hate everything you are and I won't be anything like you!" She whirled and went crashing off through the trees.

Laurie looked stunned, but then started after her daughter. "Alyson, wait!"

Never get in the middle, Tim had told himself over and over, but it seemed he wasn't going to heed his own advice. "Laurie," he said quietly, "you stay here. I'll go after her."

CHAPTER FIFTEEN

ALYSON HAD MOVED at a good clip, and it took Tim a few minutes to find her. He surmised, however, that she wanted to be found. You didn't make a grand exit like that without wanting some kind of follow-up.

"Go away," Alyson said from among the pines.

"I have a better idea. Come back and apologize to your mother."

Alyson stepped out from behind a tree. "This doesn't have anything to do with you. Butt out."

"Sure. As soon as you stop acting like a brat," he said.

She gave him one of her accusing stares. "Obviously you're on *her* side."

Tim was about to say he hadn't taken anybody's side, but then he stopped himself. "Yeah, I guess maybe I am. I don't like to see her hurt. And you're probably the only person who can hurt her, Alyson."

She bent her head and he thought he'd gotten through to her. But then she looked at him again and her face was impassive.

"What about *you*, Tim? I have a pretty good idea you could hurt her, too."

He hadn't expected this line of attack. "Your mother and I..." he said, searching for the right words, "we know we're going to go our separate ways."

"That's convenient, isn't it? You can take what you want and then you can just leave. Peter did that. I'm pretty sure my father did, too."

"I'm not like them," Tim said brusquely. "Laurie and I...we haven't exchanged any promises."

"Like I said—convenient. Would you just leave me alone now?"

Tim couldn't think of anything he'd rather do. But he remembered that wounded expression on Laurie's face and he had to do something about it. At least he had to try.

"Alyson, for what it's worth, don't back yourself into a corner. No matter how you feel about this Nichols, don't let him pressure you into anything."

For just a second she looked uncertain. But then she put on the world-weary front. "What makes you think he'd pressure me—about anything?"

"Because I know a little something about guys," Tim said dryly. "Particularly guys that age. And it's a pretty safe bet he *is* pressuring you."

Alyson lifted her chin. "Maybe Kevin and I both want the same thing. Maybe we just want to be together. He's not like the men Mom has been involved with. And he's not like you. He won't just take what he wants and then disappear."

"You've been going out with him, what? A week? It's even less than that, isn't it? And already you've decided this is the grand passion of your life."

Her face tightened and he knew he'd taken the wrong tack.

"I know what I'm doing," she said. "I can look

out for myself. Besides, none of those stories about Kevin are true. *You* of all people shouldn't be listening to gossip."

"This doesn't have anything to do with gossip," Tim explained as patiently as he could. "Kevin Nichols could be the greatest person in the world and still want something you're not ready to handle."

"Why don't you just come out with it," Alyson said scathingly. "You think Kevin wants *sex.* Well, maybe I want it, too. And maybe there's nothing wrong with that!"

Never get in the middle, Tim reminded himself. He should turn and walk away—but something in Alyson's expression stopped him. Uncertainty still hovered underneath the bravado.

"Listen," he said, "just be sure you're making your own choices. Don't let anybody—not even Kevin Nichols—persuade you into something you're not certain you want. That's part of being cool, you know."

"Yeah, right," she muttered. "Like being cool is what it's all about."

"Maybe it is," he said. "It means staying in control of the situation, not letting somebody else make decisions for you."

"So I'll be cool," she said flippantly. "That means *you* won't make my decisions. And neither will my mother. Fair enough?"

She probably thought she was being clever. But Tim saw the doubts in her young face, doubts she couldn't conceal no matter how hard she tried. He hoped he'd gotten through to her, after all.

So much for not getting involved.

KEVIN PRESSED HIS FOOT to the gas and sent the Jeep surging up the narrow mountain road. Alyson clutched the sides of her seat, telling herself to relax. Immediately below the road, the cliff plunged in what seemed a limitless drop. The slightest wrong turn of the wheel, and the Jeep would go plunging, too.

"Spectacular view, isn't it?"

"Yes." Alyson couldn't look. Her throat was dry and she had a sick feeling deep inside.

"These old mining trails, they go all over," Kevin said. "I know every one of them—I could drive this blindfolded. You aren't scared, are you?" He seemed to be taunting her somehow.

"No, of course I'm not scared," she lied. It wasn't just the narrow cliff-side road that was making her stomach roil. It was the thought of what had happened last night—the night of her eighteenth birthday.

She hadn't meant it to happen. She'd gone out with Kevin and she'd expected it to be like their other dates this past week: a lot of kissing and a whole lot more of other things in the back seat of his Jeep, but always her pulling back before they went too far. Whenever she'd stopped him those other times, Kevin hadn't protested. He'd been disappointed, she could tell that much, but he hadn't pressed for anything more. But last night...

She'd tried to stop, but everything had suddenly moved too fast. Kevin had made it very clear there was no turning back. And *it* had happened. She'd been surprised at how much it had hurt. She'd almost humiliated herself completely—almost started crying right while he was *doing* it. But there had been other surprises, too. It had been over much more quickly than she'd ever imagined and she'd been left with a terrible emptiness. She'd always thought it was something that would make her feel complete and whole and happy. Instead, she'd felt only a strange and awful nothingness.

"I'm planning out a new route," Kevin said now. "For Jeep Tour number five. I'll come this way and then switch back along the Spiral. What do you think?"

Alyson thought she didn't want to be anywhere near something called the Spiral. For that was how she felt inside—as if she was spiraling out of control. And she remembered what Tim had told her only yesterday at her birthday picnic: stay cool, stay in control.

Oh, how she wished that life were like a video— that you could stop the tape, rewind it to a certain point and then play it again. If she could, she'd rewind until she came to the part where she and her mother started arguing. This time Alyson wouldn't let there be any horrible hateful words. She'd just blow out the stupid candles and eat her birthday cake. And then she'd go home with Mom and Tim, and everything would be safe and ordinary. There wouldn't be any Kevin...

But life wasn't like that. If you did something, you couldn't change it. The reality of what you did just grew and grew until it threatened to engulf you.

"Feeling okay?" Kevin asked. "You look a little pasty."

"Pasty—what's that supposed to mean?" Her voice was doing peculiar things, wobbling all over the place. But at last they'd reached the summit, the ground leveling out around them, and Kevin stopped. He climbed out and came around to Alyson's side, undoing her seat belt as if he thought she couldn't handle it herself. Then he helped her out of the Jeep.

"The first time up here scares a lot of people," he said. "You're not the only one."

"The first time..." she echoed as if that was all she could do anymore, parrot what he said. She saw the satisfied way he looked at her, and in a flash she knew something more about last night. He *liked* that it had been her first time. He liked that she'd been a virgin and that he'd done something about it.

She wasn't a virgin any longer. She'd always thought losing her virginity would make her feel wise and knowledgeable. Instead, it just made her feel small and insignificant. And, yes, scared.

Kevin took hold of her hand, an oddly innocent gesture after what had transpired between them. "Look at the view," he said. "Go ahead, take a look. Nothing can happen to you while I'm holding on."

Almost involuntarily she curled her fingers in his. And she did look. The view was stunning. The mountains with their red earth and their unforgiving rock faces swept all around her, while far below the buildings of Grant were scattered like a child's toys. She gripped Kevin's hand as if she was in danger of tumbling down at any minute. He gave that satisfied smile and then he kissed her.

"It gets better," he murmured. "Trust me."

She felt that roiling in her stomach again, and for a second she longed with all her heart to be at the bottom of the mountain...to be home safe with her mother, for things to be the way they used to be. But then, as Kevin pulled her close to him, she felt something else. She felt the pull of a dark confusing desire. And she knew, with frightening certainty, that there was no turning back.

DAY FOURTEEN of the campaign. Only one week to go, and Laurie didn't know where she stood in the polls. According to the latest informal count taken by the *Grant Sentinel,* several people had decided to vote for her, several more had decided not to, and the rest of Grant was apparently keeping its own counsel until the day of the election—

She stopped, struck by the absurdity of her thoughts. Now she was worried about polls, of all things. With an exasperated sigh, she dropped a patient file onto Bess's desk.

"You'd better call Mr. Stempel and round him up for another appointment. We're not just talking peptic ulcer here. I'd say Mr. Stempel drinks too much."

"Good luck informing him of that," Bess said. "Men don't listen. For years I've tried telling Jonathan Garrett to cut down on his scotch and soda, but has he ever paid any attention? A big whopping no."

Laurie was getting used to this. No matter what the subject lately, Bess seemed to turn it around to Doc Garrett—more often than not, to the doc's disadvantage. Gone were the times when Bess spoke about the man in almost reverent hushed tones. These days all she could do was find fault with him.

Laurie glanced at the waiting room—no more patients for the time being. She tried to ignore the fact that most who had come in today had, as usual, requested an appointment with Tim—not her. What was the source of his appeal, dammit?

Just then he emerged from the small area in back where the clinic kept a few beds for overnight patients. He tossed his own patient file down on Bess's desk.

"We'll need to observe Ms. Padilla for another few hours," he said. "She has asthma. We'll run a pulmonary function on her, but right now I'm using Doc's time-tested method—the old-fashioned vaporizer."

"Hah," Bess said. "Jonathan Garrett thinks he has the answer for everything. And it generally *is* old-fashioned."

Tim gave her a considering glance, then focused his attention on Laurie. "How's the campaigning?" he asked. "I hear you're getting a committee of women together for a vaccination drive. Smart move. Very smart move. Bring 'em on board, make 'em feel useful."

Laurie frowned. "It's not just a campaign ploy. This whole area needs a vaccination drive. I have plans for Edgewood and Digby, as well."

"Digby," Bess said in tones of deep disgust. "Why don't you just recruit Estelle, while you're at it. She might as well make a contribution to society for once, instead of—" Bess broke off when she noticed that both Tim and Laurie were gazing at her. "Never mind," she said, disappearing behind yet another patient file.

Tim focused on Laurie again. "Something's different about you today," he murmured with a glint of the humor she found maddening and provocative at the same time. "Now, let me see, Doc Russell, what is it? Your hair, I'd say. Looks like you're trying to batten down the hatches."

Defensively her hand went to the barrettes she had, indeed, clamped on her hair. "I'm trying a new style. What's wrong with that?"

"Nothin'. Except I'd say you're tryin' to look proper and subdued for the townfolks of Grant. Anything to win a few more votes."

She wished he'd keep that drawl to himself. The sound of it was enough to send a tantalizing shiver down her spine. One thing for sure—he had a charming bedside manner. It didn't matter who he was dealing with, the easy charm just seemed to come naturally. It was so effortless she wondered if he even knew he had it. He won people over without trying— and meanwhile she was bending over backward for little enough results.

"It's ludicrous," she said. "At the debate you let the whole town know you have misgivings about this job. And what happens? Nobody gets offended. Instead, everyone takes it as a personal challenge. People have been streaming in and out of here for days just to list the advantages of Grant for you."

"Clean air, quiet living," Tim said with only a trace of irony. "I've heard the spiel, all right."

Bess spoke up. "Tim, you have Dr. Russell to thank for all the public support you've been getting. She's the one who squelched those rumors about you and her daughter. Believe me, it's not a piece of cake, squelching a rumor in this town."

Laurie glanced at the older woman in surprise. This was the first time Bess had offered her any sort of approval. Bess, however, already seemed to regret the vote of confidence. She pulled out her calculator and made a great show of being involved with patient billings.

Tim studied Laurie gravely. "It's true you stopped those stories and you went out of your way to do it—practically buttonholing folks on the street to tell them I was an upstanding citizen. I do owe you a hefty thanks for that." No humor in his voice now.

"I did it for Alyson's sake," Laurie said quickly. "And because...because I can't stand falsehoods anymore. Not of any kind." That was true, but deep down there was something else. She knew that Tim, for all his reluctance to establish roots, possessed a rock-solid sense of honor. And somehow she hadn't been able to tolerate anyone's questioning it.

"Thanks, anyway," he murmured.

"You're welcome." She felt foolish standing here having this conversation. She glanced into the waiting room again hoping a few patients would conveniently materialize to keep her busy. "This is the first time it's slowed down in a while," she observed unnecessarily. "At least *you've* been busy, Tim."

"Doing what?" he said, almost to himself. "Treating asthma and heartburn. Not to mention pinch-hitting as a marriage counselor. Exciting times all right."

"You're adding marriage counseling to the roster?" Laurie asked skeptically.

"That's right. Shirley Patterson came flouncing in here this morning asking why I'd made her husband take up jogging. Says it's transformed him and she doesn't like the transformation. Says he's always out and about now, instead of home where he should be. Says he looks like an idiot in those new jogging shorts of his.''

"I hesitate to ask what you told her."

"I told her that if you can't beat 'em, join 'em.'' Tim grimaced. ''I'm sure that's one more piece of advice that'll backfire on me somehow. I'll be plagued by the Jogging Pattersons wherever I go.''

"I'll tell you what's backfired,'' Bess announced. ''You telling me I should try to make Doc Garrett jealous.''

"Hold on,'' Tim protested. ''I never said anything—''

"Well, you didn't try to stop me, and you should have. It hasn't done me any good! He's spending more time in Digby than ever.''

"Your social life has picked up,'' Tim said.

"What's the use? When the one man you want won't even look at you—'' Bess stopped and addressed Laurie. ''You might as well know, too,'' she said testily. ''I'm in love with the old coot. Heaven help me, but I am.'' With that, she stood and vanished toward the back of the clinic.

Laurie stared after her. ''It seems so obvious,'' she said. ''Why didn't I put it together before? Bess and the doc.''

"Too bad he hasn't put it together. He's still busy chasing Estelle.''

Love. It hit you sometimes and maybe there wasn't anything you could do about it. Like the way Laurie felt about Tim. The way she couldn't seem to stop thinking about him or wanting him or needing him to hold her in his arms—

"No," she exclaimed.

"What is it?" Tim asked. She turned away from him, saw with alarm that her hands were shaking. She couldn't believe what she'd just been thinking. For a minute there, she'd assumed that everything she felt about Tim added up to...love.

But, no. Of course not. It couldn't be. She wouldn't *let* it be. It was only the stress of these past few weeks adding up. This ridiculous campaign and her all-encompassing worries about Alyson—the way Alyson had confronted her at the ill-fated birthday picnic and claimed actually to hate her. Perhaps it was understandable that Laurie would try to escape all that by centering on Tim. Understandable, but not acceptable. Now more than ever, she had to avoid depending on him.

"Laurie," he said, "what's wrong?"

She heard the concern in his voice, noted again how it seemed to come so naturally to him. Wasn't that how he spoke to his patients, regardless of his misgivings about a small-town practice? He was a healer, after all. And so, naturally, he expressed concern for her. She shouldn't take it as something personal, something unique meant just for her.

"I'm fine," she said.

"I've said that myself plenty of times—when I wasn't fine."

"I really am okay," she insisted, only to have him place his hand on her shoulder. It took all her willpower not to turn around and go straight into his arms. "Please, Tim...just don't."

"You keep telling me that."

"With good reason," she said, amazed at how

steady her voice sounded. "We both know we have no future together in Grant. There's only room for one of us here."

If secretly she'd hoped for a denial, she wasn't to be rewarded. He didn't say anything, just left his hand on her shoulder.

"I can't be distracted," she said. "Too much is at stake. With my daughter...with everything."

He stayed where he was for another moment, but then dropped his hand and moved away. And Laurie tried as hard as she could not to feel the loss.

Two EVENINGS LATER, Laurie put the finishing touches on the dining-room table. Place settings for four, a vase of wild violets as a centerpiece. It was the first time she'd used the table. Large and solid and made of walnut, it was much too formal for everyday meals. It was also an heirloom, having once belonged to Doc Garrett's father. But tonight seemed to require something imposing.

Tim appeared in the doorway. "Looks like you're ready," he said.

"I can't think of anything else. Casserole's in the oven, salad's made." She gave a shrug of resignation. "Despite what Alyson believes, I do know how to cook."

"Seems like you have everything under control," Tim said, his tone noncommittal, like that of a stranger just passing through.

Laurie gazed at him. "You don't have to stay, you know. That's what I've told you all along. This isn't your fight—it's mine." After great deliberation, Laurie had decided to invite Kevin Nichols to dinner. She needed to know more about him, to find out if he was as great a threat to her daughter as she imagined. What better way to do that than to invite him into her home? So far when he came to pick up Alyson for a date, he stayed outside in his Jeep waiting for her. Well, enough of that. Now he'd have to come inside and be inspected. Laurie had looked up his telephone number and called to invite him personally.

"Alyson's furious with me," she said. "I'm accused of going behind her back even though Kevin agreed to dinner."

"So let her be furious," Tim said. "You're only doing what any parent would do."

She hesitated. "You still think it's a good idea?"

"I'm lousy at giving advice, but, yeah, I think it's a good idea. Get him on your own territory—that's what you have to do."

Without quite knowing how it came about, she'd ended up discussing the matter with Tim. He'd listened to the pros and cons, put in his own two cents' worth. But all along, Laurie had sensed his discomfort. Now she realized how foolish she'd been involving him in her family matters. He didn't want a family. What would it take for her to remember that?

"You know," she said now, "I think it would be better if you didn't stay. I think I'd prefer it."

She had the distinct suspicion that he'd prefer to leave, too, but he got an obstinate look on his face. "Too late," he said. "I changed for the damn occasion."

It was true he wore slightly newer jeans than usual and a nubby blue-gray jacket in a Western cut. He'd even polished his cowboy boots. He was more handsome than ever, if such a thing was possible.

Laurie took an unsteady breath, wishing the mere sight of him didn't affect her like this. "Tim, really, there's no reason you should suffer along with me."

"I know you want to handle everything on your own, but I'll be here," he said. "I'm your backup."

"You make this sound like it's the shoot-out at the OK Corral."

"I'm just here," he said. "If you need me."

She gazed at him in exasperation. How did you ever know where you stood with someone like Tim? He'd made it so clear he didn't want a family, didn't want entanglements. But here he was, refusing to do anything but stay by her side. Which was the real Tim? The devil-may-care cowboy who never settled down—or the man who almost made you believe you could rely on him? Almost...

Alyson appeared in the dining room and sent a scathing glance over the table. "How cozy," she said. "Do you think any of this will fool Kevin? The happy family, gathering him into the fold?"

More and more, Laurie's daughter sounded like a stranger. And Laurie couldn't forget those words Alyson had flung at her: *I hate you. I hate everything you are.* The words were burned in Laurie's memory. She'd tried to tell herself that Alyson hadn't meant them, but she wasn't so sure.

"This is something families do all the time," Laurie said. "They invite people to dinner."

"There's only one small problem. *This* isn't really a family." Alyson gave Tim a pointed glance. "It's just more pretending."

Tim didn't seem perturbed. "Your mother already tried to get rid of me. I'm staying, kid."

"Would you stop calling me that?"

"As soon as you stop acting like a kid, glad to," he said evenly.

Alyson glared at both him and Laurie. Tonight she presented an unsettling mixture of youth and precocious maturity. She wore a sleeveless blouse with a fitted bodice, the top few buttons left daringly undone. Her skirt, however, was the loose flowing kind she'd always favored. It was as if Alyson had tried to put together new and old parts of herself and hadn't quite known how to make them match.

Laurie wanted to tell her that it was okay not to grow up too fast. But Alyson was eighteen now, determined to be an adult even if Laurie wasn't ready for it.

The doorbell rang and Alyson jumped. "That's him," she said. "Oh, this is going to be awful, just awful! Don't do anything to humiliate me, Mom. *Please.* Aren't things already bad enough?"

"Relax," Tim said. "It's just dinner, not the guillotine." He came over to stand beside Laurie as if allying himself with her. And somehow it worked out that both Tim and Laurie answered the front door together.

Kevin Nichols greeted them with just a shade too much deference. "Dr. Russell, Dr. Miller. Thanks for having me here tonight."

Laurie and Tim ushered Kevin into the living room, where he ended up sitting on Doc Garrett's shabby old sofa.

"How about a soft drink?" Laurie asked. She was

trying to be polite, even though her instinctive dislike of Kevin Nichols hadn't changed. He sat there on the sofa too respectfully, back held straight and both feet planted in front of him, a parody of the anxious suitor.

"A soft drink would be great," he said. "Something in lime, if you have it."

Alyson was the one who hurried to the kitchen, then rushed back again with the drink. She handed it to him and then sat gingerly beside him. Tim and Laurie remained standing.

"How's the tour business?" Tim asked in a brusque tone.

"Going along pretty well," Kevin answered, still overdoing the respectful-guest bit. "Things are picking up. They always do this time of year."

"We were very busy today," Alyson said. The conversation went into a lull after that and there didn't seem any help for it.

"If you'll excuse me," Laurie said, "I'll go check on dinner."

"Sure thing, Dr. Russell," Kevin said.

In the kitchen Laurie pulled open the oven door. The casserole was bubbling. Perhaps while they ate she could take a better measure of Kevin. For Alyson's sake, she kept wanting to believe he wasn't the little creep everybody said he was.

"Dinner's ready," she announced a few minutes later, and everyone filed into the dining room and sat down. Passing the food around took some time, and then Laurie had to suffer Kevin's unctuous compliments.

"This sure is delicious, Dr. Russell. I'll definitely

be asking for seconds. Did you make these rolls from scratch? They sure taste like you did."

Alyson gazed at Kevin with a peculiar expression—half fascination, half reluctance. Laurie felt a stirring of hope; maybe her daughter's emotions hadn't been totally swept away by this boy.

"So, Kevin," she said at last, "does your family live in Grant?"

"My parents are in Durango. My sister married and moved away to Denver. She just had a baby—great kid. Wish I could see the little tyke more often."

Laurie still had the feeling Kevin Nichols was playing a part—this time taking on the role of doting uncle to his "little tyke" of a nephew. But at least now she knew one thing for certain. She didn't like Kevin. She didn't like him at all.

"This dinner is the best I've had in a long time, Dr. Russell," he said. "Home cooking, that's what I miss most." He treated her to an insincere smile. She merely looked at him, making certain he knew exactly where he stood with her. His smile faded.

"Sure wouldn't mind another one of those rolls, Dr. Russell," he said after a moment, his voice a trifle too hearty.

The bread basket was empty, and Alyson practically shot out of her seat. "There's more in the kitchen," she said breathlessly. She went to get the rolls, returning with them only seconds later. Standing beside Kevin, she leaned down and placed one almost reverently on his plate. Kevin smiled again. Then he reached up and ran a finger down Alyson's neck, straying along all those open buttons. It was a telling gesture, brazen in the intimacy it displayed. Alyson froze and a look of mingled delight and shame suffused her face. Kevin just looked insolent as he glanced deliberately at Laurie.

He was sending the message loud and clear: he'd been sleeping with her daughter. And he wanted to make certain—very certain—that Laurie knew.

A hard cold fury possessed her. She pushed away her plate of half-eaten food and stood, almost knocking her chair over. "You little shit—get out of my house," she said. "Get out right now. And stay the hell away from my daughter."

CHAPTER SIXTEEN

WHAT HAPPENED AFTER THAT was a blur, only a few images throwing themselves into sharp relief: the expression of utter horror on Alyson's face, the satisfied look on Kevin's, the authoritative way Tim stood and took charge.

"I think you'd better leave," he said to Kevin in a manner that allowed no alternative. In only a matter of seconds, Tim ushered Kevin out the door and prevented Alyson from following him. With a single inarticulate cry, Alyson bolted up the stairs and disappeared into her room, slamming the door behind her. Suddenly the commotion was over, leaving Tim and Laurie to preside over the wreckage. The dining-room table was strewn with uneaten food; only Kevin Nichols had managed to clean his plate.

"I played right into his hands," Laurie said even as fury threatened to overwhelm her again. "He wanted me to know what...what he's been doing with my daughter. He wanted me to react just the way I did. Damn him."

"It's over," Tim said. "He's gone. But if that isn't enough, I'll go beat the crap out of him for you."

Laurie almost smiled. "No. We've done more than enough damage. It's time for something else." She went to the staircase and began to climb it. She held on to the bannister. No mountain could have presented more difficulty than these stairs.

Tim followed her. "Like I say, I'm lousy at giving advice. But maybe you should just leave her alone for a while, let everything cool down."

"No, Tim," she said. "I know what I have to do. Just...let me do it."

He didn't try to stop her again. She climbed the last few steps, went down the hall and knocked on Alyson's door. She knew there wouldn't be any answer, and after a moment or two she opened the door and went in.

Alyson was huddled on the window seat, her knees drawn up tightly to her chest. She didn't turn to look at her mother, but she spoke in a clear brittle voice.

"Go away. That's all I'm asking—just go away."

Laurie sat down in the chintz armchair. Almost buried beneath the cushion was a ragged one-eared stuffed rabbit that had once been Alyson's favorite companion. Laurie thought the rabbit had been lost long ago. She held it in her lap.

"I've made a lot of mistakes," she began quietly. "A lot of what you've said is true, Alyson. I *have* tried to make a world where nothing harmful or hurtful can ever touch you. Believe me, I finally see how unrealistic that is. But I did it all because I love you. And because...because I never wanted you to end up making the same mistakes I did. Falling in love with someone who couldn't love me back, getting pregnant so young..."

Alyson still refused to look at her. "I'm not like you," she said rigidly. "That's what I've been trying to tell you all along."

"But you are having sex with Kevin Nichols."

Alyson didn't move a muscle as she sat huddled there. And she didn't bother to deny Laurie's statement. Laurie smoothed the one ear remaining on the little stuffed rabbit.

"Kevin Nichols is a user," she said. "A user and a manipulator. He's probably very pleased with himself right now. He knew what buttons to push with me. He pushed them all right and I exploded, just the way he wanted. It was his way of showing he had power."

At last Alyson moved, twisting her head to glare at Laurie. Her eyes seemed very large and dark. "How can you say that? *You're* the one who invited him to that hideous dinner! He was just trying to be polite and friendly and get along."

"He's a manipulator," Laurie repeated. "And unless I miss my guess, he's manipulated you."

She saw the emotions struggling across her daughter's face. Defiance, misery, doubt. But then Alyson swiveled back toward the window.

"I haven't done anything I don't want to," she muttered.

"Are you using birth control?"

"I can't *believe* you're doing this!"

"If you're old enough to have sex," Laurie said, "you're old enough to take responsibility for it." She heard the calm in her voice and didn't understand where it came from. She knew only that she needed it to get through this ordeal.

Every line in Alyson's body denoted outrage at her mother's intrusion. But at last she gave in.

"He's taking care of it," she muttered. "He says

he won't get me pregnant. He uses condoms, all right? Is there anything else disgusting or embarrassing you have to know?''

Laurie very nearly did lose her calm then. Her daughter, having sex with that little creep...

She still held on to the stuffed rabbit, as if only it could prevent her from abandoning control. ''Alyson, all I've ever wanted was for you to have something better than I did. To make a better start. Pregnancy isn't the only danger. Falling in love with the wrong person, that can cause more than enough damage. I should know.''

''I'm not *like* you,'' Alyson burst out. ''Why won't you see it? I'm not like you at all. I'm not going to marry Kevin. I'm not going to make the same mistakes you did!''

Laurie knew the moment had come, but she quailed from it. She almost wasn't brave enough. But then she set down the little stuffed rabbit. She allowed herself nothing to hold on to as she spoke.

''Alyson, there's something I have to tell you. I should have told you a very long time ago...but I didn't. I was afraid of hurting you. I was wrong not to tell you, though.''

Something in her tone must have gotten through to Alyson. Her daughter gazed at her almost fearfully. Laurie knew she had to go on no matter what the words cost her.

''Alyson, I was never married to your father. There was no wedding, no divorce. He never even wanted to marry me. He walked out the day I told him I was pregnant.''

Alyson shook her head as if she couldn't believe

what she'd just heard. "Why?" she whispered. "Why did you let me think…"

"I didn't want to hurt you." Laurie ached inside with all the guilt and regret, but still, she had to go on. "I wanted you to believe you'd had at least the semblance of a normal beginning…."

"Normal." Alyson repeated the word as if it was something dirty. "What's normal, Mom? Do you even know? And didn't you think I was strong enough to have the truth?"

"It wasn't that," Laurie said. "I didn't want anyone or anything ever to harm you. I wanted to keep you safe—"

Alyson gave a harsh laugh. "That's quite a way to make me feel safe. Hiding the truth from me. *Lying* to me all these years. You know what's really funny? Lately I've been wishing, deep down, that we could go back to the way things were before. Back to the time when we trusted each other and we did keep each other safe. Only now…now I find out there was never a time like that. It was all a lie. All of it!"

The ache inside Laurie threatened to engulf her. She thought she'd known pain in her life, but it had been nothing compared to this. How could anything hurt more than the hate and the disillusionment she saw in her daughter's eyes?

"Alyson," she said, her throat raw with unshed tears, "Alyson. The way I've loved you, that hasn't been a lie."

"Save it. After tonight, after everything, I'll never forgive you. Do you understand? I'll never ever be able to forgive you."

LATE THE NEXT EVENING, Grant's small medical clinic was a scene of chaos. A young woman named Stacey Eldridge was about to give birth to her first child, and it seemed that every relative and every friend she'd ever had filed into the clinic. Bess tried to keep all the in-laws and sisters and ex-college-roommates at bay, while Tim and Laurie went about their work in the labor/delivery room. It wasn't entirely clear which of them was Stacey's doctor, so they'd both ended up in here. Oddly enough, to Laurie it didn't feel like too many doctors. It felt just right, in a way she couldn't entirely explain.

"Cervix effacing, but only four centimeters dilated," Laurie said after conducting yet another examination. Stacey moaned; she'd been having contractions for several hours.

"Looks like we're going to have to rupture the membranes," Tim said.

"I agree," Laurie said.

"Rupture—what does that mean?" Nathan Eldridge asked anxiously, gripping his wife's hand.

"It's nothing to worry about," Laurie assured him. "We're just going to help Stacey along a little."

"Ready?" said Tim.

"Ready," said Laurie.

It was more hours yet before Nathan Alexander Eldridge, Jr., deigned to make his appearance, but at last, shortly after midnight, the baby's head crowned.

"Come on, Stacey, one more good push," Tim urged.

"That's right—just one more push!" Laurie exclaimed. It didn't matter how many births she'd attended. Each one seemed special and extraordinary, as if it were the first ever to hit the planet. Only a few moments later the Eldridges were two proud and shaky parents. Still working together, Laurie and Tim accomplished the weighing and measuring of the little boy and delivered him safely to his mother's waiting arms.

"Dr. Russell, Dr. Miller," Nathan Senior said fervently. "How can I ever thank you?"

"Your wife did most of the work," Tim said.

"You know what? Come election day, I'm going to vote for both of you. That's what I'm going to do." Nathan went over to his wife and son and promptly forgot the presence of the two doctors.

Laurie watched the young family. "You know why people have children?" she murmured to Tim.

"A little something about continuing the human race?"

"That's the farthest thing from their minds. They're thinking of a fresh start, that's all. A new beginning, new hopes, all wrapped up in eight pounds, three ounces..." The tears smarted in her eyes, but she hadn't allowed herself to cry yet. Even last night she hadn't allowed herself to cry.

Tim reached out and took her hand, his fingers tightening around hers. Tonight they'd shared a small miracle together, welcoming another human being into the world. That kind of thing could create a false closeness between two people. Laurie knew she had to guard against it.

But the emotion welled up in her nonetheless, emotion that told her, quite simply, that she was in love with Tim Miller.

She tried to fight it as she stood here, clinging to

his hand. She tried every argument she knew. She was only feeling vulnerable because of her daughter and because of the long labor she'd just assisted. And Tim, admittedly, was a very attractive man.

But the knowledge stayed with Laurie, insistent and irrevocable. She'd gone and fallen in love with a man who was only passing through her life. He wasn't the staying kind—he'd made that very clear.

At last the tears spilled over.

It was Ulysses S. Grant Day. This was nothing unusual for the town, however. As far as Tim could tell, Ulysses S. Grant Day was declared several times a year on an as-needed basis. With the election only two days away—the election that would decide whether he or Laurie remained—the town council had decided to whip up a little extra community spirit. Hence the booths set up in the town park, hence the barbershop quartet and the square-dance caller and the two fiddlers who played one old-time duet after another.

Tim wandered restlessly through the park. He saw a booth selling apple and cherry pies, another offering three varieties of pickle relish, another where you could purchase Ulysses S. Grant key chains, Ulysses S. Grant mugs and Ulysses S. Grant sweatshirts. Lord, there was even a kissing booth. Tim felt stifled by all the down-home atmosphere. He'd spent way too much of his life knocking around small towns, going nowhere. That was the problem with Grant—it was another go-nowhere town. So for the hundredth time he asked himself what he was doing here. And for the hundredth time he didn't have an answer.

He kept on wandering, stopped now and then by citizens who either wanted to assure him of their votes or give him their own solutions to the two-doctor dilemma. Why not have Tim and Laurie draw straws or play a good game of poker to decide the outcome...

Tim smiled and listened with only half an ear. He kept scanning the crowd, looking for Laurie. He knew that was the only reason he'd shown up here today. He wanted to see her—as if living in the same house with her wasn't enough.

Their time was running out. Two more days, and the crazy election would take place. That would be the end of everything between them. Tim was good at endings. So why was he out here, scanning every face and wanting it to be Laurie's?

He saw her at last after he'd doubled back and come upon the kissing booth again. She was talking to the guy inside the booth, and meanwhile, a small group of people had gathered around. With a very formal gesture, Laurie set down a few dollar bills. She presented her cheek to the guy, who surprised her by craning his head around and kissing her on the mouth. The small crowd cheered.

That was enough for Tim. He came up to Laurie and tucked her hand into his arm. "Sorry, folks," he said genially. "My fellow candidate and I are wanted elsewhere." Then he escorted her as far away from the kissing booth as they could get.

"What do you think you're doing?" she asked.

"Just didn't want you to take your politicking too seriously."

"It was perfectly innocent—but why am I explaining myself to you, anyway?"

"Beats me. All I know is that you seem mighty earnest about building your constituency. Little by little you're even changing the way you look. I'd watch it if I were you, Doc Laurie. This politics business is running away with you."

They'd reached a bench next to a cluster of shrubby pines. Laurie sat down on it, giving Tim an exasperated glance. "And what, may I ask, is wrong with the way I look?"

He allowed his gaze to travel over her. She wore the kind of dress he'd never seen on her before: a country sort of dress made of cotton and patterned with sprigs of flowers. Laurie could probably make any dress look appealing, but this unsophisticated style just wasn't her.

"If you're trying for the milkmaid effect, you're missing the cow," he said.

She flushed. "What I'm wearing is perfectly appropriate."

"At least you didn't batten down your hair today."

"I have the barrettes in my pocket. I may still decide to use them."

"Don't," he murmured. "I like your hair loose…refusing to do what you want."

Self-consciously she smoothed a stray curl away from her face. "What is it, Tim?" she asked. "Are you a fashion consultant now, along with everything else?"

He grinned slowly. "As a matter of fact, I once worked—"

"*That* I don't believe. I really don't."

"Okay," he admitted, "I've stuck more with the outdoor vocations. But I can tell you something, Laurie. Don't let this town change you. Don't try to be something you're not."

She plucked at the skirt of her dress. "I'm just trying to show people that a woman doctor can be...trusted. That she's not someone who's going to steal away everybody's husband."

"Yeah, I guess the little demonstration at the kissing booth will help convince them, too."

Laurie's flush deepened. "That man happens to be single. And he's perfectly respectable. He's Phil Cline's nephew."

"Great," Tim muttered. "Is that how you'll end up, Laurie? Keeping company with the likes of Phil Cline's nephew?"

"From the way things are going, I won't end up keeping company with *anyone* in Grant. You'll probably be the one who stays. You'll start stepping out with the likes of Phil Cline's *niece*, only she'll get fed up with you because you'll refuse to commit. But some other girl will be lined up to take her place, and you'll start all over again."

"Seems pretty unlikely to me," he murmured. "Does Phil Cline even have a niece?"

She stared at him. "You're doing it again," she said.

"Doing what?"

"Making a joke so you can push me away. You always do that, you know. You want to make damn sure I don't get the wrong idea. You're...you're infuriating, Tim." Her voice was low and intense. "One minute you provide a shoulder for me to lean on, but then, just in case I've gotten too comfortable, you bring out the humor. Don't worry. I won't be leaning on you any longer.''

He didn't feel too humorous at the moment. ''Laurie, it's not just me. You've made damn sure there's no room in your life for anything but your career and your daughter.''

''There isn't any room,'' she said tightly. ''So maybe we're two of a kind.''

''Maybe so,'' he admitted, but it didn't make him feel any better. In fact, he was feeling lousier by the moment. ''You have to understand one thing, Laurie. When it comes to family life, I'd rather not do it at all than blow it.''

''I haven't *asked* you to be part of my fam—''

''Maybe it's smart to realize ahead of time that you don't have what it takes to be good at something. And a family…I've known for a long time I wouldn't be any good at that.''

Everything he said only seemed to make her angry with him. ''What is this—true confessions?'' she snapped. ''You've already made your point, Tim. You don't want to settle down. You don't want to end up with a wife or a teenager who'll drive you to distraction. I get it, all right? What you're doing now is…it's a *non*proposal. It's a nonproposal, if I ever heard one.''

He rubbed that crick he still got in his back sometimes. ''What are you talking about?''

''It's exactly the opposite of a proposal,'' she said. ''You're asking me *not* to marry you. *Not* to spend the rest of my life loving you and all the rest of it. Well, Tim, I accept. I accept your nonproposal wholeheartedly!'' With that, she scrambled to her feet and strode off.

She disappeared among the crowd and it took him a minute to catch up to her. The fiddlers had been joined by a bass player, and several people were already dancing to the rather sonorous music the trio produced.

"Care to join me?" Tim asked Laurie as he reached her side.

"I thought we were finished."

He didn't know how to finish this time. Before, he'd always just walked away from women. No promises, no regrets. But now all he could do was take Laurie in his arms and waltz with her in the town park.

"Dammit," she said. "Why do you have to be a good dancer, along with everything else?"

He pulled her closer. No matter that it was broad daylight, no matter that the townspeople of Grant seemed to be looking for something new to gossip about. Laurie Russell was warm and womanly in his arms and he didn't want anything else to intrude. Not even the promises he couldn't give her.

But there were intrusions all right. The music faltered to a stop as a man dressed somewhat grandly in a double-breasted suit came up to consult with the fiddlers. The musicians nodded at whatever he was telling them, then broke into a brief impromptu rendition of the wedding march, the bass providing a booming counterpoint. The man in the double-breasted suit made an announcement to the crowd at large.

"My good friends, I'd like to ask all of you to

celebrate with me. Bess Thompson has only this minute agreed to be my wife! Where is she? Bess! Bess, come over here, sweetheart.''

From all appearances, Bess was trying to duck her way through the crowd and make an exit. She didn't look like somebody who'd just agreed to a proposal of marriage. She looked like somebody who wished she'd received a *non*proposal, instead.

Despite her efforts, Bess ended up next to the man in the double-breasted suit. He put his arm around her.

''Kitten, I want everyone to know how happy we're going to be!''

Laurie shook her head. ''Did that man just call Bess 'Kitten'?''

''Afraid so.'' Tim wondered what the hell was going on, and apparently so did Doc Garrett. He appeared at Tim's side.

''Tim-o, what do you know about this? What right does she have agreeing to marry Max Worley?''

''First I've heard of it,'' Tim said. ''If you ask me, it's the first Kitten has heard of it, too. She looks taken aback.''

''Max Worley is a fool,'' the doc pronounced. ''And she'd be an even bigger fool hooking up with him.''

''Why don't you tell her so yourself?'' Laurie suggested.

The doc scowled at her. ''None of my business,'' he said, and stalked off.

Well-wishers crowded around Bess and the elegantly tailored Max Worley. ''They make quite a pair, don't they?'' Tim asked. Now Laurie was the one who scowled.

"You and Doc, you both refuse to get involved, don't you? You'll both let love pass you right by."

Something in her tone made him give her a hard look. "What are you saying, Laurie?"

"Nothing. I'm *not* saying I love you—you'd better be darn sure of that much. Now, can we finally be done with each other?"

It seemed that his nonproposal was being followed up by a nondeclaration. Tim felt uneasy, but before he could get to the bottom of it another interruption occurred. Alyson made an appearance.

"If you'll *excuse* me, Tim, I'd really like to speak to my mother alone."

He saw the hope that flared in Laurie's expression. And then, from a distance, he watched as Alyson spoke very quickly and intently. He also watched as Alyson turned and hurried away, and as Laurie's face crumpled. In a few strides he was next to her.

"Laurie, what is it?"

She stepped back. "You can't give me your shoulder to lean on this time." Her voice sounded utterly hollow. "Because my daughter—my Alyson—says she can't bear to live in the same house with me anymore. She says she's going to move in with Kevin Nichols...starting immediately."

Tim didn't think much else could happen on Ulysses S. Grant Day. But that was before he glanced up and saw who was approaching across the park: an imposing gray-haired gentleman Tim hadn't seen in years.

"Hello, son," said Samuel Miller.

CHAPTER SEVENTEEN

THE AFTERNOON was ripening toward evening as Tim and Laurie arrived home from the park. Laurie immediately headed for the stairs leading up to her daughter's room. She barely heard Tim's voice as he tried to stop her.

"I think you need a stiff drink," he said. "Brandy's my recommendation."

"Not now. I have to see…" She couldn't finish the sentence. All she could do was hurry up the steps and down the hall. As she went, she prayed that it was all a mistake. That she'd find Alyson curled up on the window seat. She wouldn't mind if Alyson brooded or sulked or even said hateful things—just as long as she was *here*.

Without even bothering to knock, Laurie threw open the door to her daughter's room. It was empty. Alyson wasn't here. And in the closet half the hangers were empty. Alyson had left behind the soft lacy clothing she'd once loved, but she'd taken her jeans and sweaters and T-shirts.

Uttering a wordless cry, Laurie sank down in the armchair. Tim came into the room and handed her a glass of brandy.

"Drink," he said.

The liquid seemed to burn her throat as it went

down. "I thought if I refused to believe it...somehow it wouldn't be true. But she's gone. She's really gone, Tim. She's with that...that...,"

"Drink some more," he said.

She finished all of it. "I could march right over there. I could force her to come home with me. I'm her mother."

"She's eighteen years old. The more you try to force her, the more she'll pull away."

"Don't you see, Tim? She's already pulled away. More than I could ever imagine." Laurie finally understood the meaning of the word "heartache." It was what she felt now, a terrible weight pressing down on her so that her heart really felt as if it would break. The child she loved with all her soul...gone.

"I told her the truth," Laurie whispered. "I just couldn't go on deceiving her. So I finally told her. You want to know the sad part? I don't think she really cared about whether or not I'd been married to her father. It was the fact that all these years I didn't trust her with the truth. That was what hurt her. And that's why she's left."

Tim took Laurie's hand and pulled her to her feet. "Look at me," he said.

She didn't want to look. She just wanted to go find her daughter and bring her back home. But Tim gently tilted her face upward.

"Look at me," he repeated. "And listen. You're not to blame here. Alyson would have left no matter what—she's determined to make her own mistakes. And you have to let her do it. You don't have any other choice."

She wanted to protest every word he said. If she

could blame herself, then at least she'd feel some shred of control over the situation. But at last she really looked at Tim and she saw that he'd changed in a significant way during the past hour or so—ever since his father had arrived. He was here with her, offering her brandy and advice, but there was an immeasurable distance in his blue eyes. It was as if he spoke to her from someplace no one could reach. She had the unsettling conviction that he would no longer need to use humor as a defense; this had gone far beyond that. He had retreated behind a wall she didn't know how to break down.

"You should go see your father," she said. "You should talk to him."

"He'll be fine. He can stay with Doc Garrett or go to a bed-and-breakfast. The season's started now."

It was the lack of emotion in his voice that chilled her most. "Tim, you barely spoke to him at the park. He came all this way to see you. Why can't you at least give him a chance?"

"Leave it alone, Laurie," he said. "Just leave it."

She knew she would never reach him with words. The two of them were locked in their own separate pain. No. Words could not bridge that distance.

What Laurie did next was fully premeditated. She took hold of his hand, led him from the room, closed the door behind them. And then she led the way down the hall to her own room. She went to the window, drew down the blinds. Now only a few rays of the late-afternoon sun filtered in.

She went to stand before her bed. Without speaking, Tim came to stand beside her. She lifted her hands and linked her fingers behind his neck. She brought her face toward his, parted her lips for his kiss.

The pain inside her didn't lessen. But it seemed able to coexist with something else—the desire blooming along every nerve ending as she took what she needed from Tim. Their kiss went on, a prelude that could take its own time.

At last she moved away from him, but it was only so she could unbutton her dress. The dress fell away from her, and then she slid the straps of her slip down over her shoulders. It, too, slithered down her body and she stepped out of it. When she spoke, she was surprised at the absolute steadiness of her voice.

"I'm on the pill, so there's nothing to worry about there." She reached behind to unhook her bra. It was a simple matter to dispense with the rest of her underwear. She stood before him in the dusky light, unashamed, waiting for him to continue what she'd started.

As silent as she, Tim sat down on the bed. He pulled off first one boot, then the other, and they landed in a heap on the floor. He unbuttoned his shirt, took off his jeans and his own underwear. Those items, too, landed in a heap. Then he and Laurie stretched full length on the bed, caressing each other. Without words, Tim explored her body and she his. She welcomed the heat that flamed inside her. She didn't hide from it, didn't make excuses for it. This was what she needed now. Only this.

She ran her hands over Tim's back and he captured her mouth once again. They kissed and touched, their bodies pressed together. Laurie reveled in everything about Tim that was masculine and strong. She gave and took, and gave again. Still in silence they moved, but she sensed the quickening of his breath, answered it with her own. She opened her legs to him and he entered her. Nothing else mattered, only this passion that coursed between them. Clinging to him, she felt the sweat slick on his skin and knew he needed exactly what she did—this unquestioning unthinking surge toward fulfillment. And at last she cried out as she tumbled over the edge of passion. A groan escaped his lips a moment later.

Afterward they lay together, desire sated. Yet Laurie realized the distance between them hadn't been bridged, after all. Their bodies had touched and joined, but not their hearts.

"Tim," Laurie said, trying desperately to reach across the divide. "I...Tim, I love you."

She was afraid he wouldn't answer her. But then, "I'm sorry," he told her.

"Sorry—because you can't love me back?" She ached again with all the longings that hadn't been answered.

"Sorry for everything, Laurie." He kissed her once more, all too gently, as if it was the last time. Then he took his clothes and his boots, and he left her.

LAURIE HARDLY SLEPT at all that night. She tossed and turned in her solitary bed, the memory of what she and Tim had shared seeming to mock her. Could it have been true sharing if it had brought no true closeness? She listened vainly for the sound of his footsteps returning to her. The sound never came of course. She pictured him downstairs, sleeping on that wretched orange couch. Or perhaps lying awake just as she was doing.

More than anything, however, Laurie was haunted by worry for her daughter. In all of Alyson's life she'd spent the night away from home only a handful of times—slumber parties at the homes of her friends, the occasional camp-out. She'd never gone like this, leaving a trail of accusations behind her, running off with a boy who could only hurt her.

Finally, when the light of dawn began to find its way through the slats of the blinds, Laurie climbed out of bed and cinched her robe around her. She padded downstairs, approaching the den with an uncharacteristic nervousness. But as she peered in she saw no Tim Miller on the orange couch. And as she went through the house she realized he wasn't here at all. She hadn't heard him leave; he must have gone very quietly sometime in the middle of the night.

She was alone. Laurie busied herself making a cup of coffee and then sat to drink it at the kitchen table. The activity, however, seemed pointless. She knew that if she gave in to her real urges, she would rush about frantically looking for anything and everything to do. She'd march over to Kevin Nichols's apartment and yell at him for taking her daughter. Then she'd go find Tim and demand to know why he couldn't love her. A lot of good it would do her, too. And so she stayed where she was, desultorily sipping the coffee without even tasting it.

The front door opened and shut again. Laurie pushed her chair back and went flying out to the hall. "Tim!"

It was Alyson. "Glad to see you missed me," she

said sarcastically. Laurie was so glad to see her daughter she knew she could forgive anything Alyson said.

"You're home. Oh, thank goodness! Honey, let's just sit down and talk. We can work everything out, I know we can."

"Please, Mom. I only came to get some more of my stuff. I'm staying with Kevin. Nothing you can do will change that."

Laurie brought herself up short. She'd been about to sweep Alyson into a hug, but the look on her daughter's face was enough to squelch that idea.

"Very well," Laurie said carefully, searching her way. "I won't try to argue with you. But we could still sit down and talk."

"There's nothing else to talk about, is there? Not unless you have any more little secrets you'd like to share."

Alyson went on up the stairs with the self-righteous callousness you could have only when you were eighteen or so. Added years brought at least a little understanding of human frailty. But that made Laurie think about Tim and his father. Maybe she wasn't right about age bringing wisdom, after all. Because whatever had gone on between Samuel and Tim Miller, neither one of them was ready to forgive the other. Tim could hardly stand to discuss his father and she'd seen Samuel Miller's unrelenting stance at the park yesterday. He'd traveled all this way to see Tim, but he hadn't exactly embraced his son. A coldness struck deep inside Laurie. What if that happened to her and Alyson—years and years of misunderstandings that could never be broached? Nothing else

Laurie accomplished in her life could make up for that.

She waited in the hallway until Alyson came down again, this time dragging her suitcase. She carried her book bag—and the little stuffed rabbit, as well. That very nearly undid Laurie. But she managed to stay where she was, fingernails biting into her palms.

"Alyson, I can't stop you. God knows I want to, but I can't. If only you'd think about it a little more. Stay the morning at least. Consider whether or not you really want to do this."

"I *have* thought about it. I want to be with Kevin, nobody else."

Laurie studied her daughter, searching vainly for any sign of the doubts she'd glimpsed before. But Alyson's face was so set and determined it seemed made of stone.

"I don't want you to go," Laurie said, knowing the uselessness of her plea.

"Actually there *is* something I want to talk to you about. Kevin and I were up late last night making our plans. And we've decided we'd like to build a cabin up in the mountains. One of those kit cabins you order through the mail—he knows all about them. Anyway, that's what we'd like to do. I'll need my college money to pay for my share of it."

That was it. Laurie had tried to pick up the pieces again. She'd even tried to be understanding. But this was too much, way too much. The thought of Kevin Nichols taking her daughter's college money for a blasted *kit* cabin...

"That little snot-nose," Laurie said. "The gall to think he could get away with something like this!

He's not going anywhere near that money—and neither are you, Alyson. That college fund is sacred. You'll use it for college and nothing else. For crying out loud, you barely know this little twit! And already you want to sign over a lifetime's savings to him. *Think,* Alyson. Use your head and not your hormones. Kevin Nichols is using you and you're letting him get away with it.''

Alyson's eyes grew wide. They filled with tears. She clutched the little rabbit close to her. ''How can you say such horrible things! He…he cares about me. He cares a whole lot more than *you* do!''

Alyson went running from the house, her suitcase banging against her legs. And Laurie knew that once again she'd taken exactly the wrong path. She'd alienated her daughter more than ever.

IT WAS LATE MORNING before Tim made the decision to drive up to Doc's cabin. His truck bumped along the winding mountain road, and he knew he still had a chance to turn back. But he had to get this encounter over with sooner or later. He'd found out that his father had stayed with Doc last night. Imagine that, Samuel Miller roughing it, instead of seeking the best accommodations in town. Samuel had never liked less than perfection. Why was he settling for less now?

Tim reached the cabin a lot sooner than he wanted. He cut the engine and stayed where he was for a minute or two. He thought about what had happened last night with Laurie—the way they'd made love. There'd been no frills involved, no extras, just a taking on both sides. He'd wanted to bury himself in her, and use her to forget all the past failures that haunted him. Once, not too long ago, she'd blamed herself for wanting to use *him*. Maybe that was the only way it could be between them. Taking, neither one of them knowing quite how to give.

Except that last night Laurie had told him she loved him. She'd given herself then all right. And Tim hadn't known how to answer her. He hadn't been able to give back what she needed. Perhaps he never would be able.

He climbed out of the truck and went to the door of the cabin. It swung open before he'd even had a chance to knock. Doc Garrett stood at the threshold, his usual untidy self.

"Your dad's inside," he said. "Before you let into him, Tim-o, there's a whole lot I need to tell you."

"I'm not here for a blowup. That never was my way, Doc. My father should know that by now." Tim brushed past Jonathan into the cramped cabin.

Samuel Miller was in the kitchen washing dishes. That was something else out of the ordinary. Samuel, always proud of his status as a doctor, had rarely performed what he thought of as menial labor. He lived by himself in New Mexico and, as far as Tim knew, ate microwave dinners off paper plates—probably just so he *wouldn't* have to wash the dishes.

"Tim," he said, with a brief glance at his son. He finished rinsing one plate and started on another. It didn't sound like a greeting, but more like an imprecation. At least that was nothing new. Tim stood still and observed him. Samuel Miller hadn't changed much over the years and he was a study in contrasts with his old friend Doc Garrett. Whereas Doc was on the short side, with his comfortable paunch and bald pate, Samuel was imposingly tall and fit and still had a full head of silver-gray hair. True, there were grooves etched deep into Samuel's face, but his jaw hadn't slackened. And true, arthritis had taken its toll on Samuel's once-deft surgeon's hands, but he always managed to find ways to disguise the damage. That would explain today's washing of dishes. It was a way for Samuel to prove that his hands could still do their job—any job.

For a moment Tim felt something unfamiliar and almost welcome: a grudging sympathy for his dad. It had to be difficult for a vigorous man like Samuel to grow older and confront limitations. And no matter what, you had to admire someone who refused to accept his limitations, someone who just kept pushing and pushing against them. Tim continued to feel this sympathy—until his father stopped washing the dishes and turned and looked at him fully.

Tim knew that look all too well. It was harsh and disapproving. It raked him up and down and seemed to find nothing it could tolerate or forgive. Tim had been toughening himself against that look since he was twelve years old. By now he had plenty of practice, but he still experienced that initial tightening in his gut, that first jab of disappointment. Disappointment at himself for disappointing his father. But he'd learned to step back from it. He did that now—he stepped back mentally from his father and from all the unpleasant sensations Samuel Miller evoked.

"Dad, I guess you want to tell me why you're here."

Before Samuel had a chance to speak, Doc Garrett intervened. "Tim, that's something I want to explain.

I invited your father personally when I saw how this damn-fool election was going. It seemed to me that I needed your father here. He agreed.''

"You don't say," Tim murmured noncommittally. What was this all about? Doc was behaving in an oddly guilty manner, acting like he had to confess something. And meanwhile, Samuel just stood there with his arms folded, hiding his gnarled hands but doing his best to appear dignified and overbearing.

"The point is, Tim," Doc went on, "both your father and I had a little something to do with you coming to Grant. It's...something we planned together. So that's why I thought we should both be here—so we could explain it to you."

Tim felt the tightening in his gut increase. "Yeah, maybe you'd better explain."

"I'll do it," Samuel said gruffly. "You're taking hell's own time about it, Jonathan, and not getting anything out—"

"*I'll* do it," Doc said, sounding irritable. "You've trusted me this far, so you might as well let me handle the rest of it."

"Get on with it, then," Samuel said.

Tim just waited, not sure he wanted to hear what these two old codgers had in store for him.

"It's like this, Tim," the doc began. "Do you remember that cruise I went on a while back?"

"Right. The cruise where you and Estelle—"

"That's the one. What I never told you was that your dad came on the cruise, too. And we got to talking, the both of us. We realized we weren't getting any younger and maybe we needed to let the next generation take over for us. So your dad finally decided to let Gabe take over his practice in New Mexico, and the idea was for you to take over my practice here. There was a certain symmetry to the whole thing that appealed to us. Isn't that right, Samuel?''

"Symmetry didn't have anything to do with it," Samuel muttered. "It was time for both my boys to do something useful with their lives."

Parts of this didn't make any sense. Tim concentrated on those parts first. "Dad, in case you hadn't noticed, Gabe's been pretty useful all along. He took over your practice years ago."

"Gabe and I have been partners," Samuel was quick to remind him. "Fifty-fifty. I've been carrying a full load of patients. Don't let anyone tell you otherwise."

According to Gabe, it was otherwise. Samuel had been seeing fewer and fewer patients as the years went by, Gabe carrying the responsibility for the practice.

"Okay, forget the details," Tim said grimly. "I get the general picture. The two of you went on a cruise and had a few too many. And you agreed to arrange my life and Gabe's. Funny how you didn't consult either one of us about it. Funny, too, Doc, how you didn't tell me it was my father's idea as much as your own."

"Tim-o, if I'd told you your dad wanted you here, you would have turned me down flat. You would never have accepted the position—you wouldn't even have given it a chance. So, yes, I used a little subterfuge. It seemed permissible under the circumstances."

God, what a colossal joke. Samuel Miller had spent

a lifetime disapproving of Tim and ignoring him whenever possible, then had decided to up and meddle in Tim's life, big time.

"It's amusing when you think about it," Tim said. "The entire time I've been here in Grant, I thought I was following in Doc's footsteps. Not yours, Dad. But let me see if I can put this together. You're a small-town doctor—you thought I should be a small-town doctor, too. Just like you, as a matter of fact. I guess you thought you'd finally found a use for me, after all. Prodigal son bows down and admits Dad's way of life is the only way to go—that type of thing. Too bad you didn't consult me about all this."

"You wouldn't have listened," Samuel said brusquely. "I finally did see a way for you to make something of yourself—and what's wrong with that? It's what parents do. Look out for their kids."

Doc intervened. "Your dad was already proud of you, Tim. Graduating from medical school, getting that fellowship to the Jacobs Institute. All that meant a lot to him."

"Funny how he never told *me* that." Tim reminded himself to keep stepping back. That was the trick—you stepped back emotionally. You didn't get involved.

Samuel didn't say anything, just gave Tim that heavy disappointed stare, as if nothing his youngest son did could ever impress him. It was Doc who fumbled on.

"He's proud of you, Tim. Real proud. He just doesn't know how to show it."

"I can speak for myself," Samuel said gruffly.

"You're not saying the right things, though, are

you?'' Doc growled. "You old fool. You're not telling him you're proud of him and *that's* why you want him to follow in your footsteps.''

"Look, Doc,'' Tim said, "I appreciate the effort, but it's not necessary. I know exactly where I stand with my father. Let's just leave it, all right?''

"You don't know the whole story,'' Doc insisted. "Your dad isn't the same as before. He's found somebody, and that's why he's finally willing to open up a little—''

"Enough,'' Samuel said.

"No,'' the doc said. "Tim needs to know this. Anyway, Tim, your dad met her on the cruise. Her name is Margaret, and she's a good woman. She's made your father see that life is too short to have these misunderstandings, these bad feelings.''

"Enough!'' Samuel said again.

Never get involved, Tim reminded himself once more. And so he listened as if to a fairy tale: an old man goes on a trip, finds true love, tries to mess with his son's life.

"Interesting,'' Tim said. "Real interesting. My dad and a lady friend. It's a little hard for me to picture, though. Maybe that's because I grew up never hearing about him and my mother. She died, and it's like she never existed. Did you know that, Doc? We never talked about her after she was gone. Forbidden subject. I never could figure out why. Did she do somethin' wrong by dyin'? Was that it?''

"Enough,'' Samuel said for the third time. He stepped forward, dropping his hands to his sides. "It's always the same with you, Tim. Always. I try to give you something, try to do something for you, and you throw it back in my face—try to blame me for your mother.''

"Not blame, Dad," Tim said quietly. "Not anymore. I'd just like us to talk about her and remember what she gave us. Because she did give us something, you know. She loved us and she expected us to care at least a little about each other."

"She's gone. Nothing you can do will bring her back. And if she *was* here, don't you think she'd be ashamed? Of all the grief you've caused, and the damned ingratitude! You have no right to speak of her." Samuel's face had gone an ugly mottled color and it was as if he was talking to a rebellious teenage Tim all over again. It was as if he saw only the failures and the wrong turns and the bad choices. As if he couldn't see Tim as he was now—a grown man who'd finally left the bad choices behind and made something of his life. Made something, in fact, without any help from his father.

Tim didn't feel anger. He didn't even feel regret. He felt nothing at all as Samuel Miller stared at him with something very akin to hate in his eyes. The ability to feel nothing—maybe that was his father's gift to him. And maybe he ought to be grateful for it.

CHAPTER EIGHTEEN

IT WAS THE DAY of the election. In only a few hours the citizens of Grant, Colorado, would decide who they wanted as the town doctor—Tim or Laurie. The voting would take place at Ulysses S. Grant High School, and then the two-doctor dilemma would finally be resolved.

Laurie wished she could feel happy about it. She knew that a decision one way or the other would have to be a relief. She'd be able to get on with her life—no Tim Miller in the way. And maybe, once he was gone, she'd finally be able to convince herself that she didn't really love him.

For the moment, however, she simply marched out of the house with the clipping shears she'd unearthed in one of the kitchen drawers. Maybe the shears were another relic left behind by one of Doc's lady friends—a gardener, perhaps, who'd tried to win his heart with flowers. Laurie went straight out to the vine-choked gazebo in the side yard and started wielding the tool. She tried to ignore the fact that in a few hours she might no longer have any right to go chopping down vines.

"Gettin' out some of your aggression?" Tim remarked from behind her.

The clippers froze. Laurie listened to the pounding

of her heart. She hadn't seen Tim since the other night, when they'd made love. She didn't know where he'd been spending his time. She only knew that the house had seemed very lonely with him gone.

Slowly she turned toward him. Her eyes took in every detail: the vivid red of his hair, the soft faded cloth of his shirt, the long lean line of those ever-present jeans, the scuffed toes of his cowboy boots.

"Hello," she said, marveling at the nonchalant sound of her own voice.

"Actually I came to say goodbye," he told her, no humor in his eyes this time.

"Goodbye?" She spoke the word as if she'd never heard it before.

"Laurie, turns out I came to Grant under false pretenses. It's a long story, but my father and Doc cooked up a scheme to get me out here. The upshot is…I'm leaving."

"You don't need to leave," she said stupidly. "Not before the election, anyway."

"I'm leaving," he repeated. "I've already informed the town council and they've called off the election. It's no longer necessary. The job's yours."

She felt so cold and brittle inside a mere touch would have shattered her. "Tim…I don't understand. What will you do?"

"Same as always. Move on, find something new. I always manage to land on my feet."

The sudden flare of anger she felt was welcome. "Leaving—you're good at that, aren't you? Dammit, Tim! I didn't want to love you. I didn't ask for it. I wish with all my heart that I *didn't* love you!"

"I'm sorry, Laurie. I wish I could be the kind of

man you need. But I'm not. I never was. I tried not to make promises."

"Oh, you didn't make any promises," she said acidly. "Don't worry, you're off the hook about that. You can leave with a clear conscience. Well—go already. If that's what you really want, just go. Get the hell out of here."

He gazed at her for a long moment. She saw no anger to answer her own. She saw only that sorrow, as if Tim Miller truly regretted that he couldn't love her.

KEVIN LIVED in one of the old houses along Main Street that had been converted into a triplex. His apartment had two small rooms, a minuscule kitchen and an even tinier bathroom. Alyson kept trying to tell herself it was cozy.

Certainly she knew every corner of the place by now. She'd scoured years-old grime from the kitchen floor, polished the wooden shelves in the living room and the bedroom, swept dust balls from under every piece of furniture. There really wasn't much to do besides clean, whether she was here or at the office. Nicholas Jeep Tours hadn't had many clients, so Kevin wasn't doing that many tours, in spite of the fact that the tourist season was beginning to come into full swing. Alyson secretly suspected Kevin's lack of business had something to do with his manner. He acted as if he didn't care if people booked with him or not, and he'd probably scared some people on those narrow mountain roads. He didn't realize that you were supposed to give people a little thrill but still reassure them they'd be safe. That was how Alyson would handle it, anyway, if it was *her* business.

She'd tried to give Kevin some suggestions, but he hadn't taken kindly to them. After that she'd just stopped. She and Kevin didn't talk about much of anything. She spent most of the time in the office on her own, and when she came home to Kevin's place, he usually wasn't there, either. He only seemed to show up for the nights—and for the sex.

She shivered a little as she emptied a bucket of dirty water—she'd just mopped the kitchen floor again—in the toilet. She'd believed what Kevin had told her—that the sex would get better. It didn't *hurt* anymore, but it wasn't better. Kevin always did things so fast, like he was running a race and had to be first to the finish line. And Alyson was always left behind, feeling like she'd missed out on something but not quite knowing what it was. Having sex didn't make her feel smart or knowing or *cool*. It only made her feel small and insignificant, just like always.

She set the bucket under the sink and glanced around for something else to do. The apartment was really spotless, though; she'd even taken a toothbrush to the grout between the bathroom tiles. She wondered what her mother would say if she knew how much time Alyson spent cleaning. Mom would probably have a fit over that. Alyson remembered all the times they'd shared, watching movies on TV and laughing at the commercials where the women acted so *earnest* about cleaning house, as if they didn't have a single other thing to do. Mom had told Alyson that the two of them were lucky; they had so many other things to occupy themselves with they didn't have to worry about pointless cleaning. It didn't matter if their place got a little dusty or if they always did the laundry at the last minute. They'd had big plans, the two of them. Big dreams.

Why she was thinking about her mother, of all people? Just then someone knocked at the door. Alyson went to open it—and there stood Laurie, as if Alyson had conjured her up.

"Hello, Alyson," her mother said very politely.

She had a horrible urge to throw herself into Mom's arms and burst into tears. She frowned, instead.

"What are you doing here?" she demanded.

Surprisingly Mom gave a faint smile. "I didn't come here to argue, if that's what you're thinking. But, Alyson, it's been almost two weeks since you moved out. I've missed you—and there are some things we really do need to say to each other."

Alyson knew she had every right to slam the door in her mother's face. Mom had *lied* to her. She'd kept the truth hidden, behaving as if she couldn't possibly trust Alyson to understand. As if it made any difference whether or not Alyson's dad had signed a marriage certificate or not! The guy was obviously a creep for walking out on the two of them, no matter how you looked at it. But Laurie hadn't trusted her to realize that. It was just so typical of their entire relationship.

Alyson didn't slam the door. She gave a shrug as if she didn't care one way or the other what Laurie did. "You can come in," she said. "For a minute, anyway."

"Are you busy?"

"Yes," Alyson lied. "But Kevin's not here. He...had some stuff to do. He won't be back for a while." Alyson had absolutely no idea where Kevin was or what he might be doing, but Laurie looked relieved that he wasn't here. She stepped inside and sat down on one of the straight-backed chairs in the living room. Alyson didn't think those chairs were very comfortable, but she didn't want to say so herself. She sat down, too.

"I plan to do some decorating," she said in an offhand manner. "When I get the time, that is."

"I'm sure whatever you do will be...fine."

"People always use that word when they don't know what else to say," Alyson told her.

"I suppose they do."

Mom looked a little pale and maybe even tired, like she hadn't been sleeping well. She'd been alone in that big old house ever since Alyson had left...and ever since Tim had left, too.

"How are things at the clinic?" Alyson asked as if speaking to a formal acquaintance.

"Actually just fine—if you'll excuse the use of that word. More patients are coming in all the time. I guess they figure they don't have any choice, considering I won the election by default. They'll get used to a woman doctor sooner or later."

"I'm sure they will," Alyson said stiffly. And then she couldn't stand it anymore. "Why are you here?" she asked. "If it's just to complain about me and tell me what a bitch I am..."

Laurie winced. "I'd never call you that. And I didn't come to complain. I just wanted to tell you..." She took a deep breath as if fortifying herself. "Alyson, I know I made some mistakes. Some serious ones. I should have told you from the beginning about your father, how it really was. I shouldn't have listened to my parents. They're the ones who wanted to invent a marriage in the first place, but I could have said no. I could have stuck by the truth and the two of us would have been a whole lot better off.''

"Okay, fine," Alyson muttered. For some reason, she felt smaller than ever inside, and she didn't want her mother to sense that. "You've said it and now you can go."

"There's something else," Laurie went on relentlessly. "I think you have to know that even though I've made some mistakes, I've decided to forgive myself for them. If I don't there's no chance at all you and I can go on together some day. I have to forgive both of us."

"Forgive *me?*" Alyson said indignantly.

"Yes, exactly. Honey, we've both said some things we regret. We have to forgive each other and leave it behind." Laurie took another deep breath. "So here's the thing, Alyson. I know you talked to me about your college fund and how you wanted to use it for…for a kit cabin." She could barely seem to get those words out of her mouth, and she hurried on. "I'm still very much opposed to the idea, but I've also realized that the money is yours as much as it's mine. We worked together for years to save it up. And so, here's what I'm offering. If you still feel the same way in six months, if you don't want to go to college and you want the cabin, and you still feel the same way about…about Kevin, then I'm going to turn the money over to you. You'll be able to do what you want with it. No questions asked.''

"You really mean it?" Alyson asked skeptically.

"Yes," Laurie said. "You've made it clear that you're an adult now, making adult decisions. I have to respect that and let you make the decisions. My only stipulation is that you'll think about it for six months. After that, the money is all yours.'' Laurie stood and went to the door. For a moment she turned and gazed at Alyson with such an expression of love it was all Alyson could do not to burst into tears. But then her mother walked out the door, and Alyson had no idea how to call her back.

SOMETIMES YOU GOT what you wanted in life just by asking for it. Two weeks ago Tim had shown up at the Jacobs Institute in Chicago and inquired as to whether or not he still had a shot at that fellowship. The answer had been yes. So here he was, with his own little cubicle of an office and a three-foot-high pile of reading to do. The institute liked its researchers to be up on the very latest of data before being set loose in the laboratory. Too bad Tim just couldn't seem to concentrate on the reading. Too bad his mind kept wandering west, all the way to Grant, Colorado, and a certain lovely town doctor.

Sometimes you didn't get what you wanted in life because you knew that asking for it would be the wrong thing. Tim had no business being anywhere near Laurie. First off, it was her right to have that job. She'd earned it in any number of ways. Second, she deserved some guy who knew how to give her a real family, some guy who wouldn't mess things up for her. Third...

Tim glanced around, wishing there was a window in here, something to give him a little distraction. But he was lucky to be here at all and he knew it. He'd been given a second chance at success, and this time he had to make sure he didn't blow it.

One of the administrative assistants poked her head into his cubicle and dumped some mail on his desk. "Hi, Dr. Miller," she said.

"Hi."

He waited for her to go away, but she hovered. "Getting settled in okay?" she asked.

"Just fine."

"Well...I thought you might be feeling a little out of place. So far from home, you know."

"I'm managing, thanks," he said.

She continued to hover. "Dr. Miller, a few of us are going to try out a new bar tonight. It's a country-and-western place. The dance floor's supposed to be something special. Care to join us?"

"No, thanks," he said. He didn't offer any explanation.

"Maybe some other time."

"I'm not much for dancing these days," he said. She looked disappointed, but at last she moved on. He scanned a few interoffice memos, barely reading them. Already he was amazed at the bureaucratic intricacies of a place like this, and he couldn't say he much cared for them. He'd come here to do research. Why didn't he just get on with it?

He flipped over one envelope, and the postmark gave him pause: Grant, Colorado. The address was made out in a childish script and no wonder—inside was a letter from nine-year-old Amy Vance. The letter was short, sweet and to the point. "Dear Dr. Miller," the letter read, "my finger is pretty much all better. You made it so I wasn't scared. I wanted to write and say thank-you. Dr. Laurie told me where. I miss you, Amy."

"Lord," Tim murmured. All he'd done was stitch up the kid's finger. You wouldn't think something like that would make much of a difference. That had been his problem with Grant all along. He'd felt like he *wasn't* making much of a difference. Wasting his medical education on things like routine physicals and gastritis attacks and cut fingers, and delivering babies.

Tim set the letter aside and tried to get on with his work, but the thought of that letter kept distracting him. He picked it up and read it again. So it was now Dr. Laurie, was it? He couldn't help smiling. It sounded to him as if Laurie was finding her way in that town. She had a nickname—that was definitely the first step.

Laurie—beautiful stubborn vulnerable Laurie. Full of passion and need and trying to put the lid on both. Determined to stand on her own, but giving in now and then and leaning on his shoulder—except that his shoulder wasn't there anymore. She'd been willing to take a chance on love and he'd refused her. But suddenly he couldn't think of any good reason he'd refused.

"Hell," Tim said. He took the letter from Grant, Colorado, and stuffed it into his pocket. And then he strode out of his cubicle and out of the Jacobs Institute altogether.

To DATE, it was one of Laurie's biggest medical successes. A woman from Brayton named Esther Hobbs had come in complaining of long-term lack of energy, depressed appetite and recurring chills. After thorough testing, Laurie had diagnosed an underactive thyroid and prescribed the appropriate medication. This morning Esther had come in for a follow-up and already seemed a new person—full of zip and enthusiasm.

"I have you to thank, Dr. Laurie," she'd said fervently. "You found the problem and you fixed it. Bless you!"

That had been some benediction, Laurie thought. Now she watched as Esther went back out to the parking lot, climbed into her car and went zooming away.

"Heaven help us," Bess said. "Esther's going to be a terror from now on, roaring up and down the mountains. Just think, we'll have *you* to thank."

Laurie gave her nurse a mild look. "You're just a softie, Bess. You love it as much as I do when we have a success." Glancing into the waiting room, she saw there was a temporary lull. It didn't bother her; by now she'd learned that business always picked up again sooner or later. People really were getting used to the idea of a lady doctor. Even Bess.

"Seems a little too quiet around here, doesn't it?" Bess asked now.

"Not particularly."

"Without Tim, I mean."

"I wasn't thinking about him," Laurie said crisply. That much was true. She'd actually gone ten seconds without picturing Tim Miller—without wondering about him. It was the other fifty seconds in every minute she had to worry about. She was working on it. Surely it was only a matter of time before she got him out of her head entirely.

She'd been glad to hear he hadn't lost out on his fellowship, after all. It said something about Tim's caliber that the Jacobs Institute had agreed to take him after he'd refused them the first time around. Laurie sincerely hoped that Tim would be happy in Chicago and find what he was looking for. Otherwise he would just have to keep moving on...

"You really do miss him, don't you?" Bess asked.

Laurie picked up her watering can and doused the geranium taking pride of place on the counter. "It doesn't matter whether I miss him or not. He isn't here, is he? He left. Besides, there's no place for him."

"There shouldn't be any place for that damn geranium," Bess muttered. "And I don't much like the watering can, either."

"You'll get used to both of them," Laurie said unrepentantly. "You're just grouchy because it's your engagement party tonight and you still haven't told Max Worley you don't want to marry him."

That got a reaction from Bess all right. She started pacing in front of the counter, looking as if she was going to grab that geranium any minute and hurl it through the window.

"Of course I don't want to marry Max Worley!" she exclaimed. "I don't even believe Max wants to marry *me*. He just thinks he has to live up to his image as the great romantic when he'd much rather be watching football with his buddies."

"So tell him the wedding's off," Laurie suggested.

"If it weren't for that old geezer Jonathan Garrett, I never would have gotten engaged in the first place. What's it going to take for him to pay any attention to me at all?"

"Let's find out," Laurie murmured. For at that very moment Doc Garrett came storming into the clinic.

"What's this about?" he demanded. "I turn my back and suddenly all kinds of things happen. First it was a cockeyed election, complete with political debates and campaign slogans. Now it's an engagement party."

Bess started shuffling files. "You've known ever since Ulysses S. Grant Day that I'm going to marry Max Worley. If you had any decency, you'd be at the party to give me your good wishes."

"I didn't think you'd go through with it," he said. "A party—that makes it seem official."

"Why wouldn't I go through with it?" she asked carelessly. "Really, Jonathan, if you didn't spend so much time in Digby, you'd have a better idea of what's going on around you."

"This last trip to Digby was a pretty important one," he said.

"I'm sure it was," Bess said in a sour voice. "I'm up on all the gossip. I know Samuel Miller is still in town and the two of you are planning an oceangoing fishing trip with your ladyloves, and that you even think you'll sail around the world. All I can say is, bon voyage."

"You can say bon voyage all right. Bon voyage, Estelle. I went to Digby so I could break off with her."

Bess almost dropped the file she was holding. "You what?"

"Just what I said. I broke it off with Estelle. She cried a few crocodile tears, but by now she's probably living it up with some other old geezer. That *is* what you call me, isn't it? An old geezer."

Bess stared at him. "Why did you break up with her?"

"Why d'you think?" Doc said testily. "I can't let you marry that idiot Max Worley when you're supposed to marry *me*. I'm warning you, though, Bessie—this is my third time around with the state of matrimony. You'll have your hands full. And I sure hope you can find it in yourself to like fishing."

Bess did drop the folder now, heedless as papers scattered across the floor. The next minute she was in the doc's arms. Laurie, to give them some privacy, studied the geranium on the counter. She smiled—a bit of a teary smile admittedly. Happy endings always did make her cry, even if they weren't her own.

CHAPTER NINETEEN

EARLY THE NEXT MORNING, the sound of the front door opening woke Laurie from a restless sleep. Glancing at the bedside clock, she saw that it was barely six. She grabbed her robe and struggled into it as she padded out into the hall and halfway down the stairs. That was when she saw Alyson standing uncertainly in the living room. Laurie's breath caught, but she knew she had to behave in a casual manner.

"Hi there," she said. "I didn't expect to see you, but I'm glad you're here.

"Oh, Mom…" Alyson burst into a flood of tears. Laurie hurried down the rest of the stairs and opened her arms. The next minute she was holding Alyson close to her heart and vowing silently never to let her go.

"Honey, what's wrong?"

"Everything," Alyson sobbed. "I just can't take it anymore! He's such a slob and such a jerk. I found out he's actually been going out with somebody else, while I stay home and clean that stupid apartment.…"

Still holding on tightly to her daughter, Laurie led the way over to Doc Garrett's shabby old sofa and sat the two of them down. "Hush, sweetie," she murmured as Alyson sobbed even harder. "It'll be all right. Everything's going to be all right." How often she'd uttered these same words when Alyson was a little girl. Her daughter was no longer a child, but it seemed she could still use some maternal comforting.

It was several moments before Alyson could be coherent again. "Can you believe it? I cleaned the *toilet*, Mom. I cleaned the *sink*. And for what? He took some girl on a Jeep tour and then he started dating her. Some *tourist*. I mean, I booked the damn tour for her and I didn't even suspect. I wouldn't even have known if Susan at the diner hadn't told me."

For perhaps the first time, Laurie gave a hearty thanks to the town's rumor mill. "It'll be all right," she repeated.

Alyson shifted. "I brought most of my stuff. And if you could go over with me later to get the rest... I just don't want to do it alone."

"Of course I'll go with you. Of course."

Alyson started crying again. "Mom, I'm so sorry. So terribly sorry! All the things I said. I didn't mean them. Honestly I didn't."

"Hush, sweetie, it'll be all right," Laurie said again. She'd learned long ago that comforting phrases bore repeating. "We both said some things. We'll just go on from here."

"I'll go to college. It'll be just like we planned and dreamed. I just want everything the way it used to be."

If Laurie had learned one thing, it was that her daughter needed to make her own choices—and her own mistakes. "You'll go to college when and if *you* decide," she said. "We'll talk about it later. For now, I'm just glad you're home."

"Me, too," Alyson said. "Me, too." And Laurie went on holding her daughter safe in her arms.

TIM COULD HONESTLY SAY that Grant hadn't changed much in the few weeks he'd been away. The mountains still presided over the town in stern majesty, and the citizens of Grant were still spreading stories. He'd barely hit town before he heard the latest: Doc Garrett and Bess Thompson were tying the knot that very afternoon. After all these years, it seemed that Doc had finally put two and two together and realized that Bess was meant for him. It just took some people a little longer than others to figure out the truth.

According to gossip, Doc Garrett and Samuel Miller were both hanging out at the diner on Main Street indulging in a sort of bachelors' farewell luncheon. Tim entered the diner, and sure enough, there were his father and Doc finishing up the meal with the house specialty: strawberry shortcake doused in whipped cream and sprinkled with chocolate shavings, also known as the "mother lode" in honor of the town's mining heritage.

"Didn't I tell you to watch your cholesterol, Doc?" Tim said as he came up to the booth.

"Tim-o," the doc said, hardly acting surprised to see him, "don't you start. Isn't it bad enough I'm going to have Bessie watching my diet?"

"About time she looked after you," Tim said.

"Speaking of which, I'd better go down the street and check on my tux. You never do know with Loretta's Formal Wear. If I don't watch out, Loretta will outfit me in one of those powder-blue affairs, even after I told her I needed something spiffy to match the bride." Doc scooted out of the booth and strolled casually from the diner. That, of course, left Tim alone with his father.

"You might as well have a seat," Samuel said. "I'm damn sure you're not worried about *my* cholesterol."

Tim sat down opposite him. "From the sound of things, you're looking ahead to a steady diet of fish."

"We've chartered a boat," Samuel said, seemingly reluctant to divulge the details. He looked down at his gnarled hands, then placed them under the table as if to hide their infirmity from his son.

Tim searched for something to say. "Aren't you going to allow the doc a honeymoon?"

"He gets a few days alone with Bess. And then the four of us'll set sail."

"Margaret...she must be somebody special," Tim said. "I'd like to hear more about her."

"Like hell you would," Samuel muttered.

Tim ignored this comment. "What's she like?"

"If you think I'm running around with some young model type, think again. She's almost seventy." Samuel paused. "She does have one heck of a tennis backhand, though," he added.

"Like I say, she sounds special," Tim said. "Don't suppose I could meet her."

"She'll be coming here from Denver to hook up with us pretty soon. But don't worry, I'm not going to follow Jonathan's example. I don't have any marriage plans in the offing. There. You know enough." Samuel appeared defensive. That was something new—the patriarch sounding concerned that his son might judge his choices.

"I'd like to meet her," Tim repeated.

"What are you doing back in town?" Samuel asked brusquely.

Tim gave a wry grimace. "Guess you could say I'm following the family tradition, after all. I can't seem to get away from being a small-town doctor."

"The job's taken, I hear."

"Yeah, that's a little matter I'll have to clear up." Tim slid out of the booth. "Just wanted to say hello, Dad. Just wanted to tell you I'm back." He started to head out of the diner only to hear his father speak again. Samuel's voice was so low Tim had to strain to catch the words.

"Nobody can take your mother's place, Tim. Not Margaret, not anybody. Not a day goes by that I don't think about her. Not a day passes without me wishing she was back beside me. And...if she were here, she'd be proud of you." The implication was there, unspoken. *I'm proud of you, too, son.* Tim knew it would be asking too much for his father to say the words out loud. But he didn't need to hear them. He only needed to know his father felt them.

"Thanks, Dad," he said softly.

TIM WENT UP THE WALK of the doctor's house and right away he was struck by how festive it looked. White streamers hung over the door and were looped around the roof of the gazebo. Tim supposed it wasn't every day that Laurie got to host a wedding. He knew he was early; the ceremony wouldn't start for another hour or so. Just as he was about to knock on the door, it opened and Laurie's daughter came outside.

"Well," said Alyson. "Heard you were back in town."

"Hello," said Tim. "How's it going?"

She gave an elaborate sigh. "For your information—no, I'm not with Kevin anymore. And yes, I realize what a jerk he is. And, *yes*, I'm going to college in the fall, but just as far as Boulder. Anything else you want to know?"

"That'll about do it."

Alyson gave him the once-over. "You're not going to break my mother's heart again, are you?"

"Not if I can help it."

"Good. Because I don't like to see her hurt. By the way, she's in the kitchen finishing the hors d'oeuvres. I told her we should just order a bunch of stuff from the bakery, but now and then she actually thinks she has to display her cooking talents. Try to set her straight, will you?" Alyson darted past him and down the porch steps.

Tim went inside. He poked his head into the den and saw that the orange couch was still there. Satisfied, he made his way to the kitchen. Laurie seemed totally immersed in her task—slapping little sandwiches together. At the sound of his footsteps, however, she turned around. She put a hand to her throat and she looked a bit shaken, but that was all.

"So," she said. "You came back for Doc's wedding."

"I didn't even hear about it until today. I guess Doc decided he'd already used enough ploys to lure me to Grant." Tim couldn't take his eyes off her, and it occurred to him she'd never looked sexier. He was glad to see she'd abandoned the country-style dress for one of her tailored sophisticated dresses, this one made of a silky material that moved with her body. He took a few steps toward her, but the expression on her face warned him to stay right where he was.

"If you're not here for the wedding, why *did* you come back?"

"For you, Laurie," he said simply. "Only for you."

He decided he'd better elaborate. "I tried to think of all the reasons I shouldn't be near you," he said. "But in the end...they all just faded away. And I knew I had to be with you." He took another step toward her.

"Stay right where you are, Tim," she ordered, "because *I'll* give you plenty of reasons. For one thing you don't have a job here anymore. I'm the town doctor."

"I've been thinking about that. We could pool our resources. Maybe we could turn this place into a two-doctor town, after all. It'll take some creative budgeting, I admit, but I think we could do it. At least we could try."

"There's something else," she said, refusing to acknowledge his answer. "You don't have a house here anymore. This is my place now—official residence of the town doctor."

"I was thinking about that, too," he admitted. "And I figured maybe we could do some creative sharing. That orange couch, you know—it's good for my back."

She looked as if she was about to give in, but then she forged ahead. "This town isn't exciting enough for you," she said. "What you really want is to be a hotshot research physician."

At least here he had some physical evidence. He took a creased letter out of his pocket and handed it over to her. "Exhibit number one," he said. "A certain Miss Amy Vance has convinced me that small-town doctoring has its own rewards."

Laurie read the letter and then passed it back to him. "Very nice," she said. "Amy told me she was going to write to you. But if I were you, I certainly wouldn't allow a nine-year-old child to sway my career plans. Where was I? That's right, more reasons why you can't stay in this town—"

"I love you," he said. He was almost convinced that would do the trick, but she only shook her head.

"The way I understand it, the only woman you ever really loved was your sister-in-law. Even though you knew she was meant for your brother, she's the one you loved."

"No, Laurie. I used Hallie as an excuse *not* to love. You're the one. The only one. What can I do to convince you?"

"Say it again," she whispered.

"I love you. With all my heart I love you, Dr. Laurie."

It seemed he'd finally gotten through to her. Because Laurie came to him, put her arms around his neck and kissed him. She kissed him for a very long while.

He held her close, wondering how he'd ever gone all this time without her. He'd never go without her again if he had anything to say about it. "Oh, Laurie," he murmured against her cheek, "being away from you—that's what told me just how much I need you. Will you give me a chance? I don't know if I'll be very good at this family thing. But I don't want to fail at it, that's for damn sure.''

"You know what's great, Tim? There's plenty of room for mistakes. As long as the love is there, that's what'll keep us going.''

He tilted her face to his, lost himself in her dark eyes. "Here's the thing. If we're really going to make this a two-doctor town, we'll have to pull together.''

She looked thoughtful. "Let me see. We've already shown we're a pretty good team at delivering babies. With Bess about to go off sailing the seas, we're minus a nurse, but we'll work that out. That just leaves a few problems with our budget. How on earth will the town support *two* doctors?''

"We'll just have to wrassle up some more business. We'll have to pool our resources.''

"Like the orange couch," Laurie murmured.

"Definitely the orange couch." He kissed her again...and again. But there was something else that needed doing. "Dr. Laurie," he said solemnly, "I would like to deliver the opposite of a nonproposal.''

"What are you talking about?" she asked in a suspicious voice.

"Just what I said—I'm here to do the exact opposite of *not* proposing. In other words, will you marry me?''

She studied him. "Tim, you have that look in your eyes. That devil-may-care look." She grinned. "Only this time it's not pushing me away. Not a bit.''

"Darlin', you'd better believe I'm not pushin' you away. And I'm never leavin' again." He held her closer yet. "So, Doc Laurie, what's it to be? What's your answer?"

"The answer, my love, is yes."

HARLEQUIN SUPERROMANCE®

COMING NEXT MONTH

#758 BEAUTY & THE BEASTS • Janice Kay Johnson
Veterinarian Dr. Eric Bergstrom is interested in a new
woman. A *beautiful* woman. He's volunteered his services at
the local cat shelter she's involved with. He's even adopted
one of the shelter's cats. But he still can't manage to get
Madeline to go out with him. That's bad enough. Then Eric's
twelve-year-old son comes to town, making it clear that he
resents "having" to spend the summer with his father. Well,
at least Eric's new cat loves him....

#759 IN THE ARMS OF THE LAW • Anne Marie Duquette
Home on the Ranch
Morgan Bodine is part-owner of the Silver Dollar Ranch;
he's also the acting sheriff in Tombstone, Arizona.
Jasentha Cliffwalker is a biologist studying bats on Bodine
property. Morgan and Jaz loved each other years ago, but it
was a love they weren't ready for. *Are they ready now?*
They'll find out when a stranger comes to Tombstone,
threatening everything they value most.... By the author of
She Caught the Sheriff.

#760 JUST ONE NIGHT • Kathryn Shay
9 Months Later
Annie and Zach Sloan had married for all the right reasons.
They'd fallen in love and neither could imagine life without
the other. But those reasons hadn't been enough to keep
them together. Then—six years after the divorce—a night
that began in fear ended in passion. And now there's a
new reason for Zach and Annie to marry. *They're about to
become parents.*

#761 THIS CHILD IS MINE • Janice Kaiser
Carolina Prescott is pregnant. Webb Harper is the father.
After his wife died, he forgot all about the donation he'd left
at a fertility clinic. Due to a mix-up, Lina is given the wrong
fertilized egg—but that doesn't make her less of a mother!
Both Lina and Webb have strong feelings about the baby
she's carrying and the ensuing lawsuit. Can their growing
feelings for each other overcome the trauma of the battle
for custody?

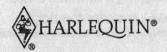

HARLEQUIN WOMEN KNOW ROMANCE WHEN THEY SEE IT.

And they'll see it on **ROMANCE CLASSICS**, the new 24-hour TV channel devoted to romantic movies and original programs like the special **Romantically Speaking—Harlequin™ Goes Prime Time.**

Romantically Speaking—Harlequin™ Goes Prime Time introduces you to many of your favorite romance authors in a program developed exclusively for Harlequin® readers.

Watch for **Romantically Speaking—Harlequin™ Goes Prime Time** beginning in the summer of 1997.

If you're not receiving ROMANCE CLASSICS,
call your local cable operator or satellite provider and
ask for it today!

ROMANCE CLASSICS

Escape to the network of your dreams.

See Ingrid Bergman and Gregory Peck in *Spellbound* on Romance Classics.